THE
SOUTH BANK
MURDERS

An absolutely gripping crime mystery with a massive twist

BIBA PEARCE

Detective Rob Miller Mysteries Book 5

Joffe Books, London
www.joffebooks.com

First published in Great Britain in 2022

Cover art by Nebojsa Zorić

ISBN: 978-1-80405-023-1

CHAPTER 1

The house phone rang.

"I'll get it," yelled Rob. The only people that called him on this number were the utility companies or his elderly neighbour, Mrs Winterbottom, who used to dog-sit for him.

"Rob, it's Sam," came a booming voice down the line.

Retired Detective Chief Superintendent Sam Lawrence, his old boss and mentor. Sam had become a good friend over the years, although he'd never mastered the art of speaking softly.

"Sam, this is a surprise. Why didn't you call me on my mobile?" He shifted Jack, his four-month-old son, onto his other shoulder.

"I did," he barked. "Several times."

"Shit, I'm on baby duty. I didn't hear it."

Jack reached out and tried to grab the cordless phone.

"Ah," came the gruff response. "Listen, I need a favour. Can you meet me tonight at the Vic?"

Rob eyed the dribble running down his son's chin. "Sorry, Sam. I'd love to, honestly, but I can't. Jo needs a break. She's worn out." Jack, unable to reach the device, started crying.

"Shh . . ." Rob jiggled him the way he'd seen Jo do. It had absolutely no effect. Jack kept on crying.

1

"I can hear you've got your hands full." Sam chuckled. "I don't miss those days, I can tell you — or the sleepless nights."

"Thanks." Sam's two daughters were grown up and at university now.

"How are you two coping?"

"All right. Jo takes the brunt of it. I help out at night." He scoffed. "I never knew it was possible to function on so little sleep."

"Parenting is not easy," Sam agreed. "Particularly at this age. If it's any consolation, it gets better. Soon he'll be sleeping through the night, and hopefully, so will you."

"That's a relief." He wasn't sure how much longer they could go on like this. As it was, they were both stumbling around like zombies most of the time. Thank God for Tanya, his new cleaner. He'd hired her after her last employer, Judith Walker, had been murdered in her home near Box Hill. Tanya kept the house in order and even took on some babysitting duties while he and Jo were getting used to being new parents.

"I'll let you go."

"Thanks, Sam. I'll call you when I'm free."

"Good luck, matey."

Smiling, Rob hung up.

"Come on, little man," he crooned. "What's up? You want to play with this?" Rob handed Jack the phone, which immediately went into his mouth.

He carried the baby into the living room and sat down on the sofa. Trigger, his golden Lab, glanced up from his position on the rug then went back to sleep again.

"What do you want to watch?" Rob positioned Jack on his lap and reached for the remote. He switched on a kids' programme and leaned back, closing his eyes. He'd got back relatively early — around four this afternoon — thanks to a quiet day at the Homicide and Serious Crime Command's Putney office. There were four major investigation teams, but his wasn't on call this week. No sooner had he entered the house than Jo had handed him the baby.

"Thank God you're home," she'd breathed. "I've got to take a bath and get some shut-eye. I'm a mess."

She had looked ragged. Her blonde hair was tousled, her usually clear blue eyes glazed with fatigue, and she had numerous unidentifiable stains on her blouse. He knew how hard it was to be on baby duty all day, and while he had the escape of the office, she was on maternity leave. There was no respite from the feeding, bathing and crying. Jack wasn't a great sleeper, and it was considered a small victory when he finally went down for a nap.

"Give him to me," he'd said. Jo had kissed him on the cheek, then disappeared upstairs. That was the last he'd seen of her.

The new living arrangement was working out well. Jo had moved in a few weeks before the baby was born. They'd put the finishing touches to the nursery, spent a fortune on baby supplies and got ready for the new addition to their family.

At first, Jo had felt out of place, despite his attempts to make her feel at home. They'd been overly polite to each other. Afraid to say anything that might spark an argument. Living together was a new step for them both, and one they wouldn't necessarily have taken so soon, had it not been for the surprise pregnancy.

But as the days wore on, they relaxed and settled into the new status quo. Rob had just got used to having her around when Jack's arrival had thrown everything out of whack again.

The television held Jack's attention and he lay on Rob's chest, his eyes glued to the screen. The telephone slipped out of his hands. It wasn't the ideal scenario. He should probably be reading to him or doing some motor development activity, but he was just too exhausted.

Once Jack had quietened down, he lowered him into his carrycot. Jo had fed him before he'd got home and there were several bottles of expressed milk in the fridge for later. Rob yawned and stretched out on the couch. Blissful silence. He closed his eyes and within seconds had drifted off.

* * *

A shrill ringing woke him with a start. Jack started crying and Trigger popped his head up, his ears poised.

"What the—?"

Rob reached for his mobile phone, vibrating on the coffee table in front of him. "Yeah?"

"DCI Miller?"

There was something in the caller's tone, something he didn't like.

"Yes?" He sat up.

"This is DC Preston from dispatch. There's been a shooting in Clapham. Three fatalities."

"Call Galbraith's team," muttered Rob. "He's on call this weekend."

"I have, sir. It's just, I thought you'd want to know."

"Why?" Jack's crying grew louder.

"One of the victims is Detective Chief Superintendent Lawrence, sir."

•

CHAPTER 2

Time seemed to stand still. Jack's crying faded into the background, the television became a muted murmur. The loud, arterial throbbing in his ears drowned out everything.

"What?"

Had he heard right? She couldn't possibly have meant Sam Lawrence. He'd just spoken to him earlier this evening.

"One of the victims was the Chief, sir. I know you were close . . ."

Were close . . .

"Are you sure it's him?" he rasped, his mouth dry. *There must be some mistake.* It couldn't be Sam. Sam had gone for a pint at the Vic. What was he doing in Clapham?

"Yes, sir. The first responder identified him."

He frowned, shaking his head. "But, how?"

"We don't know the details yet, sir. All three men died of gunshot wounds. The murder team is on its way, along with Forensics."

"Thanks for letting me know."

He pocketed his phone, then charged upstairs, leaving Trigger looking at a screaming Jack.

He burst into their bedroom. Jo was curled up on the bed, dead to the world. He hated waking her, but this was an emergency.

"Jo." He shook her shoulder. She murmured, then buried deeper into the pillow.

"Jo, wake up. Something's happened."

She opened her eyes. "What's up? Is Jack all right?"

"He's fine, although I think he's hungry. Listen, I've got to go. There's been a shooting in Clapham."

"You're not on call," she moaned. "Let someone else go."

"It's Sam, Jo. He's been involved in a shooting. He's . . . dead." The words tumbled from his lips. A gasping sob followed. Now he'd said it, it must be true.

Jo sat up and clutched his arm. "Oh, God. Sam? What happened?"

"I don't know. Dispatch just called me. Do you mind taking over? I have to be there."

"Yes, of course. Go."

He squeezed her hand, then ran down the stairs two at a time. He was out the front door before Trigger had time to come and see what all the fuss was about.

It was a windy night. Burnished leaves flung themselves across the road, illuminated by his headlights. The clock on his dashboard read ten to two in the morning. What the hell was Sam doing in Clapham at this hour? What was he doing there at all?

A chill shot down his spine. Was this what Sam had wanted to ask? For Rob to accompany him tonight?

Listen, I need a favour. Can you meet me tonight at the Vic?

If only he'd asked more questions when he'd had the chance.

He cringed, blinking away the sudden moisture. There was still a chance it was a mistake. The first responder may have got it wrong. Chances were, it was a man who looked like Sam Lawrence. There were a lot of scraggly, broad-shouldered, bearded sixty-year-olds in London. It could be anyone.

He saw the flashing lights as he turned into Northcote Road. They'd cordoned off a section of the road. Uniformed officers were keeping out the growing crowd of onlookers. It was a Friday night in vibey Clapham, so there were several people still out.

He didn't see the HAT vehicle, the special Homicide Assessment Team car deployed by the murder squad in the event of a suspicious death, which meant Galbraith and his team weren't here yet. That was a surprise. Neither was the Forensics van.

He flashed his warrant card and ducked under the cordon. His heart was hammering so hard it felt like it might burst out of his chest. What would he find inside?

Was it Sam?

An officer at the entrance gave him a sombre look. Rob rushed past him and into the restaurant. It was a Thai place, by the looks of things. Fairly narrow, with rows of red-clothed tables, hanging lanterns, and the smell of noodles in the air.

The first body lay about four feet inside the front door. A Thai man, thrown back against the counter, a hole where his eye should be, and another in the middle of his chest. Quick, efficient, definitely premeditated.

Rob turned to his left. At a table near the back slumped another body, this time of a younger man leaning back in his chair. Dirty-blonde hair, skinny frame, rough-looking, mouth open in a frozen gasp. Was that a gold tooth?

Rob approached cautiously. The victim appeared to be staring up at the ceiling, his eyes glazed like marbles. Tattoos snaked up both arms. Not the sort of guy the Chief would normally hang out with. This guy had been facing the door. The last thing he would have seen was the gunman or -men entering the restaurant and opening fire.

Rob could barely bring himself to look at the man on the floor. Heart pounding, he forced himself to study the face, swallowing back the bile in his mouth.

It was Sam. No doubt about it.

The shock of white hair, the ox-like shoulders, the beard speckled with his own blood.

Jesus. Rob closed his eyes, fighting the urge to puke. When he opened them again, his pulse had slowed to a quick but decisive rhythm. He needed to memorise as many details as possible. He took out his phone and snapped a few shots, ignoring the "I'm not sure you should be doing that, sir" from the first responder.

Two bullet wounds. One in the shoulder, one in the head. The shoulder shot would have been unlikely to kill him, but the head shot made sure of it. Judging by where Sam had been sitting and where he now lay, it looked like he'd stood up, spun around, taken the first bullet in the shoulder and the second in the forehead. He'd fallen backwards, his arms out to his sides, eyes shut.

It was a cool October night and the Chief had been wearing his coat. It had fallen open on the one side. Rob leaned over, ignoring another shout of protest from the policeman standing guard. *What's that in his pocket? A mobile phone?*

"Sir, please can you move away from the bodies," came the insistent voice. "I must ask that you remain outside."

Rob gave him a look that said he wasn't moving. At that moment, Galbraith and his team arrived. Sirens blared and then cut out with a deflated whoop. Blue lights created a strobe effect outside and ricocheted off the walls in the restaurant. Heavy footsteps fell, then the burly Scot burst into the restaurant.

"Bloody hell, Rob. I heard you were here. You're contaminating the crime scene."

"It's the Chief," he said bleakly.

"I know. The Super's on her way. The whole blasted team is coming."

Another police car screeched to a halt and in rushed DS Will Freemont, DS Jenny Bird, DC Mike Manner and DC Jeff Clarke.

The first responder threw up his hands and stomped out.

"Is it true?" Jenny was hiding behind Galbraith.

He nodded. She stifled a sob.

The rest of the team stared at the bodies of the three men in horrified silence. That was their chief lying on the floor.

Galbraith cleared his throat. "SOCO is outside. Once you lot clear out, they can process the scene."

Rob thought out loud. "Looks like an organised hit. First one to drop was the owner." They all turned to look at the Thai man lying closest to the door. He still had a look of surprise on what was left of his face. "Next was the blonde guy the Chief was talking to. He was facing the door. It looks like Lawrence got to his feet, turned around and was hit in the process."

"It's a massacre." Mike ventured forward to stand beside Galbraith. Blood was pooling under the two bodies on the ground and dripping off the seat where the blonde guy sat. It gleamed black in the red-hued light of the restaurant.

Jenny retched and darted outside. Will followed, along with Jeff. Only Galbraith and Mike stood side by side, gazing at the crime scene.

"At least it was sudden," the Scot said.

Rob grunted.

"Who was he meeting?" asked Mike. "Do we know who this guy is?"

Rob shook his head. He didn't know. Had no clue. Sam wasn't supposed to be here. He was supposed to be in the tiny Victoria Arms pub on Richmond Hill, laughing with the other locals, his booming voice regaling them with stories from his past.

He gazed at the still figure of the Chief, forcing his brain to accept the awful reality. He was dead. Gunned down in a hail of bullets. It was fucking surreal.

Heels clacked on the wooden floor. Superintendent Mayhew was here in all her fiery glory. "Get out, all of you," she barked, her Irish lilt more pronounced than usual.

Neither Rob, Galbraith nor Mike moved.

"Did you hear me? This is a crime scene. You can't be here."

"It's the Chief, ma'am," said Galbraith.

"I know." She paused. "I'm sorry for your loss. It's tragic, but you have to let Forensics do their job."

"This is our case." Rob turned on her. "He was *our* chief. This is *our* case."

Mayhew stared at him for a long time before answering. "I'm not taking this case, DCI Miller. Central MIT can deal with it. You're too close. You all are."

"What?" blurted Mike.

"Ma'am, with all due respect—" began Galbraith.

"No," snapped Rob. "There's no one better equipped to deal with this than we are. We knew him. He was our chief, for God's sake."

"Exactly." She put her hands on her hips. "That's why we can't take this one."

Rob turned back to the body of his mentor. No fucking way was this case being taken away from him.

"I'm calling Forensics in now." She turned on her heel. "I want you all out."

Rob took a step closer to the body.

"What are you doing?" hissed Galbraith.

"There's a phone in his pocket."

"So? That's evidence."

"We need to see what's on it. If another team takes this case, we won't have access to that information."

"It'll break the chain of custody," Galbraith hissed. "It won't be admissible in court. It could call into question the validity of all the other evidence."

"It could tell us who he was meeting." Rob glanced at them. "We need this to find his killer."

Mike glanced at the door. "Five seconds. They're coming."

Galbraith exhaled. "Okay, but this stays between us. We could get into serious shit if this gets out, and I mean that. End-of-career shit."

"Mike?" Rob needed all of them to be on board.

He didn't have to think about it. "Do it. It's the Chief."

Rob reached forward and snatched the mobile phone out of Sam's pocket. He straightened up just as the white-clad SOCO team marched through the door.

Rob stepped back. "It's all yours." He passed the pathologist. "You might want to take my prints and DNA. I leaned over to feel for a pulse."

He got a hard look in response but ignored it and kept walking.

Once outside, the team assembled beside the specialist homicide vehicle. The blue lights pulsed over them. Rob glanced at their ashen faces, dilated eyes and haunted expressions. He was sure he looked the same.

"What are we going to do?" whispered Will.

Jenny swiped at her eyes. "I can't believe he's dead. What was he doing here?"

"That's what we need to find out." Rob's head was spinning. Sam's phone was burning a hole in his pocket. He'd never, under normal circumstances, consider taking evidence from a crime scene. It had been risky, and it could have serious consequences for the prosecution's case, but without it, they were in the dark.

"We're not handing the case over, are we?" Jeff raised an eyebrow.

Galbraith snorted. Mike looked grim. Rob shook his head.

Jeff nodded. "Didn't think so."

CHAPTER 3

Nobody went home. It was nearly 4 a.m. when Rob got to the Major Investigation Team's Putney office, their base of operations. He'd called Jo on the way and told her he wouldn't be back until later that day. She said she'd take Jack to visit a friend in Guildford and not to worry.

"Take as long as you like," she'd said. "This is Sam."

That was one thing about having a cop for a partner. She understood. He never had to explain why he was late or try to make her comprehend how important a case was, or why he had to act now while the evidence was fresh. Yvette, his ex-wife, had never got it. She'd resented his job. Hated everything about it. He should have realised that from the beginning.

That's what he loved about Jo. She was so uncomplicated.

"Let's see the phone," Galbraith said, once the team was assembled in the incident room. The rest of the squad room was eerily quiet, the workstations in darkness, computers off. The only light came from the room they were in.

Rob placed the Chief's mobile phone on the table. They all stared at it.

"You took his phone?" Jenny gasped.

"I had to. It'll tell us who he was meeting."

12

"Shit, guv. It's evidence. That's illegal."

Even Jeff looked shocked. Rule 101 of policing was 'Never interfere with a crime scene.' It had been drummed into them ad infinitum at the police academy. Rob was usually a stickler for such things. It was completely out of character for him to resort to something this drastic.

"I know, and I understand the implications. If there's a blowback from this, I'll take it. None of you were involved, okay?"

They all stared at him.

"We agreed," insisted Galbraith. Mike nodded, jaw firmly set.

"It was my idea." Rob shot them a hard look. "End of story. Let's focus on what the Chief was doing there."

Galbraith sighed. "Okay, so let's have a wee look."

"First, there's something I have to tell you." They all looked at him. "The Chief called me yesterday evening."

Jenny's mouth dropped open. "The night he was killed?"

"Yeah."

"What did he want?" asked Will.

"He asked me to meet him for a pint. Said he had a favour to ask."

"Shit. I take it you didnae go?" Galbraith arched an eyebrow.

"No, I was looking after Jack." Rob bit his lip. "If only I had . . ."

"Don't." Jenny shook her head. "You weren't to know."

"She's right," agreed Will. "This isn't your fault."

Rob took a deep breath. They could say what they liked, but if he'd gone to meet Sam, he might have been able to talk him out of this meeting, whatever it was about. Or arranged backup. Or gone with him. Except then he'd also have been at the restaurant and would probably also be lying in a pool of his own blood right about now.

He picked up the phone. There was no point in using gloves. His prints were all over it.

"What about the code?" asked Will.

13

"Sam was a creature of habit. He used his wife's birthday on all his devices."

"Seriously?" Will blinked.

Rob typed in 2-1-0-5-6-2.

"*Voila.*"

The screen sprung to life.

"Well, I'll be . . ." Galbraith muttered.

"You'd think a chief superintendent would know better," said Will.

Rob scrolled to the recent call log and looked at the top number. It was his. *He* was the last person Sam had rung.

He swallowed, then moved on to the next. It was unrecognised. Could that be the man he was meeting? Had the rendezvous been set up before he'd spoken to the Chief? It would make sense. That's why he needed a favour. Perhaps he'd wanted Rob to be his wingman, to watch his back. He clenched his fists. Now he'd never know.

"This could be it." He showed the number to Will, the tech whizz of the team.

Will jotted it down. "I'll look into it. Hey, can I see that for a minute?"

Rob handed him the phone.

Will frowned, then double-clicked the button at the bottom. "You do realise the voice-memo function is activated?"

"Huh?" Rob peered at the screen.

Will's face reddened. "The Chief was recording his conversation at the restaurant. Look at this. It stopped after two hours."

"No way!" Rob's pulse ticked up a notch. "You mean everything he said to the person he was meeting is on his phone?"

"Looks like it." He glanced up. "The only way to find out is to listen to it."

"Do it."

They all sat down around the boardroom-style table, the phone in the middle. Will pressed play. The Chief's voice was loud and clear. *"Ant, I have to admit, I was surprised to get your call."*

The hair on Rob's arms prickled. It was like Sam was in the room, talking from beyond the grave.

"I know. I'm sorry. I didn't know who else to talk to." The blonde man's voice was higher pitched, anxious.

"Let's sit down."

There was rustling as they sat down at a table. The one at the back.

"Kitchen's closed," said an accented voice. *"But I can get you a drink if you want?"*

"No thanks, Zhou. We're good."

"They know the owner," muttered Galbraith. "It's not the first time they've met there."

Rob had been thinking the same thing. What on earth had Sam been into? He was retired, for Christ's sake. Why was he attending clandestine meetings in Northcote Road after closing?

"What's this about, Ant?"

"Ant? Ant who?" whispered Jenny.

There was a pause. *"There's something big going down, Sam. Not drugs. Something else."*

"What do you mean?"

Ant lowered his voice. *"I'm not sure, exactly. Maybe girls . . . trafficking. I don't know."*

Galbraith raised a bushy eyebrow.

"What makes you think there's something going on?" continued Sam.

"Torch. He's acting strangely. Late-night meetings off the estate. He goes alone, not even his closest gang go with him. I followed him. He went to a place in Southwark. Looked like a 'massage parlour' — if you know what I mean. Dodgy as fuck."

Will wrote *Torch?* on his notepad.

"Did he speak to anyone?" enquired Sam.

"He went inside, came out an hour later. I waited until he'd gone, then went inside. They took one look at me and kicked me out. Said I

couldn't afford what they were offering." He scoffed. *"I know I look rough, but that place wasn't the fucking Hilton."*

Rob remembered the tattoos down the man's arms and on his fingers, his gold tooth and his greasy hair. He could have priors. He might be on the system.

"Who did you speak to?" Lawrence again.

"A bald guy with an Eastern European accent. Big mother."

There was a grunt. Rob could picture the Chief thinking this through.

"So why come to me? Why not go to Cranshaw?"

Rob nodded at Will, who wrote *Cranshaw* beneath *Torch*.

"Cranshaw . . ."

Ant's voice petered off as a loud bang could be heard. Rob pictured the intruder bursting through the door, perhaps using his boot to kick it open.

A shout, then shots fired. Rob counted them in his head.

Bang. Bang.

Bang. Bang.

Bang. Bang.

Six shots. All fired one after the other, like a deadly heartbeat. No hesitation. Not a shot wasted. A pro.

Silence.

Jenny sat with her hand over her mouth. No one else spoke. They were all processing the moment the Chief's life was taken from him.

"One thirty-seven," whispered Will, still looking at the phone. "Time of death."

CHAPTER 4

Jenny brushed the tears from her eyes. "I'm sorry," she sniffed. "I can't help it. I can't get my head around the fact that the Chief is gone. He was always so full of life. To think of him lying there . . ." She shook her head.

Jenny wasn't prone to melodramatics. She was a fine sergeant, experienced and gaining a reputation for herself as an effective interrogator. She was tough and practical, but this was testing them all.

Will patted her hand. "It's okay. We're all in shock."

Rob gritted his teeth. Now that it was beginning to sink in, a seed of anger began sprouting in the pit of his stomach. Left unchecked, he feared it could grow into inconsolable rage. Rage against the man who'd done this. The shooter who'd gunned down his former boss, his mentor, his friend. The man who'd taken the life of a husband and a father. Christ, what was he going to tell Diana?

"Excuse me." He got wearily to his feet. "I must go and see Sam's wife."

"We'll get started with what we know," Galbraith said. It was his team who were officially on call, although they were two men down. Evan, the soft-spoken American, had taken his English wife and young children back to the

States. They'd had a farewell party for him a couple of weeks back.

Harry Malhotra was on annual leave. Rumour had it he'd landed a bit part in a national soap opera, but that hadn't been confirmed.

Mike and Jeff nodded. They'd migrated over as temporary replacements, while Jenny and Will had stayed with Rob. To be honest, they could have done with taking on another investigator, but Rob hadn't broached it with Mayhew. Since his almost-suspension earlier in the year, he tried to stay out of her office as much as possible.

"I'll stay too." Jenny glanced at her watch. "It's almost morning, anyway."

Will grunted in agreement.

"Okay, thanks." Rob gave them a curt nod. He wasn't relishing the task ahead. "I'll be back as soon as I can."

* * *

The sun was well up by the time Rob made it back to the station. Diana had not taken the news well. She'd crumpled right there on the doorstep in front of him, and he'd had to help her into the house.

Diana Lawrence was a strong woman. She'd stood by Sam's side throughout his thirty-year police career, from beat cop in uniform, to detective and then rising through the ranks to chief superintendent. An interior designer, she'd run her own business while raising their two daughters. Rob recalled the Chief saying her only rule was that he leave work at work, and Sam had always respected that.

"He managed to survive thirty years in the force only to die in a shooting the year he retired." Diana's eyes mirrored her grief. "How unfair is that?"

It was tragic. There were no words to ease her pain. Instead, he held her while she sobbed, giving way to the tears that ran down his own face. Then he made them a cup of tea and told her, as best he could, what had happened.

"I didn't know who he was meeting," she said. "He didn't tell me, and I've learned not to ask. I wish I had now. It might have helped you catch whoever did this."

"Oh, I'm going to do that," Rob promised her. "You can count on it."

* * *

He felt strung out when he got back to the office. Raw. Like someone had ripped a plaster off his soul and it was bleeding out.

Mayhew was in her office. He could see her sitting at her desk, the blinds up and the light on. Unlike her predecessor, the fleeting Superintendent Hodge, who'd kept the blinds drawn, Mayhew liked to keep an eye on her officers. She met his gaze and beckoned to him.

Great.

He'd known this was coming. Steeling himself, he crossed the office and opened her door. "You wanted to see me?"

"Come in, DCI Miller." She was wearing a red skirt suit that clashed with her orange hair. Her voice was tight with tension, and she sat upright in her chair. She looked prepared for battle. What she didn't know was that Rob wouldn't back down.

"Look, I'm sorry if I came across as unsympathetic at the crime scene. I'm truly sorry for your loss. I know Sam Lawrence was a friend."

"He was more than a friend," Rob said. "He was my guvnor for five years. My mentor. I'm not going to give this case to another department."

She sighed. "The decision is made. Central is taking it on. The Deputy Chief agrees with me. Your team is too close."

Rob glared at her. An icy silence enveloped them. "God forbid you might have to get your hands dirty," he hissed, after it had stretched on for a long, uncomfortable moment.

"What did you say?"

19

He took a step closer to her desk. "When was the last time you did some real police work, other than driving a desk?"

Heat rose into her cheeks. "Might I remind you who you're speaking to, DCI Miller. I could have you reprimanded for this."

"You do what you have to. I'm going to find the Chief's killer." He left her office without another word.

* * *

The rest of the department were similarly in shock when they got in. Most had worked with Lawrence and knew and respected him. Celeste spent the first hour hiding in the loo. When she emerged, her face was blotchy and her eyes overly bright. "I want to help," she told Rob. "I know you're not going to hand this over to Central."

Celeste was a young DC, but she was gaining in confidence and experience with every case they worked. Rob had come to know her well, and had let her into their inner circle.

No one else knew the team were investigating the murders, or that they had the phone evidence. That was something they'd have to take to the grave with them. They'd met at a coffee shop across the road with big glass windows overlooking the River Thames. It was high tide and the water had burst its banks, yet again, flooding the towpath.

"What do we know about the restaurant owner, Zhou?" asked Rob.

"Raymond Zhou, although that's not his real name. He changed it when he arrived in the UK twenty years ago. He's originally from Bangkok," said Will, referring to his iPad. "He opened the Thai Kitchen the year he arrived. He's got a clean record. No arrests, no suspended sentences, no warnings. There's nothing on file about the restaurant either."

"He definitely knew the Chief," pointed out Galbraith.

"What about this Ant character?" asked Rob.

Jenny pursed her lips. "We traced his number to a burner phone. Without a surname, we'll have to wait for the fingerprint analysis to find out who he is."

"If he's in the database," remarked Rob.

"I've got a contact in Central," said Mike, who was a South Londoner. "We worked at Southwark nick together. I could ask him to keep us posted."

"Couldn't hurt," said Rob. "Celeste, why don't you look into the Chief's old cases. See if there's anyone who might have a vendetta against him."

She nodded.

"When's the post-mortem?" Jenny asked.

He sobered. "I don't know, but I'm going to be there. Liz wouldn't dare keep me away from this one." Liz Kramer was a Home Office pathologist and had worked on many cases with Rob over the past few years. She was a brisk, no-nonsense woman who was brilliant at her job.

"How's the Chief's wife taking it?" asked Celeste.

"Not good." Rob swallowed over a lump in his throat. "She didn't know where he was going or who he was meeting. She'd learned not to ask."

"Copper's wife," snorted Galbraith, who'd been married for over twenty years himself.

Rob reached for his coffee. Was that what Jo was? Would she one day open the door to find Will or Jenny standing there? He shivered and took a gulp, scorching his throat. It didn't bear thinking about.

"I looked into the guy Ant was talking about, 'Torch'." Will glanced down at his iPad. "Real name, Shamar Williams. Torch is his street name — and he's got form."

"Oh?" Rob arched his eyebrows.

"Yeah, and plenty of it." Will scanned down the screen. "He was arrested for burglary and GBH seven years ago. Spent two years inside. Was released and arrested again that same year for a domestic disturbance, but his girlfriend withdrew the charges. Three years ago, he was booked for possession, but his solicitor got him off. Apparently, he had a prescription."

Mike snorted.

"Do we have an address for him?" enquired Rob.

"Beaufort Estate, Lambeth," replied Will.

"Did you say Beaufort?" Mike leaned in, hands on the table.

"Yeah, you know it?"

"I fucking grew up there."

Rob turned to him. "Right, you're coming with me. I want to get eyes on this Torch character."

* * *

Beaufort Estate was a sprawling council estate consisting of fifteen tower blocks and lots of smaller units. Part of it had been scheduled for demolition and the windows were boarded up, the residents relocated to newer units. This section had a derelict feel to it, but as they drove through, Rob saw people entering the abandoned buildings.

The newer section had CCTV, street lighting and communal spaces for people to come together. Right now, those spaces were occupied by uncouth kids standing in small groups playing loud music and smoking weed.

"How long did you live here for?" asked Rob. Mike had always been on Galbraith's team, and despite working together, they hadn't really got to know each other.

"Until I was seventeen. Then I left and joined the army."

"You served?" Rob hadn't read his file.

"Yeah, five years. Did two tours, then chucked it in and joined the police force."

Rob pursed his lips, impressed. "Southwark?"

He nodded. "My old hood."

"Couldn't have been fun getting called out here as a copper."

Mike shrugged. He didn't need to answer. Rob glimpsed the jagged scar that started below his ear and ran down his cheek. "How'd you get the scar?"

Mike scowled. "Tried to stop a fight from escalating into a gang war. My face got in the way of a switchblade."

Rob winced. "Here, on the estate?"

He tensed his jaw. "Long time ago now."

"Do you know this Torch guy?"

"No, must have been after my time. I stopped coming here when I transferred to the crime squad. My mother died the year before and my brother—" He stopped.

Rob waited for him to continue.

He cleared his throat. "My brother got arrested for armed robbery. He's doing six to eight at Scrubs."

"Sorry to hear that." Rob didn't react, although he was surprised. Mike's brother was a criminal, while he was a cop. Two completely different paths. Was one a result of the other?

Another shrug. "That's life. Idi was older than me. He got in with a bad crowd. Not hard to do around here. Joined a gang. Started dealing drugs. It escalated. By the time I was sixteen, he'd already been arrested twice and was looking at his third strike." His voice cracked. "I promised my mother I wouldn't take the same path."

Rob nodded. "I'm sure she'd be very proud of you."

He grunted. "So what are we doing here? We can't just walk up and speak to him. He'll be surrounded by fellow gang members. Protected."

"That's exactly what I'm planning to do," said Rob. "If he's involved in something outside of the gang, he's not going to want them to overhear."

"How do you know he is?"

"Ant said he left the estate at night. Alone."

Mike hesitated, then nodded. "Okay, but watch your back."

"Which block is it?"

"C, over there."

Rob looked where he was pointing. A cluster of dark-brick apartment blocks stabbed the overcast sky. He parked in a spot between a beaten-up Toyota Yaris and a white panel van. A group of kids stopped what they were doing and stared at them.

Rob took a deep breath. "This place is patrolled, right?"

"Yeah, a couple of times a day. Don't ask me when, though."

They got out of the car and approached Tower Block C. The base was dank and smelled faintly of urine. Water and dead leaves had collected in the gutters, overspilling into puddles on the ground that refused to dry. The boys watched silently, suspiciously. They knew.

"What floor?" said Rob.

"Eleventh, flat 106."

They approached the elevator only to discover it was out of order. Great. As they headed to the stairwell a deep voice behind them said, "Can I help you?"

They turned. Standing there was the biggest man Rob had ever seen. At least six foot eight with wide shoulders and biceps the size of coconuts. His ebony skin was made even darker by the gang tattoos covering his arms and hands. A crowd of locals, presumably his gang, had gathered behind him.

"If you're Torch, then yes." Rob met his gaze. Hard, tough and ruthless. Yes, this guy could easily have put the kill order out on the Chief.

Mike bristled beside him. The Southwark copper was by no means a small man — neither was Rob — but this guy towered above them both.

"I'm Torch," he said. "And you are?"

He knew full well they were police. "DCI Miller and DC Manner from Putney Major Investigation Team. We'd like to ask you a few questions about a man called Ant."

The dark eyes narrowed. "Ant who?"

Nice try.

"I don't know yet." Rob came clean. "I believe he used to live here. He was shot and killed last night at a restaurant in Clapham."

Torch's eyes widened ever so slightly. Was that a reaction to the fact that Ant, whoever he was, was dead, or that the police knew about it? He couldn't tell.

There was a faint murmur among his posse. Definitely news to them. So, if this wasn't a gang hit, then what was it? Had Torch been acting alone?

"Don't know him," snapped Torch. He glanced around at the group that had formed behind him. "How about you guys?"

Everybody shook their head.

Rob smirked. "Nobody knew him, that's great." He looked at Torch. "Where were you last night between midnight and two a.m.?"

"In bed."

Rob looked for signs he was lying, but there was no hesitation. Not so much as a flicker. Either Torch was very good at pretending or he was telling the truth. Still, that didn't mean he wasn't guilty. He could have given the order, even if he hadn't pulled the trigger.

"Can anyone vouch for you?" he asked.

"Yeah, Chantelle, my woman."

"Can we speak to her?"

Torch lifted a hand and clicked his fingers. A slender woman wearing skintight jeans and a defiant smile sashayed forward. "Yeah, I was with him all night." She stressed the 'all'. There were a few sniggers from the group.

"Will that be all, policeman?" Condescension dripped from his tongue.

"For now."

They turned to go back to the car when a scruffy white guy in his thirties walked past. "Fucking hell, is that you, Mikey?"

Mike stiffened.

The man stopped. "I thought it was. Jesus Christ, it's been a while."

"You know this guy, Si?" growled Torch.

"Yeah, man. This is Mikey Manner. He used to live here. Block E, innit?"

Mike nodded in greeting. "Good to see you, Si."

"How's your bruv?"

Mike shrugged. "You know."

"Yeah, well send 'im my best, won't ya?" And he strode off across the car park.

Torch looked at Mike as if seeing him for the first time. Interest, mingled with a hefty dose of suspicion. Mike met his gaze head on.

Rob tapped his colleague on the shoulder. "Come on, let's go."

Mike bristled but followed Rob to the car. The whole gang watched them leave.

CHAPTER 5

"Where have you been?" demanded Superintendent Mayhew as soon as Rob walked into the squad room.

"Had something to check out." He walked past her to his desk. Mike followed, refusing to make eye contact. Mayhew was left standing in the middle of the room.

Rob wasn't the only one giving her the cold shoulder. None of his or Galbraith's team had said a word to her since the night the Chief's body had been found.

"Okay, I get it," she huffed. "You're all pissed at me for not taking the restaurant shooting case. I know he was your chief, I know you're loyal to him, but can't you see? You're all far too emotional."

"No other team on this planet is as motivated as we are to find out who did this," said Rob. There were several nods and murmurs of agreement.

Mayhew's gaze roamed over them, lingering on Rob. "You're still investigating, aren't you?"

No point in lying. "Yes, ma'am."

"A mutiny, that's what this is." She sighed. "Okay, I'll tell you what. I'll have a word with the Deputy Chief and see what I can do."

Immediately, everybody perked up.

"In the meantime, a body has been found in the river next to the London Eye. Rob, I want your team over there. This one is ours."

"What about the South London team? That's their jurisdiction." The last thing Rob felt like doing was diverting his attention to a new case when this one was still hot.

"They've got their hands full with this latest surge in knife crime. We're going to help them out. Come on, the clock is ticking. Southwark Police have cordoned off the area, but they're waiting for you before they move the body." She raised her eyebrows. "It's frightening the tourists."

God forbid.

"Rob — now, please. You need the breather."

"But, ma'am, you just said—"

"I said I'd see what I can do. Right now, you're wanted on the South Bank."

Will grabbed his jacket off the back of his chair. "I'm ready."

"Me too," said Jenny.

Rob sighed. None of them had slept a wink last night, and this was turning into a very long day. He locked eyes with Galbraith.

"We'll keep working on the recording," the Scot said under his breath.

"I'll dig up what I can on Torch," added Mike, his eyes glittering. "I want that fucker taken down."

Rob patted him on the shoulder. "Thanks, guys. See you later."

* * *

They blue-lighted it across town to the South Bank. As they approached, they could see the giant Ferris wheel arching into the sky, its glass bubbles shimmering in the weak afternoon sunshine. Was it really only four o'clock?

They parked in the Southbank Centre car park, off Belvedere Road, which was as close as they could get to where the body had been discovered. They had to fight their way through a rapidly growing throng of onlookers, most of whom had their phones out, filming.

"Christ, is a corpse really what they want to remember when they look at their holiday snaps?" muttered Rob. "Get rid of this crowd," he growled at a uniformed officer who'd cordoned off the section of the river path closest to the grisly discovery. "I want this entire walkway cleared."

The policeman spoke into his radio and soon more officers appeared and began moving the crowd even further back.

"Are Forensics on their way?" Rob asked.

"They're here, sir." A female police officer pointed to the stairs leading down to the embankment beside the Festival Pier. "You'd better suit up." She handed them disposable forensic suits complete with shoe covers and gloves.

They kitted up. The steps were slippery and covered with moss. They clutched the handrail as they descended, careful not to slide down and land in the mud. The tide was low, exposing several metres of riverbank, which was how the body had been spotted. It was tangled in some rope, entwined with seaweed and lodged in a section of the wall that jutted outwards.

"Liz, what have we got?"

The Home Office pathologist turned, her eyes sombre. When she saw it was him, she got to her feet. "Rob, what are you doing here? I was so sorry to hear about DCS Lawrence. What a terrible loss."

"Thanks." It was funny how everybody still called him the Chief Superintendent, or the Chief, even though he'd left the force almost a year ago. That was the calibre of the man. Unforgettable. "We'll get whoever shot him."

She squeezed his arm. "I know you will."

He gestured to the body lying face down on the rocky bank. It was a black male, slender build, below average height, but he couldn't tell more than that.

"He's young, Rob," she said. "A teenager. Sixteen, maybe seventeen at a push."

"Shit, really?" Rob frowned. "Do we have an ID?"

"Not yet. There's nothing on him, and we'll have to get him back to the lab before we run his fingerprints and DNA."

"Cause of death?" Drowning would be the most obvious, but he'd learned not to assume anything.

Liz separated the boy's hair, displaying a glistening red wound. "Shot in the head. Single bullet wound. The killer knew what he was doing. The poor kid didn't stand a chance."

Jenny grimaced. "How long ago?"

"About twenty-four hours, judging by the condition of the body, although in water, it's hard to tell." She nodded to her assistant. "Help me turn him over."

They gently rolled the body onto its back and Rob stared at his face. He *was* young. His skin was still smooth, with a smattering of fuzz along his jawline. He wore torn jeans and a T-shirt with some sort of garish logo on it.

"Are those bruises?" Rob pointed to his face. "Or is he just disfigured from the water?"

Liz bent over the body. "Right first time. It looks like he was beaten before he was shot." She grimaced. "Quite badly, too. There's a large contusion beneath his right eye, swelling and bruising on his left cheek, and he's got a split lip."

"What's that?" said Will.

"What's what?"

"There, on his wrist."

Liz made an irritated noise in her throat. "Hang on. I haven't got there yet." She inspected it. "It's a stamp, like the kind you get in a nightclub. I can't make out what it says. Most of it has come off."

She nodded to the crime scene photographer who'd been snapping away at the body in situ. He came in close and took several shots of the stamp.

"Let's have a closer look." Will moved forward, then shook his head. "It's not legible."

"I wonder where he went in." Jenny glanced upriver.

"That I can't tell you," Liz said. "It could be anywhere."

Rob thought back to the day before. "They dumped him after they shot him."

"Looks that way."

"That puts the time of death around four o'clock yesterday afternoon."

"Give or take a few hours. I can be more precise after the PM."

"Which is when?" asked Rob.

She stood up straight. "Possibly Monday, but more likely Tuesday. There's been a spate of knife crimes, and I've prioritised your chief tomorrow. Orders from the Police Commissioner herself."

"I'll be there," said Rob.

She nodded, accepting that as a given. "Get some sleep. You look awful."

He grunted. "Thanks. See you tomorrow."

Jenny looked a little shell-shocked as they walked back to the car. Rob couldn't blame her. It had been one hell of a day. "A young kid, beaten and shot, then thrown in the river." She glanced at him. "Who could do something like that?"

"There are a lot of sickos in the world," said Will.

She scoffed. "Why do you think I don't do online dating?"

"Let's wait for the post-mortem," Rob said. "We can't do much until we ID the body. Once we know who he is, we can look at who wanted to kill him."

"That stamp was interesting," remarked Will. "Pity we couldn't make it out."

"Yeah, that was strange. It might not have had anything to do with his death, though."

"It might be where he met the killer," Jenny said. "Perhaps he was into something dangerous. Drugs, dealing, something like that. Who knows? It could be any number of things."

"Let's go back to the office," Rob said, when they got to the car park. "The others may have found out who Ant is."

31

CHAPTER 6

"Anthony Price was a confidential informant," Galbraith told them as soon as they walked through the door.

Rob threw his jacket over his chair. "A CI? Whose?"

"Lawrence's, back in the day. More recently, his handler was DCI Morris Cranshaw, at Southwark CID."

Cranshaw, the name on the recording.

"The Chief never mentioned a CI," mused Rob.

"No, it was before your time," Galbraith said. "You know, now that I think about it, I do recall a junkie that the Super helped out. Got him into a programme. Helped him clean up his act. Perhaps it was this guy."

"Let's find out," said Rob. "That would explain how he knew him. If they go way back, he probably felt he could trust him with this. Whatever *this* was."

"'Something big'," quoted Jenny. "Not drugs."

Jeff looked up. "I'll get hold of Cranshaw and—"

"No, let's go and see him," cut in Rob, glancing at the neon-blue digital clock in the squad room. It was almost six. Bugger. He couldn't go now, he had to get back to Jo. "First thing tomorrow morning."

Galbraith raised an eyebrow. "That's not like you."

"I've got to get home," he said. "Jo's been alone with the baby since two o'clock this morning."

"Ah, yes. I forgot about the wee bairn. How's he doing?"

"Good. He eats a lot and doesn't sleep enough, but we can't complain."

Galbraith laughed. "Got a healthy pair of lungs, has he?"

"You have no idea, mate."

"Off you go, then. We all need some sleep. Let's pick this up tomorrow."

Rob got home and walked in the door, straight into Jo's arms. She hugged him hard. "I'm so, so sorry," she murmured. "Are you okay?"

He'd had time to process it now. It wasn't as raw as when he'd been at the crime scene. "Yeah, I will be." She took his hand led him into the living room.

"Where's Jack?" He looked around for the carrycot.

"Miraculously, he's fast asleep upstairs."

Rob stared at her. "How did you manage that?"

"I think he wore himself out. It probably won't last long, so if you want some sleep, now would be a good time."

"I'm exhausted," he admitted. "We had a hot lead and followed it to a housing estate in South London."

"You have a suspect?" Jo asked.

"A guy called Torch. Some local drug dealer on the estate."

Jo frowned. "Torch . . ."

"You've heard of him?" Jo's old job at the National Crime Agency meant she kept tabs on a lot of nefarious characters, drug dealers in particular.

"Yeah, the name rings a bell. I think we looked into him as part of our county lines operation two years ago."

"Was he involved?"

"No, not at that point. We suspected he might be supplying the local area, but we didn't have sufficient evidence of his connection to the wider network. Of course, that might have changed now, it has been a few years. These guys don't downscale. They either expand or get busted."

"Do you have any information on him?" Rob asked.

"I'll see what I can dig up."

"Thanks." He felt himself sagging.

"Have you eaten?" Jo asked.

He shook his head. Countless cups of coffee were all that had sustained him during the day. Now he felt ragged and a little shaky.

"Your neighbour brought round a casserole," she said with a smile. "She's a sweet old dear. It's pretty good too. Let me get you a plate, then you can collapse."

"I'm too tired to eat." He sat down on the couch and patted the seat beside him. Jo curled up next to him. He put an arm around her and sighed. "This was what I needed. How come you always make everything okay?"

She snuggled into him. "I was going to ask you the same question."

Rob put his feet up on the coffee table and they stayed like that until he began to drop off. "I'd better go to bed," he murmured. "I can't keep my eyes open."

"Come on, then." They turned off the lights and went upstairs. Trigger snorted as they left the room but didn't get up. The house was quiet. They checked on Jack, smiling as they gazed down at his angelic, sleeping face.

Rob squeezed Jo's hand. After the day he'd had, he was grateful he could come home to this. His little family. As he fell into bed, Jo beside him, he felt like the luckiest man alive. This was exactly what he needed to rejuvenate his spirits and mend his soul.

* * *

The warm, safe feeling he'd had at home disappeared the moment Rob walked through the glass doors into the squad room. Even though it was Sunday and the office was deserted, the tension was there, hanging over him like a sword about to drop.

Jack had almost made it through the night, waking at four thirty for a feed. Since he'd also slept well, Rob had got up and given him a bottle, put him back in his cot, made some toast, then showered and got dressed, careful not to wake Jo.

By seven o'clock he was in the office. When they were on a case, particularly in the first twenty-four hours, the days tended to blur into one another, and weekends ceased to exist. Today was no exception.

Will, who was also an early riser, walked in half an hour later, laptop bag over his shoulder. He never went anywhere without it. "Did some research on Anthony Price last night," he said. "Guy's got quite a history."

"Let's hear it." Rob, who was writing reports on yesterday's activities and filing them on the system, reached for his coffee mug, but it was empty. He couldn't even remember drinking it.

Will sat down and opened his laptop. It booted up almost immediately. "Back in 2009, when the Chief was still a DCI, he ran a joint op with the vice squad, as it was known back then. It was a contract killing. An investment banker jumped to his death from his four-storey townhouse in Mayfair. In addition to the obvious internal injuries, the post-mortem revealed blunt force trauma to the head inflicted prior to his leap, which suggested foul play. Lawrence opened a murder inquiry."

"What has this got to do with Price?"

"Anthony Price was the small-time drug dealer who sold him the coke that he was high on at the time."

"Ah, I see." Rob sat back in his chair.

"He was arrested and was looking at a manslaughter charge on top of the drug charges, so he gave up his supplier. In return, he got relocated to the estate in Southwark. For some reason, the Chief took a liking to this kid. According to the notes attached to the file, Lawrence took him to a cheap hotel, got him clean, then put him into a rehab programme.

The kid stayed off the gear, got a job as a brickie and was placed in social housing on the Beaufort Estate."

"Where he continued to report back to the Chief."

"Yeah." Will consulted his screen. "Their relationship continued until Lawrence was promoted to superintendent, after which Price was handed over to Southwark CID. Cranshaw took over as his handler."

"We need to talk to him," Rob said.

"Talk to who?" asked Jenny, who'd just arrived. She was wearing casual clothes, jeans and a floppy jumper, and her hair was up in a messy bun.

"DCI Morris Cranshaw," said Will.

She gave a small nod. "The informant's handler, right?"

"Yep. Will, check to see if he's working today. If not, get his home address."

Will immediately got on the phone. Galbraith's team arrived, with the big Scot striding in first, followed by a beefed-up Mike, who looked like he'd just come from the gym, and Jeff, whose hair was still mussed up from sleeping. Even Celeste, who really didn't have to be there, rushed in flushed and out of breath. "I want to help."

It was a relief not to have to look over their shoulder for Mayhew all the time.

"Thanks for coming in," said Rob. "It means a lot."

They all nodded. "We want to get justice for the Chief as much as you do," said Galbraith. Rob had forgotten that he'd known Sam for longer than all of them.

"Will and I are going to speak to DCI Cranshaw this morning. He might be able to shed some light on what Anthony Price discovered."

"We'll keep looking into Torch and his background," said Galbraith.

"I thought I'd go and talk to Si. Get the low-down on Torch and what's going on at the estate." Mike had a determined scowl on his face.

"Is that safe?" Rob hadn't liked the look on Torch's face when they'd left.

"I know where his mother lives," said Mike with the faintest hint of a grin. "He always goes there for Sunday lunch. I checked, she's still alive and living in the same place."

"Okay, fine. But don't put yourself in unnecessary danger."

"I won't." He squared his shoulders. The young detective constable still seemed to be seething with animosity towards Torch. "That scumbag needs to be put away. It's men like him who lead the kids in those estates down the wrong path."

Like your brother, Rob thought.

* * *

DCI Morris Cranshaw lived in a two-bedroomed mews cottage in Vauxhall. All around him high-rises were going up, the skyline rammed with cranes, scaffolding and half-finished buildings, but somehow, his little street remained untouched by the recent surge in development.

A young girl in a dressing gown opened the front door. Behind her, a stocky figure loomed. "Greta, what have I told you about opening the door?"

She gave a toothy grin, then skipped off down the passage. The man shook his head. "Can I help you?"

"DCI Cranshaw?" Rob held up his warrant card.

"Yes?" The detective frowned.

"DCI Miller and DS Freemont from Putney Major Investigation Team. We'd like to ask you a few questions about an informant of yours, Anthony Price."

Cranshaw's shoulders slumped. "Sad business, that." He opened the door wider. "Come in. We can talk in the kitchen."

"Ant was one of the rare success stories," he said as they walked, then gestured for them to take a seat around the breakfast nook. Rob squeezed in, tucking his long legs under the bench. Will, who wasn't quite as tall, slid in beside him.

"Yes, I believe DCS Lawrence recruited him back in 2009."

"Yeah, got him off the gear, cleaned him up. The kid was bright, got a job, made a fresh start. When I took over, he was well into his stride. Easiest snitch I've ever worked with."

"What exactly did he do for you?" enquired Rob.

"Nothing too hectic," said Cranshaw. "Fed us information on what was going down at the estate. Who the main players were. Who the gang members were. Any big deals going down."

"How did he know all this?" asked Will.

"He'd been living there since he ratted on his previous supplier, a ruthless bastard whose name escapes me right now."

"Was he close to Torch and his gang?"

Cranshaw frowned. "How'd you know about him?"

"We're looking at him for the shooting."

The detective arched an eyebrow. "Yeah? We wanted in on that, but orders from above were that Central were taking it on. Where do you guys fit in?"

"The Chief Superintendent was our old boss." Rob's voice was firm. "We're going to be investigating the shooting."

Cranshaw pursed his lips. "If you say so. Ant was my CI, but I don't think the shooting had anything to do with Torch's gang."

"What makes you say that?" asked Will. "The CI was meeting with a retired police officer of high rank. Surely that would imply it had something to do with his death?"

"Torch has cleaned up his act recently." Cranshaw shrugged. "He's part of this community drive to uplift the estate, get the kids into development programmes — football clubs, art clubs, stuff like that. It's an initiative implemented by the new mayor, Raza Ashraf."

Rob gave him a look that said he didn't believe a word of it. Guys like Torch didn't just change.

"Seriously, Torch has been doing some good work. The kids look up to him, he's the closest thing they have to a role model in that community. The perfect person to implement change."

"If it's for real," said Will.

Cranshaw gave a stiff nod. "Ant seemed to think it was. There's even a tutoring programme to help the kids with their schoolwork. It's run by a group of teachers every Sunday. They'll be there now. You should check it out." He checked his watch. "Nine till two, at the community centre."

Rob glanced at Will, who nodded. They may as well go and see Ashraf's new initiative in action. Raza Ashraf had been a prime suspect in a recent investigation, but due to a hastily implemented press injunction, it hadn't damaged his reputation, or his political ambitions. The guy had a murky past, but Rob was glad to see some good had come out of his mayoral election.

"Is Torch still dealing?" asked Will.

"As far as I know. Ant said Torch wanted to put all that behind him, start a legitimate business, but he hasn't got there yet. There's still a shitload of coke being sold in that place, along with weed and occasionally H, but that's the drug squad's remit. We pass on what we know, but our main concern is crime on the estate and in the nearby area. If anything goes down, we're usually the first on the scene."

Rob got it. Knife crime was out of control. The kids were armed, it was easy as hell to get weapons, and young lives were being lost every day. Policing them wasn't an easy job.

"Why do you think he went to Lawrence with this, and not to you?" asked Rob.

Cranshaw shrugged. "He knew the Chief well. They went way back."

"Yeah, but the Chief had retired. If Ant had something to report, it would have made more sense to bring it to you, as his handler."

Cranshaw put his hands flat on the table. "The truth is, we have limited powers at CID. Ant knew that. We investigate street crime, burglaries, stabbings. If someone dies, the murder squad takes over. Lawrence would have had more sway."

That made sense.

"Could you send us any files you have on Anthony Price?"

"I'd have to check with my boss. That's classified information."

"Fine." Rob's tone left no doubt that he would get those files, one way or another.

"Anything else you can tell us about Torch? Real name Shamar Williams, right?" Will was making notes on his phone.

Cranshaw nodded. "That's the name we've got on record for him. He appeared on the scene a couple of years ago."

"Why's he called Torch?" asked Rob.

"The information I have is that he grew up in the foster system, jumped around from place to place, couldn't settle. Then one day, the house he was staying in caught alight and burned to the ground."

"Was he hurt?" asked Rob.

"No, he managed to get out in time." Cranshaw glanced up at them. "Fire investigators determined he started the blaze."

CHAPTER 7

Rob and Will stared at him.

"Arson?" asked Rob.

"Yep. His foster parents died in the fire. Shamar was taken into custody and put in a detention centre. He was fourteen at the time."

"Christ," muttered Rob.

"There was talk of abuse, but nothing came of it. Shamar did his time, then was released. When he turned eighteen, he was allocated a council flat on an estate in Barking. That's where he made his Albanian drug contacts. There's talk of him running with a gang called the Hellbanianz."

"I've heard of them," said Rob.

"Aren't they the ones who posted those music videos featuring guns, money and Ferraris all over social media to recruit youngsters?" said Will.

"Yeah, that's them. They're street dealers and enforcers for the Mafia Shqiptare, the Albanian mafia. According to my sources, they've tied up the cocaine trade in the city."

"Shit, so Torch is playing with the big boys."

"Yep. That's who he gets his drugs from. He has his own network of dealers on the estate, and we suspect beyond. The National Crime Agency is watching him. At some point, they'll raid the place and bring him in, but they'll be lucky if they can pin anything on him. Now with his community-serving reputation, it'll be even harder."

"Smart guy," muttered Rob. "He knows what he's doing."

Cranshaw nodded. "So it would seem. Sorry I can't be of more use."

"You've been extremely helpful." Rob elbowed Will to get out of the breakfast nook before his legs went into spasm. They stood up.

"I hope you catch whoever did this," Cranshaw said, as he walked them to the door. "Ant was a good guy, as was your chief. Neither of them deserved to die this way."

"Nor did the restaurant manager," added Rob. "He was an innocent bystander in all of this." *And the first to die.*

"Let me know if I can do anything else," the Southwark detective said.

"Will do."

* * *

The Beaufort Estate seemed like a completely different place from the day before. Maybe it was the sunshine, or the fact that the centre quad was filled with people. Kids were playing in the square, their laughter echoing off the surrounding tower blocks. Mothers with prams chatted outside the community centre, while teenagers strolled in and out, bags slung over their shoulders.

Rob glanced at Will. "Shall we go inside?"

"Yeah. It doesn't look that bad."

Rob didn't reply.

They walked into the squat, prefab-like community centre. It had a row of windows along the front and a bright red door. There was an entrance hall, about the size of a living room, with a front desk and a middle-aged woman with her hair in dozens of tiny braids sitting behind it.

"Can I help you?"

"Yes, we're looking for Torch. Is he here?"

"What do you want with him?"

Rob flashed his warrant card. Her jaw tightened. "I ain't seen him today."

Yeah, right.

"Don't worry, we'll just have a little look around."

She was about to jump up when Rob held up his hand. "Don't trouble yourself, ma'am. We won't be long."

They walked down a wide corridor and into a spacious studio. Tables and chairs were lined up in rows with a handful of kids hunched over books. There was a whiteboard at the front with an equation on it. A tall, lanky man with locs walked around, supervising the kids. The volunteer tutor, no doubt.

"Not busy today?" remarked Rob, as he looked up.

"Some days are better than others," he said, with a Jamaican accent. "But when the sun's shining, it's hard to get them in here."

"Still, at least you're helping these ones." Will nodded to the three girls and two boys who were studiously writing in their notebooks.

"They're regulars," he said proudly. "They want to learn."

"Torch here today?" asked Rob.

The eyes darkened. "I've not seen him."

Was he afraid of him? Maybe things were more peaceful when Torch wasn't around. Rob wouldn't be surprised.

"Okay, thanks. Keep up the good work."

The tutor nodded and watched as they left the classroom.

* * *

Mike pulled up outside a pharmacy in Southwark, a short bus ride away from the Beaufort Estate. Mrs Greaves, Simon's mother, lived in the flat above it.

Mike swallowed. It had been a while since he'd spoken to Si and longer since he'd talked to his mother. He remembered her as a savvy, no-nonsense type of woman. A strict mother, instilling a sense of discipline in her boys. Si was the youngest of two, but Mike didn't have much of a memory of his older brother.

Si had always been Idi's friend, but when Idi had got involved with the gang, they'd lost touch. Mike suspected it was Mrs Greaves's influence. She'd probably told her son not to have anything to do with Idi — and rightly so.

Si had a father who lived across town, as he recalled, and Si's mother's solution to keeping her son alive and out of jail was to send him off to his father every weekend.

It must have worked because Si was a construction worker or a handyman now. His van was parked two cars down from Mike's with a ladder attached to the roof. That was the best you could hope for growing up on a South London estate.

He took a deep breath and pressed the buzzer. The entrance was on street level, beside the pharmacy. A masculine voice sounded over the intercom. "Yeah?"

"Si? It's Mike. Mike Manner."

A pause.

"Jesus, Mike. What are you doing here?"

"I want to speak to you. Can I come in?"

"I'm having lunch with me mum."

"I know."

Another pause, longer this time. Then a sigh. "Yeah, okay."

The door clicked open, and Mike pushed it. A damp smell assailed his senses, and he crinkled his nose. An automatic hall light went on as he stepped over the threshold. He glanced down at the dirty carpet and then up at the short flight of stairs ahead. There was nowhere else to go.

He climbed the stairs and knocked on the door. It was opened almost immediately.

"Fuckin' hell, mate. This is a surprise."

"I know. I'm sorry to barge in like this."

"Nah, come on in. Mum will be glad to see you."

Mike wasn't sure about that.

He walked into the living room. Simon's mother had aged. Instead of the dark-haired, straight-backed woman he remembered, she was now bent over and grey. Except she still had those sharp eyes.

"Good afternoon, Mrs Greaves."

"You're Idi Manner's younger brother, the policeman," she said, standing up.

He embraced her. "That's right. How are you, Mrs Greaves?"

She shrugged. "Oh, you know. Old age is never kind to anyone."

"This is Mike, Mum." Si gestured for him to sit down.

"Actually, Si, I was wondering if we could have a word in private?"

"Won't you join us for lunch, Mike? How is your dear mother?"

Mike hesitated. He didn't want to be rude, but he needed to get back to the office.

"She passed away several years ago, ma'am."

"I'm so sorry to hear that. She was a good woman."

"Yes, she was."

"Sit down," said Si, taking his seat.

Mike sighed internally. It was clear he wasn't going to get that private moment until he'd engaged in some small talk.

"Are you hungry?" Mrs Greaves asked. "You must be. Si, fetch Mike a plate."

"Oh, no. I'm fine, really."

"Nonsense," she sniffed. "A big lad like you has to eat. When did you last have a family roast?"

Actually, he couldn't remember. Reluctantly, he sat. Si came back with a plate and his mum dished up some roast beef and vegetables, then plonked a Yorkshire pudding next to them. Everything was cooked to perfection. He remembered she always had been a good cook.

Despite himself, he tucked in.

Mrs Greaves smiled knowingly. "How's that older brother of yours?"

Si cut in. "He's still in prison, Mum. Remember?"

"Still? But that was years ago."

"He got arrested again, ma'am." Mike swallowed over a potato. He hated talking about Idi. "He's still got a few years to go."

"Poor thing," she mumbled. "He was always so charming. It was heartbreaking seeing him go off the rails like that."

Not half as heartbreaking as for his family.

"Mum, I'm sure Mike doesn't want to talk about that."

He'd got that right.

"Yes, yes. Of course. I'm sorry, Mike. I just have fond memories of Idi and Si playing at my house. You know, when they were little. You boys were inseparable."

Si looked down at his plate.

"You've done well for yourself." Mike changed the subject. "I saw your van outside."

"Yeah, I do odd jobs for people in the neighbourhood. A bit of carpentry, some painting. It pays the bills."

His mother puffed out her chest. "Yes, he's his own boss now. Beholden to no one."

An accomplishment by anyone's standards. "That's great."

"But so have you. You're a policeman now." She looked him up and down as if surprised to find he wasn't in uniform.

"I'm a detective," he corrected. They didn't need to know for whom. "And it's Sunday, so I'm off duty." A small lie. He was working, but they weren't to know.

They chatted about the old times and his parents for a while, and then he stood up. "I'm sorry to be rude, but I really must go. It was lovely seeing you again, Mrs Greaves."

"Likewise, Mike. Stop by anytime you need a good meal." She chuckled. "You know where I am."

"I will do, ma'am."

Simon walked him to the door. "Sorry about that. She does like to talk."

"That's okay. Listen, I wanted to chat to you about Torch and his crew. Do you have a minute?"

"Sure, I'll come down with you. I wouldn't mind a smoke. I'm trying to quit, but . . . you know . . ." He shrugged.

They went outside. "Torch runs things on the estate," Si said, between puffs. "He's the main man around there. You want drugs, he can get them for you. Anything that goes down on that estate, Torch is involved."

That's what he figured.

"How dangerous is he?" he asked.

"Why?" Si frowned. "You're not thinking of taking him on, are you?"

"No, but we're looking at him for a homicide. Do you think he's capable of something like that?"

Si's eyes widened. "Murder? Shit. I don't know. Maybe."

"You haven't heard anything? Any rumours?"

"Nah, brother. I keep to myself. I don't mix with that lot. And I live in Block A, which is the furthest from theirs."

"Your mother's old pad?"

"Yeah, they passed it on to me. Keep it in the family, so to speak."

"Nice one."

He shrugged. "The place has gone to the dogs, to be honest with you. I'm thinking about moving on. It's just so handy not having to worry about rent, you know?"

"Yeah, I know."

It was a common problem. Why move out when you got free housing? Never mind the location.

"What can you tell me about his crew?"

"Not much. His girlfriend, Chantelle, is decent. She also took over her mother's place. She's dead now. Diabetes, I believe."

Mike recalled the sexy young woman in the short skirt who'd vouched for Torch the night of the murder.

I was with him all night.

That knowing smile. The sniggers from the group.

"What's she doing with a thug like that?"

"He's the boss. The dude. He's the one with the power. I guess that's attractive to some women." He gave a little shrug. "Personally, I think she can do much better."

Mike got the impression Si was a little infatuated with Torch's girlfriend. "What about the others?"

"Well, he has two guys he's always with. Ali and Shane. They're dangerous motherfuckers. Ali's psycho. I once saw him beat a kid to a pulp in the Underground because he disrespected him." He shook his head.

"Anyone else?"

"There's Declan. He's not the sharpest knife in the drawer, but he's got a good heart. Looks after his mum. She's got emphysema."

"Part of Torch's crew?"

"Yeah, they've been friends for years. Ever since Torch first arrived on the estate."

Mike shook Si's hand. "Thanks, mate. It was good speaking to you. And your mum."

"Be lucky." Si waved him off and closed the door.

Mike went back to the car and wrote everything down before he forgot it. At least they had some background info on the gang. It would help to put things in context.

* * *

Once back at the station, Rob told the rest of the team what they'd discovered about Ant Price and Torch, aka Shamar Williams.

"Did DCI Cranshaw send through any files?" asked Rob.

"Yep." Jenny nodded. "They came through a short while ago. I printed out a copy and put it on your desk."

He gave her a thumbs up. She knew he preferred a hard copy to take home and mull over rather than a digital version. He still hadn't got used to working on an iPad or a laptop.

"You want to give me the gist?"

"It's a tragic tale," she said.

Like so many were.

"Torch repeatedly complained to his social worker about his foster parents," Jenny explained. "But she didn't take him seriously. The couple were as clean as a whistle, attended the local church, and were respected members of the community. They said Shamar was making it up. 'Attention-seeking' was the phrase used."

"He ran away twice," Jeff added. "Only to be picked up and taken back again."

"There was no escape," Rob muttered.

Jenny nodded sadly. "Fire experts found he'd started the blaze during the night by stuffing paper into the toaster. His school homework book, no less."

"Bloody hell."

"He waited until the fire had spread before climbing out of the window and legging it. He was picked up at a friend's house early the next morning."

Rob let out a low whistle.

"It gets worse," Jeff said. "The bedroom door where the foster parents slept was locked. The key was never found, so Forensics couldn't determine whether it was locked from the inside or the outside."

Rob stared at them. "You mean Torch may have locked them in to burn?"

"It's a theory." Jenny leaned back in her chair, arms folded across her chest.

That it was. The young Shamar must have really hated his foster parents if he'd done that. Still, there was no proof. Innocent until proven guilty and all that.

Galbraith's phone rang and he excused himself to take it. When he came back, he said, "They've IDed the teenager found on the South Bank. He goes by the name of Benny. He's an unaccompanied asylum-seeking child, or UASC, to use the official term. They don't know his real name."

"A refugee?" Rob frowned. "How'd they get an ID?"

"He was processed at an asylum intake centre in Kent last month, then transferred to London for placement with a foster family. He was living in a children's home for displaced kids."

"And they didn't realise he was missing?" Jenny raised an eyebrow.

"They did, and they contacted the authorities, but without his real name . . ." Galbraith shrugged.

"Where's he from?" asked Rob.

"Eritrea," said Galbraith.

"He came here all by himself?" Celeste bit her lip. "That's quite a journey for a teenager, isn't it?"

"Where is Eritrea anyway?" asked Mike. "I'm guessing Africa, but I don't have a clue whereabouts."

"Yeah, it's between Sudan and Ethiopia," supplied Will, who had an IQ over 150. Rob only knew that because Will had told him once when he'd gotten very drunk, after being duped by a journalist who had seduced him to pump him for information on a case. "Current hotspot, I believe."

"So this kid is about to be housed, when he runs away, gets beaten up, shot in the head and then his body is dumped in the Thames?" Rob looked up. "What the hell was he into?"

"Maybe someone was taking advantage of him?" suggested Jenny. "He probably didn't speak English. When he realised what was happening, he ran, but they got him." She winced at the thought.

"The children's home should have been looking out for him," said Jeff. "They had a duty of care."

"Well, something went wrong," said Rob. "First thing tomorrow, we'll pay the children's home a visit" Rob picked up the folder and stuffed it into his rucksack. "Right now, I'm heading over to the mortuary for the PM on the Chief." The mood instantly darkened, as if a light had gone out. "Why don't we all go home and regroup tomorrow?"

"Good work today, guys," called Galbraith, before turning to Rob. "A word, mate?"

"What's up?" Rob walked with him to the windows that overlooked Putney high street. The traffic wasn't as frantic as on a weekday, but cars and buses whizzed past regardless.

"Perhaps we should think about splitting up the cases," he said. "I feel like we're all trying to do everything, which is perhaps not the most effective way forward."

"Yeah, you're right," agreed Rob. They needed to assign tasks properly. Luckily the team was well versed in working together and automatically splitting the tasks among them. "Although, until we're officially given the Chief's case, we're only supposed to be investigating the river death. The Clapham shooting is still with Central."

"What about the phone?" Galbraith lowered his voice. "We can't put it into evidence because it won't match with the crime scene photos, nor will it be on the official evidence list."

"No." Rob could see his colleague was worried about that. "We have to keep it out. It's not a big deal. We don't need it to prove causality. We would have identified the Chief's CI without it, his fingerprints were on the system. From there, it's not a great leap to Torch, the man Ant Price was told to watch by his own handler."

Galbraith tugged at his beard. "We'll be bloody lucky to get away with this, Rob."

"I know." He patted the burly Scot on the shoulder. "If there's any comeback, we'll say the phone was logged as property as opposed to evidence."

"They won't buy that once they hear what's on it."

Rob met his gaze. "Then let's hope they never find out."

CHAPTER 8

Rob didn't want to be at the post-mortem. He would rather be anywhere but here, looking down on his friend and mentor's body. Yet he had to. If Sam were his guvnor right now, he would expect no less.

Leave no stone unturned, Rob, he would say. *Find out who did this to me, and subject them to the full wrath of the law.*

So that's what he would do. For the Chief.

Liz Kramer glanced up. She was ready. Both she and her assistant were wearing fresh scrubs, gloves and masks. He nodded from the viewing gallery.

"The victim is retired Chief Superintendent Sam Lawrence, age sixty-one years old. There is evidence of a gunshot wound to the left shoulder and another to the head."

Rob listened as Liz went on to describe the wounds in more detail, gave diameters and made assumptions based on the nature of the wounds.

"There is no gunshot residue on the body, which means the shooter was at least ten feet away when he pulled the trigger."

That made sense. If the intruder shot Zhou first, then turned the gun on Ant Price and then Sam, he needn't have come any further into the room. A visual of Sam lying in a pool of blood flashed before his eyes, and he took a sharp breath.

"It was the gunshot wound to the head that killed him," Liz was saying, leaning over the body. "Death would have been instantaneous."

Thank God for that. He hadn't suffered. Much.

He would have got a good look at his killer, however. Pity he hadn't said anything on the recording that could identify him or at least give them a clue.

"Who shot you, Sam?" he whispered.

"I've retrieved both bullets." Liz looked up at Rob. "I'll send them to Ballistics. They might be able to tell you which gun they came from."

He gave her a thumbs up. He didn't hold out much hope. A professional wouldn't have used a gun with a history. Certainly not one the police could pick up on.

"The time of death—" she referred to her notes — "was a little after one thirty a.m."

If Rob had needed proof that Liz was great at her job, that was it. She didn't know, but that was almost the exact time on the recording when the sixth gunshot was heard.

"Right, I'm going to open him up," she announced a few moments later.

He depressed the audio button so she could hear him speak. "Thanks, Liz. I'll leave you to it. If you find any anomalies, let me know."

She looked up and nodded. "Will do."

Rob exhaled as he left the gallery. He couldn't wait to get outside and away from the stench of death and loss.

* * *

The children's home was a run-down, dirty Edwardian monstrosity. With its heavy windows, faded mock-Tudor cladding and missing tiles over the front porch, it looked as tired and broken as its inhabitants.

The paved pathway leading up to the peeling front door glistened in the weak autumn sun, thanks to the rain that had fallen overnight, and dead leaves fluttered in the unkempt garden on either side.

Will shivered. "It's not the most welcoming place, is it?"

Rob knew what he meant. He also got the feeling something had happened here, and not good.

They went inside. The hallway was dimly lit, with a reception nook on the one side, behind which sat a young woman, probably in her early twenties, with pale skin highlighted by a slash of red lipstick.

She looked up as they walked in. "Can I help you?" The way she pronounced "help" made Rob think she was Russian.

There was a glass panel between her and the entrance hall, with a gap underneath it like a teller at the bank or post office. The only entrance into the cubicle was via a side door that was closed and probably locked.

Protection? From whom? Visitors or residents?

Rob and Will held up their IDs. "We'd like to speak to someone about a missing boy, Benny. His body was found in the river on Friday night."

Her forehead furrowed. "One minute. I get the manager."

She picked up her phone and thumbs whirring, shot off a text message. Then she got up from her desk and emerged from the cubicle. "You wait in the lounge. This way, please."

"Thank you."

Rob and Will followed her into a communal living room with sofas, chairs, a pool table and a tea and coffee station on the side. "You want something to drink?"

Rob glanced at the coffee flask and shook his head. "No, we're good."

The furnishings were old and threadbare, but it was warm and cosy. Not altogether unpleasant. Even though it was empty, there was the faint stench of body odour in the air like too many unwashed bodies in the same place.

The receptionist returned to her station, and they sat down to wait.

Five minutes later, a middle-aged woman with sparkling eyes and a ready smile walked into the room. "Hello, sorry to have kept you. I'm Margaret Pavić. I run the hostel with my husband, Bruno."

They got to their feet and shook hands.

"DCI Miller and DS Freemont," said Rob. "We'd like to speak to you about Benny."

Her expression changed. "Yes, we were sorry to hear what happened to him. He was a lovely boy. Damaged, of course, like all of them, but still managed to smile. Please, sit down."

They sank back into the overly soft sofa. Margaret sat on the chair opposite.

"What do you mean by 'damaged'?" asked Will.

She shrugged. "Traumatised. Anxious. Uncertain. Some of them act out."

"Did Benny?"

"No, he seemed relieved to be here. You must understand that all the children are damaged to some extent. They've travelled long distances to get here, they're missing their parents, they're displaced, and we try to help them acclimatise. It doesn't always work. Some children don't want our help. They feel they're better off on their own."

"Did Benny run away?" asked Rob.

She bit her lip. "That's what I can't understand. He seemed happy. Well, as happy as a child in his situation could be. But then, who knows what's really going on in their heads? We do what we can, but this isn't a prison."

"When did you first notice he was missing?" Rob studied her, trying to get a read. She was warm and motherly, but he sensed a toughness underneath the skin. He supposed she had to be, dealing with a bunch of traumatised and displaced children. It couldn't be an easy job.

"It was Friday evening, when we did our final roll call. We check on all the children before they go to bed. He wasn't in his room."

"No one saw him leave?"

"No." She shook her head sadly.

"Why didn't you report it?" he asked.

"It's a fairly common occurrence. We can only do so much. If they really want to leave, they'll find a way. Sometimes they come back, other times they end up on the street or simply disappear." Her eyes clouded. "It's tragic, but there's nothing we can do."

It was tragic. They'd travelled so far, risked so much to get here, and finally, when they were safe, they took off, putting themselves at risk all over again.

Was that what had happened to Benny? Had he tried to make it on his own, got into trouble, got beaten up and shot? Maybe he'd stolen something? That was the most likely scenario.

A shooting. An accidental death. A rushed attempt at hiding the body.

He scratched his head. Would they ever find out what had happened?

CHAPTER 9

"What made you get into this line of work?" Rob asked Margaret.

She gave a knowing smile. "You're thinking how difficult it must be caring for all these damaged children."

He nodded.

"I was like them once," she said softly. A faint blush crept into her cheeks. "I lost my parents very young. They died in a car crash."

"I'm sorry," murmured Rob.

She pursed her lips. "I was one of the lucky ones. I was fostered by two kind and generous people. I went to a decent school, on to college, and finally graduated with a degree in social work. It's been my life's ambition to help others like me."

"That's a very noble ambition." He couldn't do it. It took a certain type of person. Emotionally strong, dedicated, passionate. Margaret seemed to be all those things.

"Do you work with the children?" asked Will.

"Not in an official capacity, but I use my skills every day with this bunch."

"I can imagine." Rob thought for a moment. "You don't know Benny's real name, do you? Or what caused him to emigrate?"

"No, unfortunately not. He arrived like most of them do — in a bedraggled state, exhausted and dehydrated. The unaccompanied asylum seekers are processed at the intake centre in Kent or Croydon and then brought here. We have several volunteers who help us clean them up, give them fresh clothes, prepare meals and make sure they're not ill. We even have a GP who comes in twice a week to check on them."

"Where is everyone now?" Rob looked around. The place was deserted. He hadn't heard so much as a whisper.

"They're at breakfast next door. We own both properties. This one is primarily for housing and recreation, while next door is the dining room and kitchen, the TV room, where most of them hang out, and the library, which is really just a room stacked with donated children's books. Most of them have never read a book in their life, so it holds a great deal of fascination."

"Do you have volunteers monitoring them?"

"Oh yes, there's always someone on duty. The children are never left alone."

"How did Benny get on with the other kids?" asked Rob. "Did he have any altercations with them? Or with the volunteers?"

"No, not really. He was close to one of the other boys, younger than him. I think they came over together, although we can't be sure. Immigration tries to identify them, if possible, although many of them can't speak English and don't give the interpreters their real names."

Will scribbled a note. "Do you have a contact at the processing centre?" he asked. "Someone we can talk to about Benny?"

She reached into her pocket and pulled out a card. "I knew you'd ask. This is the person we deal with."

Will pocketed the card. They'd get on to them as soon as they got back.

"How long was Benny here for, before he ran away?" Rob asked.

"Two weeks or thereabouts. I can check my records."

"That would be great."

She left them sitting alone in the lounge. Two teenagers walked in, talking in a foreign language. They checked out Rob and Will with suspicious eyes, then carried on with what they were doing. One made coffee while the other set up the pool table. Rob watched them interact. Tentative friends, thrown together due to circumstance and bonded by misery and fear. Or perhaps survival. You'd need friends in a place like this. Someone who had your back.

Margaret returned. She smiled and said something to the boys, then returned to her seat. "Benny arrived a week and a half ago with one other boy. They'd asked to be placed together. We had a few vacancies, so we took them both in. Normally, it's one in, one out."

Like a human production line. A business. He was aware that Margaret and her husband were getting hefty allowances from the government for fostering so many children.

"How many do you have here?" he asked.

"Ten is our limit," she said. "We still want to make them feel like they're in a home."

He got that. More than ten would be mayhem. You'd lose that family feel.

"How long have you been doing this?" asked Will.

"Over ten years now." She gave a proud smile. "We started with just one house, then when next door became available, we bought it and knocked through. Bruno, my husband, did most of the work himself. He used to be a builder back in Croatia."

"Have you been married long?" asked Will.

"Nearly fifteen years in December. I met him shortly after he arrived in this country. He needed a fresh start." She shook her head. "He didn't have a very happy childhood. We had that in common. I think it's what brought us together."

"I'm sorry to hear that," murmured Will.

Rob got to his feet. "Thanks for your time, Mrs Pavić. Would you mind if we spoke to some of your volunteers? It would be useful to get their perspective." The teenagers had started their game now and pool balls ricocheted off the green baize, clashing into one another.

"Of course, I'll take you through."

Margaret introduced them to a striking woman in a demure headscarf. Nurse Nima wore a pale pink tunic over her clothes with a district nurse badge on her pocket. There was a gentleness about her that Rob liked. He felt it in her handshake and in her smile.

"Pleased to meet you," she said.

Margaret nodded at them. "I'll leave you to it. You can show yourselves out when you're done."

"Thanks, Mrs Pavić," called Rob, as she left the room.

"Do you assess all the children?" enquired Will. They were in a study that had been converted into a makeshift clinic. There was a desk with a computer, but also a fold-up bed separated from the rest of the room by a curtain.

"I try my best. They're often very poorly when they first get here and need monitoring."

Rob nodded. "Did you treat a boy called Benny?"

"Benny, yes. I remember him." Her face fell. "He was a lovely boy. Bright and funny, which is remarkable considering all he'd been through."

Rob nodded. That's what Margaret had told them. "Was he difficult?" he said. "You know, damaged or unhappy?"

"Benny? No. He was dehydrated and undernourished, like most of them, but he had a good heart. He made the others laugh. I'm not sure how, but God knows they need it around here."

"Were you surprised to hear he'd run away?" said Will.

She frowned. "I didn't know he had."

"Apparently he ran away on Thursday. We found his body in the Thames late Friday night."

She closed her eyes for a long moment, her brow furrowed. "That's awful. I heard he'd died, but I didn't know how."

"When did you last see him?" asked Rob.

She thought for a moment. "I'm here every Monday and Wednesday, so it would have been last Wednesday."

"How was he then? Did he seem his usual self?"

"Yes, I think so. Although it was only the second time I'd seen him. He hadn't been here that long." She hesitated. "You might want to speak to Adam. They were friends."

"Adam? Okay, thanks. Where would we find him?"

"I'm not sure. You'd have to ask one of the social workers."

"Right." They finished up the interview then spoke to a man who was sitting at a desk in the library, reading the newspaper.

"Do you know where we can find Adam?" asked Rob.

The social worker pointed to a teenager sitting by himself in front of a rack of children's books. He was thumbing through one, glancing at the pictures, but not reading any of the words.

"Hi," said Rob, bending down.

The teenager glanced up at him.

"I'm Rob, and this is Will." Will waved but kept his distance. They didn't want to overwhelm the boy. "Do you know Benny?"

The teen's eyes flickered at the name, but he didn't respond. Rob glanced at the social worker. "Can he understand me?"

"Not really," he said. "He might recognise the name, but that's all."

"Is there anyone around who can translate?" asked Rob.

"No. Sorry, mate."

"What about the other kids?"

"No one speaks his language," he said. "That's why he's sitting here by himself. Benny was the only one who could understand him. I think they came from the same country."

Rob sighed. "This is pointless." He patted the boy on the shoulder, then stood up. "We'll have to come back with a translator."

As they were leaving, they saw a van pull up and a tall, well-built man climb out. He looked like he was in his mid-forties, ruddy-faced and thick-necked. Despite the chill, he was wearing jeans and a T-shirt, his muscles bulging beneath the sleeves.

A builder, Margaret had said.

They were heading back on the motorway when Rob's phone rang. "Miller."

"Rob, it's Jenny. You'd better get back here. We've been given the case. The Clapham shooting is ours."

CHAPTER 10

Rob punched the air. "Yes!"

Will glanced over.

"We got it," he hissed. "Let's get back to the office."

Will put his foot down and they got back in record time.

"Mayhew?" Rob asked, striding into the squad room.

Jenny beamed. "Yes, she talked the Deputy Chief around, believe it or not."

"Fucking hell," muttered Will.

Rob went into her office. She was signing a bunch of documents and looked up as he entered. "DCI Miller, I take it you've heard the news."

"Yes, thank you, ma'am. I mean that. You've no idea how much this case means to us."

"I'm beginning to." She hid a smile behind her pen.

"What did Central say?"

"They weren't too happy about it, but apart from the delay, no harm was done. All the files have been transferred to us. DS Bird has everything you need."

"We'll get right on it." He turned to leave.

"What happened at the children's home?" she asked.

"It looks like Benny ran away. Nobody saw him leave and we can't question the other children because of language issues. We're going to have to go back with a translator."

"Arrange it."

He gave a curt nod and left her office.

"Everybody in Incident Room One," called Rob, addressing his and Galbraith's team. They jumped up and followed. He shut the door and grinned at them. "Right, now that the case is officially ours, we can do this properly. Let's have a quick update and we can take it from there."

Galbraith nodded.

"Where are we with the phone records?"

They'd requested Lawrence's call logs as well as those from Ant Price's burner phone and Zhou's, just in case. Rob had signed off on the warrants, even though he hadn't been the SIO at the time. Clearly Central hadn't got around to it yet, which worked in their favour.

"The phone companies have sent them through," Jeff said. "I was about to go through them."

"Let me know if anything stands out."

He nodded.

"Jenny, I want Uniform to question everyone in that street. It was a Friday night in Clapham. Someone must have seen something."

"Yes, guv." She picked up the phone.

"Celeste, what about CCTV? Anything?"

"I've got a team going through it now," she replied. They'd just started outsourcing the CCTV analysis to eagle-eyed professionals who'd been trained in what to look for. Consequently, if there was something to find, they'd spot it. Trawling through CCTV footage used to be a task reserved for the rookies but now was a specialised field in itself.

"Where's Mike?" Rob asked Galbraith.

"He's tailing Torch with a plain-clothed copper. They're keeping close tabs on him."

"Okay, good. Anything yet?"

"Low-level dealing, but nothing relating to the shooting."

"What do you say we bring the whole gang in?"

The Scot stared at him. "What? Arrest the bunch of them?"

"Yeah. That way we can question them individually. Torch is our biggest lead. Ant Price said he was involved in whatever it was that was going down. Ant was snitching on him. He's a badass gangbanger. You put it together."

"We still don't have anything on them." Galbraith raked a hand through his hair. "We can't hold them."

"We don't need to. I just want to shake the tree and see what falls out. One of the other guys might talk."

"I went over that list Cranshaw sent through," chipped in Jenny. "Several of them have priors. We might be able to push them over the edge."

"I suppose it's worth a shot," the Scottish DCI said. "We can't talk to them on the estate. None of them will say anything with Torch there."

"Okay, I'll clear it with the Super, but let's aim to go in at dawn tomorrow morning."

"I'll arrange it with SCO19." Galbraith pulled out his phone.

* * *

At 4 a.m. Rob sat in his car outside the Beaufort Estate. The sky was a deep indigo, the sun having yet to poke its head over the horizon. It had rained during the night, leaving puddles on the tarmac the size of oil slicks. He watched as the firearms unit prepared to go in.

Galbraith was leading the raid. Since they'd combined teams to work the Chief's case, they were also sharing responsibility. Rob was happy to let him do it. Galbraith had seen plenty of action overseas in the armed forces and was more than equipped to handle this scenario.

By contrast, Rob had got very little sleep thanks to Jack, who'd had a bad night, and both he and Jo were bleary-eyed this morning when he'd got up at three o'clock. Before he'd left, Jo had pulled the baby into bed with her, and he'd been hit by a pang of longing, looking at them curled up together.

"Be careful, Rob," she'd whispered, as he'd left.

The men from the firearms unit moved silently into position, formidable in their dark attire, Kevlar vests and helmets, specialist rifles at the ready.

Galbraith gave the word and they spurred into action. Rob could hear everything that was happening through the comms.

"Armed police!" shouted the tactical team leader as they barged into a flat. "Get on the ground, hands behind your back."

Similar shouts could be heard from the other apartments. This was a synchronised attack. The firearms teams were going in simultaneously, so as not to warn the others. Half an hour of chaos ensued when all Rob could hear were shouts of "Get down!" and "On the floor!"

"Got Torch and his girlfriend," came Galbraith's rough brogue through the radio. "Coming out now."

There were other confirmations as the armed police officers emerged from the various tower blocks, leading their handcuffed suspects out. Lights had gone on in a multitude of windows as scared faces looked out onto the action below.

"No luck in flat 29, Block E," came a voice. "Bastard escaped through the bathroom window."

Block E? Rob squinted into the darkness. That was the fifth tower block, closest to where he was parked. He started the car, killed the headlights, and drove slowly down the street in the direction of the hulking great high-rise.

He switched off the ignition and waited. He was outside the perimeter of the estate, beyond a shoulder-height brick wall. If someone was on the run, they'd have to scale the wall to get out. Behind the estate was a ditch leading down to the train tracks. Doable, but not the easiest option. Beyond the wall on this side was a sleepy residential street sporting a row of identical Victorian terraced houses, their windows in darkness.

He didn't have to wait long.

Rob saw a dark shape roll over the top of the wall and fall onto the pavement below. Not the most elegant dismount. He picked up the radio. "I've got the suspect from flat 29 on Berrydale Road. I'm pursuing on foot. Requesting backup."

He got out of the car. The man turned and saw him, then took off down the street. Rob ran after him. Damn, why hadn't he kept his gym membership? The lack of activity, the baby, the sleep deprivation had all taken its toll, and his legs burned as he raced after the escapee. Luckily, the man he was pursuing was no fitter. He was overweight and Rob could hear him wheezing as he closed the gap.

He gained on him and in a final sprint tackled him to the ground. The man fell hard, wincing as the tarmac tore at his knees and hands.

Rob wrenched his arms behind his back. "You're under arrest."

CHAPTER 11

After the suspect had been given an asthma inhaler from the police vehicle's first-aid kit, he was handed over to the armed officers, who took him down to the nearest police station for processing along with the rest of the gang.

"We're going to Brixton," Rob told the team once SCO19 had gone. That's where the nearest custody suite was located, where the suspects would be held and questioned.

"I'll head back to Putney and update the Super," said Galbraith. He rarely conducted interviews, preferring to let his sergeants handle that for him. Each SIO had a different way of working. Rob liked to be more hands-on, even though he knew, as a DCI, he was expected to take more of a high-level approach.

"It won't be easy getting them to talk," Mike said, once they'd got to Brixton Police Station. "Most of these guys are more frightened of Torch than of us."

"Let's give the custody sergeant time to process them and then we'll start the interviews. Will and I will take the fat guy. Mike, you take the girlfriend. Jenny and Jeff, take your pick."

"What about Torch?" asked Will. "Shouldn't we interview him first?"

"Let's leave him till last," Rob said. "We might get something we can use from the others."

* * *

Rob sat opposite the man he'd chased down the road. The suspect looked even bigger in the harsh light of the interrogation room. It must have been a tight fit through the bathroom window.

Will was beside him, operating the recording. "You've waived your right to a legal representative, is that right?"

"Yeah, man. What do I need one of them for? I haven't done anything."

"Let's start with your name." Rob placed a folder on the table in front of him. There wasn't much in it, but the suspect didn't know that.

He got a sullen stare in response.

Rob rested his wrists on the table. "Look, we've already fingerprinted you and taken DNA. We know who you are. It's senseless playing dumb. If you want to go home, you'd be better off cooperating."

"I don't know nothing."

"You know your name, right?" said Rob.

He glanced down at his hands. "Declan."

"Declan. Okay." At least he was talking. "Declan, how long have you been a member of Torch's gang?"

"I don't know what you mean."

"Come on. You've been part of the Beaufort Blockz for years. You grew up on that estate, didn't you?"

He shrugged. "Yeah, so what?"

"You took over your mother's apartment when she passed."

"It's allowed."

"How old are you now?"

"Twenty-three."

Rob was jumping around, trying to throw him off guard. He wanted him to talk, to answer non-threatening questions, and then he'd lead him into the more loaded ones.

69

"How long have you known Torch?"

A pause. "Since he came to the estate."

"That was five years ago, wasn't it?" Cranshaw had provided them with that information.

A shrug.

"Okay, Declan. If you don't know anything, why'd you run?"

More hand-gazing.

Rob waited.

"I don't know," he mumbled.

"We searched your apartment and found this." He placed a bag of cannabis on the table. Declan shifted in his chair, his eyes darting to the weed, then back at his hands.

"It's medicinal," he finally said.

"I doubt it's medicinal for asthma," pointed out Rob. "You do have asthma, don't you?"

"Yeah."

"Surely smoking is just going to make it worse?"

"Nah, it helps."

Now he'd heard it all. How dumb did this guy think he was?

"Well, we're willing to overlook the drug use, if you can tell me where Torch was last Friday night."

Declan stared at him, his eyes bulging in their sockets. Bloodshot, defiant and fearful. "I don't know where he was."

"Where were you?"

"In my flat."

"Can anyone confirm that?"

Silence.

"You see, Declan, there was a shooting in Clapham on Friday night and three people were killed. One of them was a police officer. Another of the victims, you might know. His name was Ant Price."

Declan's eyes flickered ever so slightly.

"He lived in Block E, like you."

"Didn't know him."

"Sure you did," said Rob. "You used to hang out all the time."

The big guy frowned. "Who told you that?"

"What, you didn't?" It was a guess, but given they lived in the same block, and both ran with Torch's crew, it wasn't much of a stretch.

Declan's shoulders slumped. "Yeah, he was a mate. I was sorry to hear what happened."

"How did you hear about it?"

"Someone told me. It was going around the estate. I didn't know he was a rat though. No one did."

And there it was. Out in the open.

"Did you feel betrayed?" Rob grabbed the opportunity to get to the heart of the matter. "Were you upset that he lied to you?"

"Yeah, of course. He was my friend and one of the—" He stopped.

"One of the gang?" asked Rob. "Part of the Beaufort Blockz gang?"

A sullen silence.

"I can imagine you were pissed off," said Rob. "You trusted him and he betrayed you. He betrayed all of you."

"Yeah." More sulking.

"Is that why Torch ordered the hit on him?" asked Rob.

Declan didn't reply. Rob's heart began to beat faster.

"Declan? Was it an organised hit?"

"No," rasped the big guy, but he was sweating, and his hands were clenched together beneath the table.

"You're sure? That possession charge is still hovering over you. I can make it go away. You just have to tell us the truth. Did Torch arrange for Ant to be taken out?"

But Declan had shut down. After the wobble, he'd decided it wasn't worth it. He'd rather face a possession charge than Torch's wrath.

"It wasn't a hit. Torch had nothing to do with it. He was as surprised as the rest of us when we heard the news."

"Did he know Ant was a CI?"

"No, I told you. No one did."

Rob gritted his teeth in frustration. He'd been so close. Declan had almost caved.

He tried one last time. "If you know something, Declan, tell us now. Once you walk out of here, your chance is over. You'll be charged with possession of an illegal substance and there won't be anything I can do about it. Talk to me now, in confidence, and you'll be back home in an hour."

But Declan was already shaking his head. "No comment."

* * *

"How's he doing?" Rob walked into the viewing room where Jenny was watching the various interviews. Mike was in the process of interrogating Torch's girlfriend, Chantelle.

"Not bad. Better than you."

Rob snorted. "I reckon Torch was behind it."

"You're probably right," she said. "But without a witness or a testimony, we have nothing."

"Did you really grow up on the estate?" Chantelle was asking Mike.

"Isn't he the one supposed to be asking the questions?" Rob turned to the screen.

Jenny grinned. "He's establishing a rapport. I think she likes him."

Rob began to pay attention.

"Yeah, but I left as soon as I could. My brother was into some bad shit, and I didn't want to go down the same path."

She gazed longingly at him.

"Why don't you get out?" he asked, picking up on her angst. "You don't have to stay there."

Rob was impressed. Mike had really come into his own these last few months. He ought to talk to him about doing his sergeant's exam. He was more than ready.

"And go where?" she scoffed. "I can't afford to rent a place of my own. No one will hire me. I didn't even finish school."

Mike frowned. "What? A clever girl like you? You could finish school, then get a job. Easy."

She melted a little more. Jenny was right, she did like Mike. "I don't know . . ."

"Come on. Surely there's something you want to do?"

"I did want to be a hairdresser at one stage," she began. Her eyes dropped to her nails. "Or a beautician."

"There you go," said Mike. "I heard Torch runs an education programme on the estate. You could go to that. Get your GCSEs."

She paused for a moment, thinking it over.

"Maybe," she said.

Mike shrugged. "You may as well. What else is there to do besides hanging around with Torch?"

She stiffened.

Uh-oh, thought Rob.

"Torch isn't such a bad guy," she said. "You don't know him."

"What's he like, then?" asked Mike.

She sniffed. "He's good to me. He treats me right."

As long as she was loyal. Rob hadn't missed the way she'd come running when he'd clicked his fingers. Neither had Mike.

"As long as you do what he says, right?"

She bit her lip.

"Listen, Chantelle. I can see you're a decent person. Were you really with Torch on Friday night, or were you just saying that because you were afraid of what he might do if you told us the truth?"

She didn't reply.

"I know you were put on the spot the other day, in front of everyone. I wouldn't blame you for lying. I would have done the same, in that situation."

Rob nodded.

"He's good, isn't he?" said Jenny.

"We'll have to let him do more interrogations," Rob said.

"You would?" she whispered, glancing up from behind her lashes.

"Yeah, course." He leaned forward. "With that lot watching, I'd have been too shit-scared to say anything else."

The bravado vanished and she blinked, suddenly vulnerable. She entwined her fingers together, long, elegant, with scarlet tips.

"Anything you say to me is strictly confidential," Mike added. "It won't go any further than this room."

That wasn't strictly true. Torch would know someone had given him up, but he wouldn't know who. Rob just hoped he'd never find out it was his girlfriend.

Finally, she glanced up at Mike.

"Okay," she whispered. "I lied."

CHAPTER 12

"Yes!" yelled Jenny at the same time as Rob slammed his hand down on the desk. Jeff, who'd just walked in, jumped.

"Sorry," Rob said.

"What happened?" He came over. "You got something?"

"Hell yeah. Mike just got Torch's girlfriend to admit she lied about his whereabouts on Friday night."

"No way." His eyes widened. "That's great, because I got nothing. Those guys aren't saying a word."

Their eyes were drawn back to the screen as Mike's deep voice resonated through the audio system. Galbraith turned up the volume.

"To clarify, you weren't with him on Friday night?" asked Mike.

Chantelle shook her head. Her glossy brown locks swept around her shoulders.

"Okay, why don't you tell me where you were?" Mike's tone was calm and casual, as if this were no more than a Sunday stroll she was admitting to.

"I was with him earlier," she said. "We made supper together, watched some TV. Then the boys came round and it got rowdy. I left at about ten."

"Where did you go?"

"Back to my place. I live in Block A. I don't like it when they start drinking and smoking weed. It makes them crazy."

Makes Torch crazy, thought Rob.

"Did you see Torch again after that?" Mike looked dejected, like he'd almost caught a fish, then discovered it had got away.

"He left right after me," she said.

"What?" Mike perked up. "He left the apartment?"

"Yeah. I heard voices and turned around. I wasn't even back at my block yet, and he was walking out with two other guys."

"Do you know who?"

"Ali and Shane, I think."

"You think?"

She shrugged. "Yeah, it was dark, but I think it was them. He goes everywhere with them."

"What did they do?" Mike was leaning right over the table now, straining to hear every word. Rob, Jeff and Jenny were doing the same in the viewing room.

"They got into Torch's car and drove off," she said.

"They left the estate?"

She nodded. "I didn't see him until the next day."

* * *

Rob swung around and paced the room. "I knew it! The fucker doesn't have an alibi for the night of the shooting."

"We got him." Will's eyes gleamed. "You want to do it now?"

"Yup, let's hit him with this," Rob said. "He'll either have to tell us where he was or admit to the shooting."

"He'll know someone talked." Jenny frowned. He knew she was worried about Torch's girlfriend.

"Yes, but he won't know who. Chantelle left his flat before he did that night. He won't think it's her. She's safe."

"I hope so." Jenny eyed the woman sitting opposite Mike. "She's lovely looking, isn't she? Even makes that custody tracksuit look good."

Rob hadn't really noticed, he'd been too engrossed in what she was saying to take in her looks.

"Mike seems to think so." Jeff grinned as Mike stood back while she was escorted out, his gaze roaming over her body.

"Dangerous, that," warned Rob.

"Could be useful too," added Jenny.

She did have a point.

Rob's phone buzzed in his pocket. He retrieved it and glanced at the screen. It was Galbraith.

"You'll never believe it," Rob said. "Torch's alibi just fell through." He listened to Galbraith for a moment, and his heart sank. "Seriously? Shit."

"What is it?" mouthed Jenny. The others were all staring at him.

"I see. Okay, thanks for the heads-up." He hung up.

"What?" asked Jenny.

He exhaled. "Guess who just walked into the office? Raza Ashraf."

"The mayor?" Will's eyebrows shot up. "What does he want?"

Ashraf had been a suspect in a homicide earlier in the year, but he'd been cleared and, thanks to an effective press blackout, managed to win the election and become mayor. Everyone was sick of knife crime in the city, and Ashraf had promised to clean it up. So far, Rob hadn't seen much proof of that, but it was early days.

"I don't know, but it can't be good."

"I'm getting a bad feeling about this," said Jenny. Rob gave a terse nod. She wasn't the only one. Whenever politics was involved, things got messy.

"Let's interview Torch now." He headed towards the door, a sense of urgency burning in his gut. "Will, are you in?"

"Wouldn't miss it." His sergeant hurried after him.

"'Bout fucking time," grumbled the gangster when Rob and Will walked in. He'd been sitting there for the better part of two hours. "Now maybe you can tell me why you arrested us? We ain't done nothing wrong." There was venom in his voice. Rob could hear it dripping off his tongue. A deep-seated hatred for the police that went back to his childhood, probably even beyond. It was so deeply ingrained, he couldn't look at Rob without his whole body bristling with hostility. Rob, by contrast, was utterly calm.

Torch's solicitor, an elegant woman in a bright yellow dress that stood out against her ebony skin, put a restraining hand on his arm.

Will started the recording. "Present are DCI Miller, DS Freemont, Shamar Williams, also known as Torch, and his solicitor—" He broke off and glanced at the woman.

"Abby Okorocha," she said.

"Right, shall we get started?" Rob asked. Torch had been cautioned and was aware of his rights. "You're here because we think you're involved in the shooting of Anthony Price and two other victims in Clapham on Friday night."

Torch made to protest, but Rob held up a hand. "Last time we spoke, you said you were at home on Friday night. Your girlfriend—" he glanced at the open file in front of him even though he knew her name — "Chantelle, confirmed it."

"If you know this, why are you harassing my client?" enquired Okorocha. She had a British accent with a trace of something else. A Nigerian influence, maybe?

"Because your client lied to us, Miss Okorocha." Rob blinked against the yellow. He wondered if she'd dressed like that on purpose to distract them. "We have a witness who says he left his house around ten o'clock that same night and along with two other men drove out of the estate."

Torch's eyes narrowed. "Who told you that?" Animosity radiated off him like rank body odour.

"What? Isn't it true?"

"No, it's not true. I was at home with my mates. Any one of them will tell you that."

"That's just it," said Rob. "One of them didn't. Do you want to explain where you were on Friday night?"

He hesitated. Rob sensed his brain working. Who had ratted him out?

His solicitor whispered something in his ear, presumably that he didn't have to answer.

"No comment," he said.

Rob gritted his teeth. "According to this witness, you left the estate around ten o'clock, which would have given you plenty of time to drive to Clapham, where you gunned down Anthony Price, Sam Lawrence and Raymond Zhou, the restaurant owner."

"No!" he yelled. "I didn't kill nobody."

"Detective, do you have something to ask my client?"

Rob leaned in. "Did you kill Ant Price and the others?"

"No," hissed Torch, the muscles in his neck flexing.

Rob held his gaze for a full minute. The dark eyes blazed into his, unspoken threats passing between them across the room.

If you killed them, I'll bring you down.

A rap on the interrogation room door broke the tension. Torch glanced away while Rob exhaled.

Will got up. "What is it?"

Jeff was standing there. "Message for the guvnor."

Rob turned around. "What? Now?"

Jeff nodded. "It's the boss. She wants you to call her ASAP."

He glanced at Will, who shrugged, but Rob thought he knew what it was about. Bloody Ashraf poking his nose in where it didn't belong.

"Interview suspended at seventeen minutes past one." Will switched off the recorder.

"Does she know I was in the middle of an interview?" Rob stomped up the passage after Jeff, Will a step or two behind them. "What's so important it couldn't wait?"

"Above my pay grade," said Jeff. "I was just told to come and get you. She said to stop whatever it was you were doing and call her back."

The bad feeling in Rob's gut got worse.

They left the custody suite, which was rather noisy and went into the police canteen, which was marginally less so. At least here they could get a cup of coffee.

He pulled out his phone and dialled Mayhew's direct line. She answered after a single ring. "DCI Miller, thanks for calling me back."

"What's this about, ma'am? I was in the middle of interrogating our prime suspect."

"I'm here with the mayor, Raza Ashraf," she said.

Here we go, he thought. Fucking politics. He pictured Ashraf sitting across the desk from Mayhew, that smarmy grin on his face. After the verbal sparring match he'd just had with Torch, he wanted to smash something, and Ashraf's face would do nicely.

"We're on speaker."

"I don't know if you're aware," began Ashraf, "but I've got an important initiative running in several of the more volatile estates in London at the moment."

Rob tensed his jaw. "I had heard."

"Good." Rob heard that smooth politician's smile. "Well, I'm pleased to say we're seeing results. We have educational programmes set up in the community centres, we have tutors assigned to help the kids finish school, and we have sport and development activities set up to keep the kids off the streets. That's how we hope to combat violence and knife crime. Too many young lives are being lost."

He could save the political speech for his constituents. "What has this got to do with our investigation?"

"Shamar Williams is a very powerful figure on the Beaufort Estate," Ashraf said.

"He's also the leader of an organised crime group, the Beaufort Blockz gang," cut in Rob. "They sell drugs, incite violence and contribute to the crime that you're so eager to minimise."

Ashraf's tone darkened. "Which is why he is so important. He influences the youngsters on the estate, for better or worse. They look up to him. If anyone can get them into the programme, it's him."

Rob remained silent. Okay, he might have a point there.

"We need him in play," continued Ashraf. "The good he's doing on the estate outweighs—"

"Don't even say it." Rob rubbed his forehead. "You do realise we're looking at him for the shooting of DCS Lawrence, along with a confidential informant and a local restaurant owner?"

"I believe he has an alibi?" said Ashraf.

"Not anymore. His alibi didn't hold up." He was hoping Mayhew would step in and back him up. "He looks good for this."

"Do you have any hard evidence?" the Superintendent asked.

"We have a witness who saw him leave the estate at ten o'clock on Friday night. The timing fits."

"That doesn't mean he did it," pointed out Ashraf.

"It doesn't mean he didn't." Rob clutched the phone to his ear.

Will came back with two coffees. Jeff was talking to someone else on the other side of the room. Jenny was nowhere in sight.

Mayhew cleared her throat. "Do you have anything else? A murder weapon? DNA? Fingerprints? Anything that puts Williams at the scene?"

"Not yet."

There was a pause. Rob's heart sank. He knew what was coming next.

"Let him go for now," Mayhew ordered. "If you find anything concrete, by all means, bring him back. At the moment, he's more use to us out there."

"More use to the mayor, you mean?" Rob knew he was out of line, but he couldn't help it. He fucking hated politics.

"Despite what you think of me, the programme is working." Ashraf's voice was tight.

Rob pictured the two girls and boy who were bent over their notepads scribbling away at the community centre. They deserved a chance. Torch was giving them an opportunity to get out of there. He might be a cold-blooded murderer, but without him, that programme would come crashing down. Their chance would be lost.

He sighed. "Fine, we'll let him go, but a word of warning. Start looking for someone else to take his place at the helm, because he's going down for this, and when he does, your little house of cards is going to tumble down too, unless you've got a Plan B."

CHAPTER 13

"You had to let him go?" Jo stopped testing the milk from the heated bottle on her wrist and glanced up.

"Fucker walked." He glanced at the baby. "Sorry."

Jo shook her head. "And you're sure he shot Sam and the others?"

"Ninety per cent sure. He doesn't have an alibi. He left the estate with enough time to drive to Clapham and gun down Sam and the others."

"Have you found the weapon?" she asked.

"No. We searched his premises and that of his gang members but found nothing. But they wouldn't be so stupid to keep them in their apartments."

"They're probably stashed at unsuspecting parties' houses," said Jo. "Vulnerable people. Elderly people. There's probably a whole armoury out there that the residents don't know about, or if they do, are too scared to say anything."

Rob grimaced. "We can't search the whole estate."

"Precisely. And they know that."

She handed Rob the bottle. He took it into the lounge, where Jack was lying on a play mat in front of the television. The sound was down, but the cartoons were on. As usual, his big blue eyes were fastened to the screen. He waved his chubby hands in the air as soon as he saw Rob.

"He hasn't been watching TV all day," Jo pointed out. "Just in case you were wondering. It's the only way I can keep him occupied while I go and get him a bottle or make supper."

"I didn't doubt you for a second." He flashed her a grin, then lifted Jack up and cradled him in his arm.

Jo squeezed his arm. "Thank you. Now if you don't mind, I'm going to take a nice hot bath before supper." She went upstairs.

Rob fed Jack and stroked Trigger's head with his foot. Immediately, the stress of the day started ebbing, and before long, he was fighting to keep his eyes open. It was hard to dwell on evil when there was such innocence in the world.

He switched the television to something more watchable, but as unwilling as he was, his thoughts kept returning to Torch. If they wanted to charge him for Sam's murder, along with the other victims, they needed something definite on him. Where had he stashed the gun? Had he disposed of it? Ballistics would have a report on the bullet casings found at the crime scene. If they could find the gun that matched those casings, there might even be fingerprints. What about CCTV? Was his vehicle picked up in the vicinity? He wondered if Celeste had heard anything from the door-to-door.

His phone buzzed. Trigger glanced up.

"It's okay, boy," he murmured, reaching into his pocket. *Liz Kramer.*

"Liz, hi. Good to hear from you."

"Sorry to call so late, Rob," came her clipped tone. "But I've written up the post-mortem report on the teenager in the river and I thought you'd like to hear it."

"You thought right. Please send it through."

"On its way," she said. "Do you want the highlights?"

"Yeah, shoot."

"Like I said, he was badly beaten prior to being shot and dumped in the river. He had defensive marks on his arms and possibly some DNA under his fingernails."

Rob sat up. "Really?"

"It was hard to tell, given all the gunk under there, but we've sent samples to the lab for analysis. I think you'll find there are some skin cells too."

"That's great." There was always a chance the perp was on the police database.

They talked for a while longer, then he hung up.

Jo came downstairs and they had dinner. She'd managed to throw together some chicken breasts and roasted vegetables. When Rob complimented her on the meal, she said, "It's all thanks to Tanya. She's been incredible, and she's good with Jack too."

"Perhaps we should think about having her more than twice a week," Rob mused. "You did seem more relaxed today."

Her face lit up. "That would be fantastic, if we can afford it."

Jo was on maternity leave from the NCA, but prior to that, she'd taken a leave of absence, and was only on a small portion of her salary.

"We'll make a plan," he said. He'd taken six weeks paternity leave, which had helped with the worst of the sleepless nights, but he'd been eager to get back to work. Perhaps it was guilt, perhaps it was seeing Jo so relaxed, but either way, the extra help would be worth it.

Rob took Trigger for a walk around the block while Jo put Jack down, then they tumbled into bed themselves. As he took her into his arms, he thought how lucky he was to have her in his life. She balanced out the bad and kept him sane. One thing he was sure of was that he never wanted that to change.

* * *

Mike and two plain-clothed officers, Glen and Chris, were in the surveillance van outside the Beaufort Estate, waiting for Torch to make a move. Mike had been in and out several times, scouting the area, blending into the surroundings. He was good at that. Even as a kid he'd been good at keeping to the shadows.

It was his brother Idi who was the showman. Charming, sociable, always cool. He'd started out with such promise, only to lose his way.

Mike still remembered his mother's face when they'd arrested Idi the first time. Disbelief, indignation — she couldn't fathom her charismatic eldest son being involved in drug dealing. Even though the drugs had been stashed in a box under his bed, his fingerprints all over it. There was no getting out of that one.

It was Mike who'd had to live with his mother's anguish, her denial, her anger. Everybody loved Idi.

He'd done two years in juvie. *Easy time*, he'd said, but Mike could tell it was false bravado. No time is ever easy.

Things had gone back to normal for a while. His mother had doted on Idi. It was all a terrible mistake, she'd tell her friends. He was in the wrong place at the wrong time. My boy would never be involved in anything like that.

She was proved wrong.

The second arrest was a few years later. Mike was fourteen, his older brother eighteen and still living at home. He was done for assault and possession with intent. They'd beaten up a boy on the estate who refused to be pulled into the gang's illegal activities. Jerome, his name was.

Jerome had a football scholarship, a chance at the big time — on condition he kept his nose clean. But that's hard to do on the estate, especially when your nose wasn't clean to begin with. Extricating himself from the gang had proved futile. He'd been bullied, coerced and finally beaten to a pulp. He'd disappeared after that. No one knew where he'd gone, but his name had never appeared in any junior or professional football leagues, so Mike guessed that never panned out.

Another dream in tatters. That's the way it was around here.

They'd led Idi away in cuffs, his hands behind his back. His mother sobbing in the doorway. Mike had tried to comfort her, but she'd turned away. She didn't want to know the truth. Didn't want to believe her son was a gangster and a drug dealer.

He got another two years, but this time, he was tried as an adult. Prison was a different ball game from the juvenile detention centre. Mike could see the change in his brother. He came out tougher and more dangerous than before.

The easy smile was gone. The sparkling eyes were jaded. He was twenty-three and he'd spent four of those years behind bars.

Instead of choosing the straight and narrow, he'd embraced the gang way of life. Prison had given him esteem among his peers. He was a big shot now. The man. He rose in the ranks and was soon calling the shots. He hadn't lost his charm, but it was laced with a dangerous edge that said, *You don't want to cross me.*

Mike had been determined not to follow in his brother's footsteps, and ironically, it was perhaps only because his brother was so high up in the hierarchy that Mike was never targeted by the gang. That was one thing his brother had done — keep him out of it. It was an unspoken rule. Mikey was off limits.

"You're not like me," he'd told Mike once in a rare moment of reflection. "You're smart. You can do anything you want. Make Mum proud."

There was movement outside Block D. Torch and his cronies were on the move. He whistled to the two cops. Glen got into the driver's seat and Chris the passenger's. Mike, who was just along for the ride, sat in the back.

They waited for Torch's car, a black Honda CR-V, to exit the estate and then pulled away in pursuit.

"He's alone," Mike observed.

The Honda merged with the South London traffic. They stayed back, a decent following distance. Nothing suspicious, nothing noticeable.

To follow someone effectively you needed more than one vehicle, ideally three. Each would take turns at cutting in behind the target, with the others falling back, thereby making sure the same car was never in the rear-view mirror for long. Unfortunately, they didn't have the budget or the clearance for that, so they had to make do with one.

"He's turning onto the A3 towards the City," Glen remarked.

"Stay with him." Mike leaned forward, peering between the two front-seat headrests, eyes on Torch's Honda.

They turned into Kennington Road. There were several cars between them and the target.

The Honda pulled over beside a parade of shops.

"Over there," said Mike.

The traffic was manic. Cars, mopeds and vans streamed along the busy road, overtaking, honking and stop-starting as the traffic lights changed. The smell of exhaust fumes was thick in the air.

"There's nowhere to park," Glen complained.

Mike glanced up and down the road. "Take the yellow line. If anyone asks, show them your badge."

They were trying not to be conspicuous, but hopefully they'd be able to see what Torch was up to before they had to show their hand.

"He's going into the mobile phone shop." Chris had the best view across the road.

"Okay, wait here. I'm going to see what he's doing."

Before they could stop him, Mike had exited the vehicle and was running across the road. He pulled his hoodie up and put on his Bosch earphones, which he kept around his neck. It made people think he wasn't listening.

Nodding his head as if in time to the music, he entered the store. Torch didn't glance up. The shopkeeper did but dismissed him as a browser. Mike turned his back to the counter and began to look at phone covers.

Torch was speaking to the shopkeeper. They seemed to know each other, although it wasn't an easy relationship. The shopkeeper was scared of Torch. Mike could hear it in his replies.

"Yeah. No problem, bruv."

Mike listened to their conversation, then moved away from the counter, further into the shop. He took a case down off the wall and studied it. A short time later, Torch left. Mike put the case back on the wall.

"You want some help?" asked the shopkeeper.

"Nah." Mike walked past him out of the shop.

* * *

Rob, who'd managed to get a semi-decent night's sleep, arrived at work just before nine. He immediately called a briefing to get up to speed with the various elements of the two active cases. It was important they stay on track with both, because with two on the go, things could easily get messy.

Galbraith took the stand first. "We've got some good news. The CCTV analysts didn't pick up Torch's car anywhere in the vicinity of Clapham on Friday night. We know he left the estate with two others in a Honda CR-V, but they must have changed vehicles en route."

"How's that good news?" Will asked.

The Scot held up a finger. "Wait, ye of little faith. Celeste has been orchestrating the door-to-door inquiries. Celeste, do you want to update us?"

She stood up but didn't go to the front. "We've been speaking to business owners in the area and last night we hit pay dirt."

Rob sat up. "Someone saw something?"

Her eyes gleamed. "Yes, there was a witness. A barman from across the street was on a smoke break when he saw a motorcycle pull up in front of the restaurant. The driver went inside, the witness heard a series of loud pops, and then the driver came out, jumped on his bike and took off."

"Did he get a plate?" Rob didn't dare hope.

"No, unfortunately not. He didn't think it had one."

Shit.

"What about an ID?" said Jenny.

"The shooter was wearing a full visor helmet. The witness didn't see his face."

"What about the bike?" asked Jeff. "Any distinctive features, decals, that sort of thing?"

"Not that he could see. Sorry. I know it's not much help, but at least we know the shooter arrived on a motorbike."

"And used a suppressor," added Galbraith. "Otherwise, half the street would have heard the gunshots."

Rob was thinking hard. "Torch doesn't own a motorcycle, does he?"

Jenny shook her head. "Not that we know of. There's no motorbike registered with the DVLA. I mean, he could keep it off-site somewhere."

"Let's look into his family and friends. See if there's anywhere he could keep a machine like that."

"I'll check for rented lock-ups and garages," said Will. "It would help if we could get hold of his bank statements."

"I'll issue a warrant," said Rob. "How's Mike doing?"

"He's still on surveillance detail. Nothing yet."

Rob nodded. It would take time. Eventually, they'd find a connection to Torch. He had to slip up eventually. Everybody did.

Rob took Galbraith's place at the front. The Scot lowered himself into a chair.

"Okay, let's talk about Benny, the boy found in the river. Liz Kramer sent me the post-mortem report last night. The tox screen was clear, there was nothing in his system. He was beaten, then shot, as you know, and his body was thrown into the river somewhere along that stretch. It's pretty tidal there, so he could have been washed up or downstream." He looked around the room. "There is, however, a small chance that he scratched his attacker. Liz found a sliver of DNA under his fingernails. It's been sent to the lab. Once we get it back, we can run it through the database."

There was a murmur of relief.

"That's good," said Galbraith. "It's something."

"I've been looking into the owners of the children's home," said Jenny. "Neither Margaret nor Bruno have any previous convictions. I've been through their bank statements, personal and business. They're getting government grants to help run that place, but on the surface, it all looks legit."

"Did we ever find out where that stamp came from?" asked Rob.

She shook her head. "I've been in touch with the asylum centre in Kent and they don't know anything about it."

"Okay, well thanks for all your hard work." He glanced at Will. "Let's run that DNA as soon as we get it and hope it brings us a result."

Will nodded.

They filtered out of the incident room and went back to their desks. No sooner had Rob sat down than his mobile rang.

"Guv, it's Mike. Torch just went into a mobile phone shop in Southwark and had a chat with the manager. I managed to catch a bit of their conversation. Something's going down. I think you should get here."

CHAPTER 14

Rob sat in the back of the surveillance van with Mike and the plain-clothed police officer, who had both been watching the Beaufort Estate since daybreak and had followed Torch to the mobile phone shop.

"What exactly did he say?"

"I only heard snippets," Mike said. "But from what I could make out, Torch said he needed four because it was a busy night."

"Four what? Four phones?" Rob looked at the others.

"Must be," said Mike. "Something's going down tonight, by the sounds of it."

Rob studied the phone shop through the front windscreen. The surveillance van had side panels and a tinted back window so nobody could see in. "Who's the manager?"

"We don't know yet. Torch left twenty minutes ago. We put a new team on him and waited here for you."

"Right. Well, let's go talk to this guy, find out what business he's got with the Beaufort Blockz."

Mike and Rob crossed the street. It was mid-afternoon and the traffic around Southwark was building up. In another hour, it would be gridlocked. There was a lot of foot traffic too, so they weaved their way around the people on the pavement and entered the store. It was hot and clammy inside. There was no one else in the store.

The owner, a turbaned man with a trimmed beard and dark, roving eyes looked up. "Can I help you?"

"Yes, we'd like to talk to the manager."

"That's me."

Rob flashed his warrant card. "Your name?"

"Mandeep Bhalla." His eyes narrowed as he saw the police insignia.

"Do you know this man?" Rob showed him a mugshot of Torch from his phone.

The manager shook his head, but the reaction was too quick. Too emphatic.

"Strange, since he came into your shop forty minutes ago."

There was a nervous pause.

"Do I need to ask you again?"

"Lots of people come in," he tried. "I can't remember all of them."

Rob snorted. A customer walked in, but Mike promptly ushered them out. He closed the door and stood in front of it.

"Right. Now, do I have to get a search warrant and tear this place apart, or do you think you can remember back to a conversation you had forty minutes ago?" He wouldn't want the police bulldozing through his accounts, finding all those little indiscretions that a cash business such as this tried to hide.

"Okay, okay—" he waved his hands in the air — "I spoke to Torch. He bought a couple of cell phones."

"Prepaid?"

"Yes."

Rob stared at him. The man shifted uncomfortably. "I swear. I sold him some phones. That's all."

Was he telling the truth? Rob couldn't tell.

Another customer tried the door, but Mike's bulk wouldn't let it open.

"Please, I'm losing business here," the man pleaded.

"Okay." Rob placed his card on the counter. "If he comes back and orders more, you let me know." It wasn't a question.

The man nodded.

Like hell he would.

Mike reopened the door, and they left the shop.

What would Torch need with four cell phones? Burners, of course. Perhaps he had a big deal going down and wanted to make sure their phones were clean.

"Back to the station?" asked Mike.

Rob spotted a homeless man sitting on the pavement opposite the phone shop. "Hang on," he said. "I won't be a moment."

He crossed the street, darting between the cars, until he came to a stop in front of the homeless guy.

He looked down. "Hi."

The vagrant grunted but glanced up. He had a shaggy beard, longish hair and startling blue eyes.

"Do you mind if I ask you some questions?" Rob bent down to show him his ID card.

The blue eyes narrowed. "What about?"

He seemed surprisingly compos mentis for a rough sleeper. Rob had half-expected him to be out of it on booze or dope, or groggy from a hangover. This man was neither of those things. He appeared to be alert, sitting up straight, his legs in a grubby but thick sleeping bag. He had a rucksack beside him, army issue by the looks of things. Retired vet?

"That shop over there—" Rob pointed to the mobile phone store — "you haven't noticed anything unusual happening there, have you?"

"What do you mean by unusual?" Again, an unexpected question.

"Strange comings and goings, people entering who don't look like customers, anything out of the ordinary."

The man pulled his legs out of his sleeping bag and began rolling it up.

"Anything you can tell us?" Rob sensed the man was about to flee.

All he got was another grunt as the man stuffed his sleeping bag into the top of his rucksack, then stood up. He was tall, nearly as tall as Rob, who was a couple of inches over six foot, although this man slouched to make himself appear smaller, or more invisible. Rob wondered what his story was.

The man hoisted the rucksack onto his back. He held it easily. There was strength in those arms, despite being thin and sinewy. He made to walk off.

"Sorry to have bothered you," Rob called.

To his surprise, the vagrant turned and said, "Come back tonight. Midnight."

Rob stared at him. "What do you mean? Is something going to happen?"

But the man had moved off, with slow determined steps, merging with the pedestrians on the busy street.

CHAPTER 15

"How do we know we can trust him?" asked Jeff, once they were back at the station. "He could be a raving lunatic."

"He didn't look like a raving lunatic to me," said Rob. "In fact, he looked pretty alert. But I agree, it could be nothing. Certainly not worth a whole surveillance team. I'll go later, just in case. I'll call if it looks like anything's going down."

"I'll come with you," offered Will.

"Are you sure?" asked Rob.

"Yeah, I haven't got anything better to do." He grinned. "It'll liven up my evening."

"I wouldn't count on that, but thanks. Meet me here at ten. We'll take the surveillance van." It was better for stakeouts. They could stretch out in the back and, with the tinted windows, would be completely invisible.

He just hoped it wouldn't be in vain.

* * *

Rob left work early to spend a few hours with his family before coming back to the office. Jo needed a break and Trigger needed a walk. After he'd fed Jack and put him down, he took a shower and prepared to go out again.

"Once this case is over, I'll be home more," he said to Jo, who was folding clothes on the bed.

"Until the next case." She gave him a tired smile. "Don't worry, I know what it's like. That's the nature of the job. We knew that when we moved in together. I promise not to hold it against you, but one day when I go back to work, we'll have to juggle the shifts."

"Have you given it some more thought?" he asked. At one point Jo had debated not going back at all, but they hadn't talked about it much since Jack was born. He suspected she was trying motherhood out for size. If she felt she couldn't go back, that was fine with him. They'd make do on one salary.

"A bit," she said, which meant she'd been thinking about it a lot. Jo never did anything in half measures. "I'm still not sure. I'd like to do something, but I'm not sure if a full-time job in law enforcement is the answer."

"Perhaps you could negotiate a part-time position?"

She wrinkled her nose. "I can't see Pearson going for that, can you? He's gunning to get rid of me."

It was true, she wasn't Pearson's favourite person. He hadn't appreciated her taking a leave of absence to work on a case for Rob's team last year, and because of that, and the fact that she'd found out she was pregnant, she hadn't been back since.

And part-time police work was almost impossible. Once a case got going, it was all or nothing. Despite his good intentions to slow down after Jack was born, here he was, fully immersed in this investigation, about to go on an all-night stake-out.

"There's always consulting," he said. "You have a great skill set and plenty of experience. Any agency would be lucky to have you."

"Thanks." She reached over and squeezed his hand. "That means a lot. Shouldn't you be heading off? You don't want to miss your midnight deadline."

"Yep." He did up his laces. "Will you be okay?"

"Yeah, as long as the little man doesn't wake up."

Rob kissed her. She was warm and soft, and he didn't want to let go. Eventually, he pulled himself away. "See you later."

* * *

Will glanced at his phone. "Five minutes to midnight."

They were sitting in the back of the surveillance van, watching the shop across the road. The pedestrian traffic had whittled down to a few stragglers heading home after a night out or couples walking home after a late dinner. The phone shop was locked up and the security shutter had been pulled down.

"Doesn't look like anyone's coming," murmured Rob.

They waited until twelve, then Rob started to get antsy. "That guy must have been full of shit. I'm sorry to have dragged you out here, Will."

But Will was focused on a grey van coming up the road. "Hold that thought."

They watched as the van came to a stop outside the shop. Rob took a photograph of the number plate. A man got out and walked around to the back. He was stocky and was wearing jeans and a black long-sleeved shirt. A cap was pulled down low over his face. Rob couldn't make out his features but fired off a few more shots anyway.

"Don't recognise him, do you?" asked Will.

Rob shook his head. "He's not from the estate."

The man pulled open the back of the van and a child jumped down. He couldn't be more than twelve or thirteen years old.

"What the hell?" murmured Rob.

Then another child jumped out, then two more.

"What's going on?" Will scratched his head.

"Four." Rob lowered the camera. "He said four."

"You think he meant four kids?" Will's voice rose in disbelief.

"Maybe, I don't know."

"This isn't good," muttered Will.

While they were deciding what to do, a second van pulled up behind the first one. The driver got out and opened the side door. Unfortunately, it was facing away from the surveillance van, so they couldn't get a photograph. The four boys, all shabbily dressed in jeans or trackpants and T-shirts with worn jackets, climbed in.

"It's a switch," hissed Rob.

"What do we do?" Will glanced from one van to the other. "Who do we follow?"

"Let's stick with the kids," said Rob, making a split-second decision. "I've got both number plates."

"Okay." Will slid into the driver's seat. Rob climbed over into the passenger seat and fastened his seat belt. They waited until the van containing the four kids had pulled away from the kerb and driven off down the street, before they followed.

"Don't lose them," Rob warned.

"I won't."

They'd all completed surveillance training and advanced driving courses. Will was as qualified as anyone to follow the white van.

"They're going back to the estate." Rob frowned. Why? Had Torch organised this? Was this his pickup? Four children? But what for? Whatever it was, it couldn't be good.

They watched as the white van drove into the Beaufort Estate. "We can't follow them in," warned Will. "Not this time of night. It's too dangerous."

"Damn it." Rob frowned. They could wait at the perimeter, but visibility was limited over the low wall, and someone had shot out all the lights on the estate, so it simmered in sulky darkness.

"I'm going to take a look." Rob got out of the van before Will could stop him. He pulled himself up on the wall and peeked over it.

The van rolled to a stop outside Block D — at least, he thought it was Block D. Hard to tell from this angle.

A big guy got out. Was it Torch? He couldn't be sure from this distance. The children jumped out of the van and followed him into the building. They had slight, thin frames and walked cautiously, like they didn't know what to expect.

"Shall we call for backup?" whispered Will, who'd snuck up beside him.

Rob bit his thumbnail. "I don't know. If those kids are at risk in any way, then yes, we should, but if not, then it might be worth letting it play out."

"How do we know?"

"We don't, that's the problem."

"What do you think he wants with them?" Will's eyes were haunted by the unwanted thoughts going through his brain.

"He's a drug dealer," reasoned Rob. "I bet he's using them as couriers."

"You mean county lines stuff? Into the suburbs?"

"Maybe."

It started drizzling, so they got back into the van. The wet streets glistened in the moonlight, but in the estate, it was eerily dark.

Will dropped his head back and closed his eyes. Rob fought the urge to doze off. He didn't know what Torch was up to, but he felt certain it wasn't over yet.

He was right. At two o'clock, they heard an engine start. Rob was out of the van in a flash and peering over the wall. "They're on the move."

The white van drove out of the estate and turned left into a road leading to the main thoroughfare. Rob jumped back into the van and they accelerated in pursuit.

"Keep on them." Rob gazed at the van's tail lights. "We have to assume the kids are inside." They hadn't seen them get in. They hadn't seen shit from outside the perimeter wall. But it made sense. Why pick them up otherwise?

The van navigated the urban streets until it merged onto the A3 towards Clapham. Will put the windscreen wipers on. The soft, rhythmic thud was strangely comforting.

"They're going out of town," murmured Rob.

At Clapham Common, the van veered left onto the A24 and continued south. It kept going, past Tooting and South Wimbledon. Will followed at a discreet distance. It would be harder to spot a tail at night, especially in the rain. All you saw through the rear-view mirror was headlights. The roads weren't busy, but there was still some night traffic. Delivery vans, postal lorries, shift workers.

After Morden, the van turned off. "He's heading to the station," Rob guessed, catching sight of a sign for St Helier. It was a British Rail and Thameslink station, which meant mainline stations like Sutton and Wimbledon were only a couple of stops away.

"That's smart," he mumbled.

"What is?" said Will.

"Watch." Rob nodded to the van, which had pulled over a couple of hundred metres from the station. The van door slid open and the four boys got out. They looked ridiculously young in the dark, unfamiliar surroundings. One even had his arms wrapped around his thin body. The rain covered them all in a fine mist. "He's dropping them off here to catch the first trains out in the morning."

Will cottoned on. "It's like a wheel radiating outward."

Rob's heart went out to them. "I think it's time we picked them up." He grabbed a stab vest and slid it over his shirt.

Will did the same. "Once they get on the train, we've lost them."

"I'll take the driver. You see if you can round up the kids. If they run, just grab one of them. I'm betting those rucksacks they're wearing contain drugs, all readily packaged for delivery."

"We could have done with some backup," gritted Will.

"Too late for that."

Rob opened the van door and jumped down. He didn't often wish he was armed, but this was one of those times. The driver could be packing, and one thing he knew about these guys is that they weren't afraid to shoot to kill.

But the man didn't climb out of the van. This was a drop-off, nothing more. The boys had obviously been briefed and knew what to do.

Rob ran along the pavement, shielded by the darkness. The boys would hang out here for the next hour or so, until the trains started, and then they'd disperse with their toxic cargo, delivering it to users all over the Home Counties.

Will did the same on the other side of the road. It was bushy with trees and foliage, and he was able to remain hidden until he'd almost reached the boys. Then one of them saw him and yelled.

All four scattered.

Will gave chase, following one of the boys over the railway bridge.

Rob held his stun gun and opened the passenger door of the van. He recognised the man inside.

"Hello, Declan," he said. "Put your hands where I can see them and get out of the car."

CHAPTER 16

Will was driving while Rob sat in the back with a wheezing Declan and one of the boys. The police sergeant had managed to catch him on the opposite platform, since the exit was still locked and there had been nowhere for him to go. Both were in handcuffs, and so far, neither had said a word.

Rob pulled on his latex gloves and inspected the boy's rucksack. "Whoa."

"You got something?" asked Will.

"Oh, yes." There were several hundred grams of cocaine in there, in individually wrapped packets. He couldn't be sure of the street value, but it was substantial.

He looked at Declan and shook his head. "Torch is not going to be happy."

Declan broke out into a sweat. The young boy fidgeted, while shooting Rob dark looks from defiant eyes.

"It'll be okay," Rob told him. "You're not in trouble."

But he got a blank stare in return. The boy couldn't understand him.

They delivered Declan and the child to the nearest police station with a custody suite, which happened to be Croydon. The suspects were processed and placed in a holding cell overnight. By then, the sun was coming up and everybody needed sleep. The interrogations would have to wait until later.

* * *

It was midday when Rob got back to Croydon. The interviews would take place where the suspects were being held. He was feeling good after a decent four-hour sleep. He'd called Galbraith and updated him on the night's activities. The Scottish DCI had said he'd inform the Superintendent.

Will and Jenny met him there.

"Here we are again, Declan," Rob said once Will had started the recording. By contrast, the gangster looked terrible. Dark rings, messy hair, and giant sweat patches under his arms. He'd stopped wheezing though, so someone must have got him an inhaler.

The boy was still in the holding cell. Officers had made sure he'd had something to eat and drink and was comfortable. Social services had been notified and were on their way. They couldn't even try to talk to him without a responsible adult being present.

Rob turned his attention back to Declan.

"You are being charged with possession with intent to supply Class A drugs, along with the exploitation of a minor."

Declan sat sullenly in the chair and stared at the table. His attorney, the same smartly dressed woman, this time in an eye-watering fuchsia dress, perched elegantly beside him.

"You do realise that this is your third Class A drug trafficking offence, which means you're looking at jail time. Minimum seven years."

"I can't go to jail." Declan was breathing heavily. "I gotta look after my mum."

"You should have thought about that before you coerced four youngsters to courier your drugs for you."

"They're not my drugs," he said.

Rob pursed his lips. "Whose are they, then? Because they were found on the kid you dropped off at the station. I bet your fingerprints are all over his rucksack."

There was a long pause, then Declan leaned over and whispered something to his solicitor.

She nodded. "My client would like to make a deal."

"Really?" said Rob. "And what makes him think we want to make a deal? We have him bang to rights. We don't need anything else to charge him."

The dark patches under his arms were spreading, and Rob could smell the desperation on him.

"I'll tell you about the drugs," he mumbled. "About Torch."

"We already know Torch gave you the drugs," Rob said. "What we don't know is where he was last Friday night."

Declan's shoulders dropped. A long moment passed.

"I don't know where he went," he said. "I didn't go with them."

"Who did?"

"Ali and Shane. They didn't tell nobody where they were going."

There was a flicker in Declan's gaze. He knew, even if he hadn't been told.

"But if you had to guess?"

The gangster glanced at his solicitor. "Will I still have to go to jail?"

The lawyer looked at Rob. "Do we have a deal?"

Rob nodded. "Yeah, if you can tell us where Torch went, we have a deal."

"No jail?" breathed Declan.

"No jail," agreed Rob, hoping he could sell it to the Superintendent.

He exhaled, slumping over the table. "Okay, I'll tell you. They went to meet the Albanian."

"Who?"

"The guy Torch gets the coke from. Once a month he meets him somewhere else, off the estate. I don't know where. He takes Ali and Shane with him for backup. They come back with the product. That's all I know."

Rob frowned. That wasn't what he'd expected to hear.

Will shot him an uncertain glance.

"Does this Albanian have a name?" asked Rob.

A shrug. "They just call him the Albanian."

Rob leaned forward. "How do you know this?"

"I heard them talking. I keep my ears open."

Rob gazed at him for some time, letting what Declan had said wash over him. The Albanian was the supplier. It had all been about the drugs. Nothing to do with the shooting at the restaurant. Unless they had taken care of that on the way home. Or outsourced it to the Albanian and his crew.

Dejected, he nodded to Declan and was about to end the interview when Jenny barged in.

"Guv, you have to come and look at this."

"What is it?" Rob and Will followed her down the passage.

"It's crazy," she said. "I don't know what to make of it."

She opened a door and walked into a holding cell. The drug courier kid was sitting on the bench in a standard-issue police T-shirt and trackpants, his hands on his lap.

"Look at his wrist."

The kid turned his hand over. On his left wrist was a stamp, just like the one found on the boy in the river.

CHAPTER 17

"Where did you get that?" Rob asked the boy. He got the same blank stare as he had in the van.

He turned to one of the police officers standing nearby. "Do you have a translator?"

"Which language?" She spread out her hands. "We haven't determined where he's from yet. He won't talk."

Rob stared at the stamp. He had a million questions and no answers.

"What does it mean?" he finally said. "Are the two cases connected?"

Will shook his head, at a loss.

Jenny shrugged. "I don't know. I've only just seen it. It's faded, like the other one. A couple of days old, at least."

The boy put his hands back in his lap.

"What was the other boy, Benny? Eritrean? Let's get someone in here who speaks Eritrean, preferably a social worker." They were still waiting for one from the council to arrive. "They might be able to get something out of him."

Jenny nodded and went over to the custody desk to arrange it. Rob and Will followed, leaving the officer to lock up behind them. They decamped to the café across the road to get a decent coffee.

"I don't get it," Rob said. "The dead boy in the river must have been one of Torch's drug couriers. That's the only explanation."

"Do you think he's targeting unaccompanied asylum seekers?" asked Will. "Kids who can't speak English, who have no contacts here and no one to turn to?"

Rob shook his head. "It's sick. They're taking advantage of those poor kids for their own gain. Forcing them to deliver drugs, and if they don't . . ."

"They beat them," finished Will.

"Or shoot them in the head and throw their bodies in the river."

They stared at one another.

"Is that what's happening here? Is that the 'something big' Ant Price was talking about? The 'something' Torch was in on?"

"Could be," said Will, warming to the idea. "And when Ant went to meet Lawrence, Torch had him taken out."

"By a guy on a motorcycle." Rob scratched his chin. "It could have been one of the gang. It could have been a hired gun."

"Probably the latter," said Will. "No accountability."

Rob nodded. His DS was right. Even if they did trace the gun back to the shooter, they wouldn't be able to link it to Torch. He was too smart for that.

* * *

The interpreter, who introduced herself as Samira, was wearing a flowing dress with a headscarf. She was first and foremost a practising social worker. "I specialise in working with traumatised children," she told them in her soft, lyrical voice. "Mostly unaccompanied asylum seekers."

She spoke many North African languages, including Arabic, Somali, Berber, Hausa, Amharic and Oromo. Rob didn't know what half of those were, but he was hopeful as he showed her into an interrogation room where the young boy was waiting. He'd eaten a sandwich and had a soft drink but hadn't said a word to anyone.

"We need to know where he's from," Rob told her.

She spoke a few words and waited for a response.

Nothing.

She tried something else. It sounded like Arabic. A flutter of an eyelash, a twitch in the cheek.

Yes.

The interpreter also clocked the boy's reaction and pressed on, her tone soft and reassuring. The boy began to respond. He glanced up at her, bit his lip and then nodded.

She raised her head. "He's from Algeria."

Not the same country as Benny.

"Does he speak Arabic?" asked Rob.

"Algerian Arabic. It's a dialect called Darja."

Okay, now they were getting somewhere.

"What's his name?"

She repeated the question. He mumbled something unintelligible, but the interpreter understood.

"Imad," she said with a smile. "His name is Imad and he's twelve years old."

Christ. A twelve-year-old travelling all this way by himself. The boy was lucky to be alive.

"How did he get here?" asked Rob.

Will was recording the interview and jotting down salient details on his iPad.

"He doesn't know," the interpreter said, after conferring with him. "His parents paid for him to come here. He didn't want to, but it wasn't safe where he lived."

Rob glanced at Will. The parents paid to traffic him to Europe to start a new life. Things must have been pretty darn desperate where he lived for them to resort to that.

"Would you ask him why he was couriering drugs?"

She turned back to the boy and asked the question. They conversed for some time, and then she looked up. "He was told he had to. That it was the payment for staying in England."

"Holy shit." Will looked up from his device.

"Who told him to do it?" Rob felt the heat rise in his face.

"A man at the house. He said if they didn't do as they were told, they'd be sent back to where they came from."

Rob shook his head. Really, there were no words. He thought of his own son, a mere baby. Nurtured, loved, protected. How would he feel about sending him out into the world to fend for himself at the tender age of twelve? It was unconscionable.

"Can he describe this man?" asked Will.

"Tall, dark-haired."

"That doesn't give us much," said Rob, thinking about Bruno, Margaret's husband.

The interpreter leaned towards Imad and asked a few more questions. He pointed to his forearm and said something.

She glanced up at Rob. "A tattoo on his arm," she said. "Of an animal. He thought it was a wolf."

"A wolf. That helps." Rob nodded at the boy. "Tell him thank you very much. He's being very helpful." He hadn't noticed a wolf tattoo on Bruno's arm, but then he'd only glimpsed him for a split second as he was getting out of his car.

The woman did as Rob asked and Imad broke into a hesitant smile. He probably didn't get a lot of compliments. The dark glare of suspicion began to lift. He became more relaxed. Rob could tell he'd taken a liking to the interpreter. He trusted her.

"Did he know the man in the van?" asked Rob.

The interpreter shook her head. "He says no. Earlier today, two men picked them up and took them to a flat where they were each given a rucksack, a map and a phone. Then they were told what to do."

"How did they communicate?"

Samira asked the boy. "One of the men spoke Arabic."

That made sense. "Did he know the rucksack contained drugs?"

There was a slight hesitation, then the boy nodded. "They knew what they were carrying, yes. If the police stopped them, they were told to run, taking the rucksack with them."

Rob let out a shaky breath, then turned to Will. "It's a county lines operation. Jo worked on something like this a couple of years back. We'll have to notify the NCA."

It looked like Imad was tiring. "One last thing," Rob said. "Did he know a boy called Benny?"

A sad nod. "He did, but Benny disappeared. He liked him. He was nice to him."

"From the children's home?"

The boy nodded again.

"Where did he get the stamp?"

Imad glanced at the woman, who translated.

"The man stamped them when they agreed to do the job. He doesn't know why."

* * *

"Right," said Rob, after they left the police station. Jenny had stayed to tie up the interview with Imad. "We need a search warrant for that children's home. They're involved somehow. If we find the gun they used to shoot Benny, then we can arrest the lot of them."

"What about the drug running?" asked Will.

"They may or may not be involved in that. It looks like they supply the kids and Torch runs the drugs. I'll speak to Mayhew as soon as we get back."

Except he didn't get a chance.

Galbraith intercepted him as soon as he walked into the squad room. "Rob, I've just had the asylum centre on the line. We've managed to identify Benny. We compared his fingerprints to their records and got a match. His real name was Biniam Yemane. He was sixteen years old and from a border town in Eritrea. Celeste is trying to contact the Eritrean authorities now in hopes we can speak to his parents to notify them of his death."

Jesus. Rob shuddered. He was glad he didn't have that job.

"We had a translator working with us in Croydon — Samira. She's excellent, and she's a trained social worker. Why don't you get her to do it? Jenny is with her now."

Galbraith took his advice and rang Jenny, who said she'd bring Samira back to the Putney office. She also told him Imad had been signed into the care of another social worker, rather than being returned to the children's home. *Good*, thought Rob. *That's the safest option for him right now.*

* * *

Galbraith led the interpreter to the incident room, where a Zoom call was being set up.

"Tell them he died bravely," Rob said to her as she passed.

She stopped. "Did he?"

"Yes. He put up a fight."

Her eyes were moist. "I will tell them."

"We're going to try to find out how he was trafficked," Galbraith said. "So we can pass it on to the relevant authorities."

For all the good it would do. That poor family. Finding out their son was dead on a Zoom call.

Rob pored over the latest reports that had come in from the lab. The DNA from under Benny's fingernails was back. He forwarded the email to Will, who would run it through the national database and see if they could get a hit. You never knew. They might get lucky. At the very least, it would help them identify the attacker, once they had him or her in custody.

That reminded him. He needed a warrant to search the children's home.

Mayhew was in her office, on the phone. He waited for her to hang up then walked over and knocked on the door.

"Come in, Rob."

Somewhere in the last few months, she'd gone from calling him DCI Miller to Rob. It felt a bit awkward, since they weren't exactly friends. Still, it wasn't worth mentioning. He still called her ma'am.

"What's this I hear about a county lines connection?"

Mayhew had a remarkable ability to know what was going on at any given time. It was almost impossible to pull the wool over her eyes, not that he wanted to. Not again. Last time he'd tried that, he'd almost been suspended. Lawrence's phone still worried him, but so far, nobody outside his team knew about that. As long as it stayed that way, they were in the clear.

"The boy we picked up the other night near Sutton had the same stamp on his wrist as the boy we found in the river. We think they were both used as couriers in Torch's drug-smuggling network."

She nodded slowly, like this wasn't news to her. "It makes sense," she reasoned. "Both young refugees, alone, vulnerable. Perfect targets for a county lines gang."

"Yes, ma'am. That's why we want to search the children's home."

Her eyebrow rose. "We have to be careful here, Rob. You know how the press get over refugees. If we put a foot wrong, we'll come off as the bad guys here."

"We still need to search the premises," Rob argued. He was aware how sensitive the situation was. "If someone at that children's home, someone in a position of care, shot the Eritrean boy and dumped him in the river, then we need to bring him or her in."

"I agree," she said. "Although, we don't know for sure it was someone from the children's home."

"We do, we just don't know who. Both boys were living at the children's home while they waited to be placed into care. Imad, the boy we brought in yesterday, told us it was a man at the hostel who told them they had to do what they were told, or they'd be sent back to where they came from."

A man with a wolf tattoo on his forearm. Rob's hands clenched as he said the words. This took emotional abuse to another level.

Mayhew flicked her fiery hair over her shoulder. "Okay, Rob. I'll grant the warrant, but please tread lightly. Be respectful. We can't be seen to be targeting refugees."

"We're not," said Rob. "We're investigating the owners of the children's home."

She sighed. "The press won't see it like that."

There was a knock on the door. Galbraith was standing there, his expression sombre.

"Sorry to interrupt," he said. "But you'd better come and listen to this, Rob."

"What's up?"

"We've just spoken to Benny's mother. She's in pieces." He paused.

"And?" said Rob.

"It turns out Benny had a younger brother who's missing."

CHAPTER 18

"A younger brother?"

The interpreter nodded. "Yes, his name is Dawit, or David in English."

Rob turned to Jenny. "What did they say at the intake centre?"

"They claim they processed them together and both were sent to the children's home. I haven't been able to get hold of anyone there to confirm."

"Okay, let's pay them a visit," Rob said to Will. "We need to find out whether Dawit was ever there, and if so, what happened to him. The last thing we need is another boy turning up in the river."

Jenny shivered.

"Did the Super approve the warrant?" Galbraith asked.

"Yeah."

"Perhaps we should wait for that. Go at the same time," he suggested.

Rob hesitated. He wanted to speak to them now, but it made sense to wait. That way they wouldn't antagonise them too much. One visit was enough. For now.

"I'll see how quickly I can get it," he said. "Gear up to go hunting, folks."

* * *

The children's home was busier than last time they'd visited. The reception room was filled with excitable youths having a pool competition. Rap music —at least, he thought it was rap music — was playing in the background.

Rob looked around for Margaret but couldn't find her. "Excuse me," he said to the woman at the front desk. She completely ignored him. He rapped on the glass. "Hello?"

She looked up, gasped and ripped the earphones from her ears. "Sorry. I didn't see you there."

"Is Margaret or Bruno in?"

"Bruno is out back, and I think Margaret is upstairs. Shall I call her?"

"Please," said Rob.

The woman sent a text, which took all of a few seconds, thumbs flying over the screen. A moment later, Margaret appeared, a confused expression on her face. "Hello again. Can I help you?"

Will handed her the search warrant. "We're here to conduct a search of the premises. I'm going to have to ask you to take all the children into the back garden."

Her eyes widened. "What, now?"

"Yes, now."

She took a deep breath. "This is very inconvenient, Detective. What is it you're searching for? We have nothing to hide here. The rooms are searched daily for drugs and other contraband. Our kids are clean."

"I'm sure they are," Rob said. "We'll search both properties simultaneously, so if you could get a message to the children in the adjoining house to go outside, that would be great."

They'd enlisted the help of the uniformed police division and had four officers waiting outside to assist. Everyone was wearing gloves and had been briefed as to what to look for. Primarily, the gun used in the shooting by the river.

Once the buildings were clear, Margaret went outside with the others.

"Right, Jenny and Jeff, you search this side. We'll go next door."

He took two uniformed officers with him and they walked through the interconnecting door into the adjoining property.

"Which one is Dawit's room?" Rob asked a social worker standing outside. He took him upstairs to a room with two bunk beds in it.

"Dawit had the top bunk over there." The social worker pointed to a bed where a picture of a footballer had been torn out of a magazine and stuck to the wall. A flimsy, paper dream.

The room was warm and tidy. A cleaner had obviously been in. The bin was empty, the mirror on the wall shone, and the beds were made. Each bunk had a table beside it with two drawers. One for each child?

Rob opened the one nearest to Dawit's bed and rummaged around. A few coins, a tube of ointment probably prescribed by the doctor, a comb and a ragged photograph. Rob took it out and had a look. It was of a young boy being cuddled by a woman in traditional attire. The same woman they'd spoken to on the Zoom call. She was smiling into the camera, but it didn't reach her eyes. Had she known then she was going to let her boys go?

He put the photo back, breathing through the heaviness in his chest. He had to find this boy. He had to let his mother know he was safe, that it hadn't all been in vain.

They searched the rest of the rooms, the attic, which was used for storage, and the garden shed. Nothing. No gun, no other weapons. The worst they found was a packet of cigarettes in one of the rooms, hidden under the pillow. They left them there.

In total, the search took two hours. They tried not to make too much of a mess. Even so, afterwards Rob went outside and apologised to Margaret and her husband. "We appreciate your cooperation," he said. "Given that Benny was placed in your care and Imad too, it was necessary."

"What will happen to Imad?" Margaret's eyes were filled with concern. "He's a sweet boy. He shouldn't be punished."

"Well, Mrs Pavić, we're still trying to work out how he came to be in that vehicle with three other young boys. According to him, someone from the children's home recruited them."

"What?" Her surprise seemed genuine. "Are you saying someone here is exploiting the children?"

It could be that she wasn't aware it was happening. "That's exactly what I'm saying," he said.

She looked at her husband. The beefy Croatian shook his head. "You are mistaken. All our staff are qualified caregivers or social workers. We have a duty of care to these kids, we'd never do anything to hurt them."

Rob would like to think that was the case.

It was a mild autumn afternoon and Bruno was wearing a black T-shirt. Rob's gaze dropped to his forearms. No tattoos. He wasn't the man who'd coerced them into taking part in the drug running.

"I understand Benny had a younger brother." Rob launched into the reason they were there. He would have preferred to question them separately and under interview conditions, but he'd have to caution them for that and so far, there was nothing to suggest they'd done anything wrong.

Margaret glanced at her husband before answering. "Yes, Dawit. Unfortunately, he ran away a couple of nights ago."

"You didn't think to report him missing?" said Rob.

"I was going to. I wanted to see if he came back first. Sometimes they do."

Rob narrowed his gaze. "Why didn't you mention it last time we were here?"

"I forgot," she said. "We're busy and we have other kids to look after. And like I said, at that point, I wasn't sure he'd run away. I still thought he might turn up. It's not a prison here, Detective. The children can come and go as they please. They're supposed to sign in and out when they leave, but they don't always."

"Dawit was twelve," pointed out Rob. "Surely he isn't allowed out unaccompanied."

"No, he shouldn't have been," she admitted. "But like I told you, we don't keep them locked up. If Dawit wanted to get out, it wouldn't have been hard."

"Did anyone see him leave?" Rob ran a hand through his hair. He was getting the impression this was a waste of time.

"Not that I know of."

Her husband shook his head. "I asked the staff, but nobody saw him. We think he must have snuck out after dark."

"Does that happen a lot?" Rob asked.

"More often than you know," she said. "These children are homeless, left to fend for themselves. We try to do the best thing for them, but some of them want to be on their own, particularly the older ones. They don't want to be here." She shrugged. "Not even until their asylum status comes through."

"How long does that take?" asked Will.

"Anything from six months to three years," Margaret replied. "It's not a quick process."

"And they're with you all that time?" asked Rob.

"Some of them, yes. We try to give them the security of a family unit. The older ones move into semi-independent accommodation."

"Dawit was twelve. What reason did he have to run off by himself?"

"Who knows?" She shrugged. "They don't always tell us what they're thinking."

"Was there any reason for Dawit to leave? Did he have an altercation with someone? A fight?"

"Not that I know of."

"What about the social workers?"

"Ask them yourself." She gestured behind her. "Louis is over there. He's responsible for the children's pastoral care. He keeps tabs on them, makes sure they're coping mentally and adjusting to British life. Then there's Cybil. She looks after the little ones and makes sure they're cared for. Mostly, they just want a mother figure they can trust. Someone who cares for them."

Rob nodded to Will and Jenny, who went over to talk to the social workers.

"Do you use a stamp on the boys?" Rob asked.

"A stamp? What kind of stamp?"

Rob showed Margaret a picture of the imprint on Benny's wrist.

Her eyes widened. "No, I've never seen that before. Have you?" She turned to her husband.

He shook his head. "What is it for?"

Rob gritted his teeth. "That's what I'm trying to find out."

* * *

"I didn't see any stamp marks on the kids," Jenny said on the way back to the station.

"Me neither." Will gave a shake of his head.

The two social workers they'd questioned didn't have anything more to add. Neither of them had seen Dawit disappear, but both were sad he was gone.

"He was a sweet boy," the pastoral carer had said, while Cybil had seemed genuinely upset. "You will find him, won't you? He needs taking care of. He won't survive out there on his own."

Rob was beginning to feel desperate.

"Now what? We found nothing, and Bruno doesn't have a tattoo on his forearm, I checked."

"Dawit went missing of his own accord, just like Benny," Jenny said thoughtfully. "Maybe they're being targeted by someone outside the children's home."

"It's possible," agreed Rob. "It could be a legal advisor, one of the educational staff, who the hell knows."

"We can't watch everyone," said Will.

"No, but we can put an alert out for Dawit. He's a missing minor. He's vulnerable and at risk. We should get every department looking out for him."

Will gave a quick nod. "I'll get on that as soon as we get back."

"It's only been a few days," Jenny pointed out. "There's still a chance Dawit is alive."

Rob prayed she was right.

* * *

Rob sank down on the couch, Jack in his arms, Trigger at his feet. God, he was tired.

"You look as knackered as I feel." Jo handed him a bottle. Jack immediately reached for it, his eyes widening in anticipation.

"Someone's hungry," he remarked.

"Always. How about you? Are you okay?"

He told her about the missing boy. "He's twelve years old. God knows what he's doing out there by himself. If he's even alive."

Jo sat down next to him. "What makes you think he isn't?"

"We found his brother floating in the Thames. That doesn't bode well. What if Dawit is dead too, but we haven't found him yet?"

She patted him on the leg. "Don't assume anything. He might have got away. He might be fine, living in a shelter somewhere."

"He's twelve," Rob repeated.

"I know, but these kids have travelled halfway across the world to get here. They're resilient. Don't give up on him just yet."

Rob stifled a yawn. "I've put out an alert."

"If you like, I can reach out to my NCA contacts. Many of them have experience in child trafficking and exploitation. They might be able to help."

"If you could, that would be great," Rob said. "Anything that might help us find this kid."

"Okay, I'll make a few calls in the morning. Right now, I think we could both benefit from going to bed."

Jack's eyes were closing. The feed had obviously satisfied him. "Come on. Let's put him down. He's ready to doze off."

Rob lowered Jack gently into his cot and turned out the light. "This case is so confusing," he said. "I was convinced it was Torch who put the hit out on Ant Price and Sam, but now we've got a county lines drug smuggler exploiting child refugees, and whoever is running that wouldn't want it getting to the authorities."

"Torch isn't running it?" Jo slid into bed beside him.

"No, he hires the kids from a third party. It's all run by some other gang. None of Torch's crew seem to know about it, and the big man himself isn't talking.

"I'll see what I can find out tomorrow," she whispered, drawing him to her.

Rob forced the case from his mind. He wrapped his arms around Jo and lost himself in her kiss. Right now, family had to come first.

* * *

Rob drove to work early the next day, opting for the river road, rather than the crowded Upper Richmond. He marvelled at the leaves changing colour and falling in their droves to line the adjacent towpath in a burnished orange carpet.

Two eight-man rowing boats passed by on the river, accompanied by a motor launch. The teenage boys rowed powerfully, gliding across the still water. The traffic was heavy and soon the two boats disappeared downstream ahead of him, leaving a silver ribbon in their wake.

"Morning, Celeste," he called as he walked into the squad room. The detective constable was sitting at her desk, nursing a coffee. The rest of the team weren't in yet. Even Mayhew's office was empty.

"Guv, I've been waiting for you to get here." Celeste jumped up, nearly knocking over her mug.

"What's up?"

"It's DCS Lawrence, sir. I've found something that might be of interest."

"Oh, yes?"

She thrust a piece of paper in front of him. "This is a list of people the Chief put away. Remember you asked me to look into his prior cases?"

"Yes." He ran his eyes down the list. She'd highlighted one name in yellow.

Kenny Holloway. "Who's he?"

"Kenny Holloway was a small-time thief and a wife beater. He assaulted his wife so badly, she ended up in A&E."

"Shit."

"He had dependency issues, but according to his statement, he'd been clean for several months before he was arrested."

"What was he done for?"

"Possession with intent to supply," she said. "Lawrence was the arresting officer. According to his testimony, they found £60,000 worth of crack cocaine in his car. He insisted it wasn't his, that it was put there to frame him. The judge didn't believe him, and he went away for fourteen years."

"Why is this relevant?"

Celeste tapped the page. "Because, sir, he was released two weeks ago."

CHAPTER 19

"Briefing!" yelled Rob, once the whole team was in the office. They all filed into the incident room. Then he got a blushing Celeste up in front of everyone to explain what she'd found.

"No way," whispered Jenny. "Are you saying that this Kenny character could have taken out the Chief?"

"It's possible," said Rob. "Think about it. He blames Lawrence for putting him away. He festers for fourteen years, finally gets out and wants revenge."

"That's the quickest way to get sent straight back to prison," said Will.

"It might be, but we can't rule it out. We need to look into this guy. Find out where he's staying, what he's doing and who his close associates are. Does he have a motorcycle? Jenny, you and Celeste keep working on him."

"Yes, boss."

"We're spread thin," Galbraith cut in. "We need to define our tasks."

"I'll stick with Torch," said Mike, who was on a rare break from surveillance. He was joining the plain-clothed team in the van around midday. "He's been good these last few days, but something's brewing, I can feel it."

"Okay, keep us posted," said Rob. "If he does anything remotely suspicious, you let me know. We know he's guilty of drug smuggling, but we still don't know if he had anything to do with the Chief's murder."

"What about the NCA?" asked Jenny. "Won't they take him in based on Declan's testimony?"

"Not if Raza Ashraf has anything to do with it," said Rob. "Besides, it's Declan's word against Torch's. Neither the rucksack nor the drugs had Torch's fingerprints on them."

"Typical," muttered Mike.

"And since Declan made a deal, we've had to release him. The story we agreed on was that Imad didn't have the drugs on him. He managed to ditch the rucksack somewhere."

"So, there was no proof?" said Jenny.

"Exactly. Which is why we let them go. Hopefully, Torch will believe it."

"Nice."

Galbraith looked at Jeff. "We'll keep digging into Margaret and Bruno's background and keep an eye on the children's home. I've got patrols driving past every two hours. If anyone picks up any kids, hopefully we'll spot it. Unfortunately, the budget doesn't stretch to full-time surveillance. Not unless we pull it from Torch."

"Give me a few more days," Mike said. "I've got a feeling something is going to go down soon."

Galbraith nodded. "It would help if we could rule out Torch or the Pavićs. Keeping tabs on all our suspects is stretching our resources."

Galbraith was more of a stickler for budgetary constraints than he was, but Rob agreed. They couldn't keep chasing everyone around. "When's Harry back?" he asked.

"Next week," replied Jenny.

He grunted. That wouldn't help them now.

"According to Declan, Torch was meeting the Albanian last Friday night," Rob said. "If nothing transpires in the next few days, we'll pull off the surveillance. As much as I don't like the guy, it looks like he's in the clear."

"For Lawrence's murder," muttered Mike. "He's as guilty as sin for drug smuggling and using young kids to do it."

"Agreed, but that's not our remit." Rob glanced at Galbraith. "Let's give Mike a few more days, then contact the NCA with what we know."

The burly Scot nodded. "I don't think he shot that wee boy either. We didnae find anything to suggest his gang was involved. Drug smugglers aye, but I don't think they're killers."

* * *

Rob spent the rest of the day reading reports on Kenny Holloway. Like a lot of criminals, he'd had a bad start in life. His father had bailed when he was a baby and he'd been raised by a mother who could barely look after herself, let alone him. At six, he'd been sent to a foster family, who'd fulfilled their basic obligation to him, but were probably just in it for the council benefits.

Kenny had performed badly at school, leaving with only two GCSEs. He'd worked as a packer, a delivery driver, an assistant in a hardware store and a trader on eBay. Then he met and married Lucy Palmer. Thin and willowy with a fragile, ethereal beauty that transcended the black-and-white wedding photograph that Jenny had found. What on earth had she seen in him?

Still, a year later she was pregnant. According to the council records, they lived in social housing in Tooting Bec and claimed benefits. Lucy had remained there while Kenny had been inside.

Rob bit his lip. He wondered how she was getting on now that he was out. Perhaps they ought to pay them a visit. A courtesy follow-up call to see how he was adjusting to life on the outside. Fourteen years was a long time to be away from your family.

* * *

He took Jenny with him.

The block where the Holloways lived was at the end of a leafy street in the South London suburb of Lambeth. It was built of monotonous red brick and instead of going up, it sprawled out. "Elmwood Place," read Jenny.

The damp road was covered with fallen leaves, clogging the gutters and mulching underfoot. Rob glanced up at the almost bare trees. There was a definite chill in the air. "Winter's coming," he muttered.

Jenny pointed. "Look."

He followed her gaze to a row of garages behind the block. Outside one of them was a motorcycle.

"Could be anyone's," he said.

They reached the entrance, a thick glass door protected by part of the wall that jutted out. There was a distinct smell of rubbish, and Rob suspected the bins were stored behind it.

He was about to ring the buzzer for number six when a woman holding a toddler by the hand appeared. "Wait," he said to Jenny.

The woman pushed a button on the inside and the door clicked open. Rob held it for her as she walked out. She smiled her thanks as her toddler gazed up at them with curious, brown eyes.

They slipped inside.

"It's a ground-floor flat." Jenny checked the numbers on the wall. "This way."

They stopped at number six.

"How do you want to play this?" she asked.

"It's a routine visit. We want to know how he's adjusting, how the wife is doing, that sort of thing. Keep it casual. Polite."

She nodded.

Rob pressed the buzzer, which choked out a tune. Footsteps could be heard coming down the passage, and then the cover of the peephole scraped back. The chain rattled and the door opened. A woman in her thirties stood there, blonde hair up in a high ponytail, blue eyes crinkling in confusion.

"Can I help you?"

"Mrs Holloway?"

"Yes."

"We're with the police. Can we come in?"

She hesitated. "What is this about?"

Jenny smiled. "It's a courtesy call. We're checking to see that everything is okay since your husband's release."

"He's not here."

"That's okay." Jenny's smile was firmly in place. "Can we have a quick word with you?"

"Um, sure." She opened the door wider and let them in. The passage was dark and on the cold side, but she led them into a bright, open-plan living room with a tiny kitchen at one end.

It was neat and tidy, although sparsely decorated. It was clear the Holloways didn't have much disposable income. The couch was old but looked comfy. There was a well-used armchair, a low coffee table with a lace cloth over it and a plastic stand with a latest-model flat-screen television on it. A Sky box sat underneath. Priorities.

"That looks painful." Jenny nodded to the deepening bruise on her cheek. Her eye was starting to swell, but she'd done a good job at hiding it with make-up.

"Oh, it's nothing." She waved her hand. "I slipped when I was getting out of the bath."

"I'm sorry to hear that." Jenny met her eye, but Lucy glanced away.

"Can I get you something to drink?" she offered.

"No, thank you," said Rob.

Jenny sat down on the couch. "We won't be here long."

Lucy perched on the armchair while Rob remained standing.

"Fourteen years," said Jenny. "That's a long time."

"Yes, but it's lovely to have him back."

"Is it?" Jenny asked.

Lucy glanced down. "Obviously, it's taken some adjusting, but we're doing okay."

"Are you sure? How is your son?"

"He's fine."

"How does he feel about having his father home?"

She shrugged.

Not great, Rob was betting. Especially since he had to watch him smacking his mother around.

"How old is he now?" asked Rob.

"He's nearly fifteen."

Rob walked to a framed photograph hanging on the wall. "That him?"

"Yes." She nodded proudly.

"Big lad."

It wouldn't be long before he took on his father, if only to protect his mum. Not a healthy situation for any lad.

Jenny was following his train of thought. "Lucy," she said. "You don't have to stay with him, you know."

She swallowed.

"If you wanted to get a place of your own, that could be arranged. You just need to speak to the council."

"I couldn't leave him," she whispered. "He'd kill me."

Jenny glanced at Rob. "Even more reason to," she said. Then she took out her phone. "Lucy, I'm going to give you the number of a friend of mine. She's a social worker. If you need help, or you decide to leave, give her a call. She'll help you with the process. You don't even need to tell your husband you're doing it."

A flicker of light registered in Lucy's eyes. Rob realised it was hope. After fourteen years of respite, she now had to deal with her abusive husband again.

"Please, think of your son. This isn't a healthy environment for him."

Lucy was right. Rob had been there. In this exact position. He'd seen his father abuse his mother. He'd been sixteen at the time. If it wasn't for his uncle stepping in, who knows what he might have done.

He took a deep breath. He'd buried those memories so effectively that he almost didn't remember it. It was like it had happened to someone else. Now, looking at Lucy and the photograph of her fourteen-year-old boy, he was hit by a sense of déjà vu.

"You don't have to live like this," he told her.

She nodded, tears springing to her eyes. "It's like a nightmare," she whispered. "When he went away, I couldn't believe it. I was so relieved, and now . . . and now . . ." She sobbed and put her hand over her mouth.

Jenny leaned forward. "Call her," she said, nodding to the card.

Rob glanced around the living room. "Where is your husband now?"

"He's at the pub." Her voice was barely a whisper.

Rob knew what that meant. Alcohol fuelled the rage. His father had been the same. His temper flared when he'd been drinking, and he took it out on his mother. Some things never changed.

Rob steered the conversation back to the reason why they'd come. "When did your husband get out, Mrs Holloway?"

She sniffed. "About two weeks ago."

"Do you remember if he was here with you on Friday the third of October?"

She scrunched up her forehead. "I'm not sure . . . Let me think."

"It would have been the first Friday since he was released."

Her forehead cleared. "Oh, yes. He met the boys at the Crown for celebratory drinks. He didn't get back until late."

"Were you with them?"

"No. I was home with Bradley."

"Do you remember exactly what time he got home?" Rob asked. "Was it after midnight?"

"Definitely. I glanced at my radio alarm clock. It was nearly three when he got back."

Three o'clock in the morning. The shooting at the restaurant occurred at roughly half past one.

"Okay. Thank you, Mrs Holloway. That's all for now."

"Why do you want to know about that Friday?" she asked. "Did something happen?"

"What makes you think that?" asked Jenny.

She shrugged. "I don't know, just the way you were asking. I thought maybe . . ."

She was hoping her husband would be arrested and put away again.

"We're just checking up on a few things." Rob motioned to Jenny. It was time to go. "Thank you for speaking with us."

She got up and wiped her eyes. "Thank you for this." She held up the card.

"Use it," Jenny said. "You deserve to feel safe in your own home."

Lucy led them down the passage, this time turning on the light. They got to the door and Rob caught a glimpse of the sideboard against the wall. He nudged Jenny. She turned to look.

There was a black motorbike helmet on top of it.

CHAPTER 20

Back at the Putney precinct, Rob told the others what they'd found. "I took down the plate," he said to Will. "Let's run it through the DVLA database and see if we can pick it up anywhere on Friday night."

"I'll get right on it."

"Do you really think this guy, Kenny, could be the shooter?" Galbraith asked.

"I really don't know. I wouldn't have thought so. Torch has as good a motive as anyone, so do the Pavićs, if they're running a child exploitation ring. But he did have a beef against the Chief, and he was released days before his death. His wife says he was out Friday night. I'm going to follow up with the pub, but he had the opportunity."

They spent the rest of the day following up leads. The Crown in Lambeth confirmed Kenny was there on Friday night. The barman was a little hazy on what time he'd left, but he said he was pretty wasted.

"If he was pissed, he wouldn't have been able to ride his bike, let alone gun down three people with military precision," Rob said to Jenny after he'd put the phone down. "Whoever the shooter was, he had training. Two shots per victim. One in the head, one in the chest, except for Sam, who was turning around. I just don't think Kenny did it."

"He could have hired someone to do it," Jenny said.

Rob thought about this. Kenny had only been out for a few days. It took time to organise a hit like that. It took money. The guy was broke. "Nah, I'm not buying it."

"Did Will pick anything up on the ANPR?"

"Will?" asked Rob. "Any luck?"

"The plate didn't flag." He looked up from his computer. "But that's not to say he wasn't there. Bike plates won't show up on front-facing cameras."

Jenny frowned. "Do you want to search his apartment? Look for the murder weapon?"

"No," Rob said. "We're overstretched as it is. Let's put him on ice, for now."

"See everyone at the funeral tomorrow," said Rob, as he left that evening. The whole team nodded. Sam Lawrence was being laid to rest in the morning, and it promised to be an emotional day.

* * *

It was a beautiful autumn morning. The trees shimmered in bronze glory while the sun smiled down on the congregation. It was as if the elements had transpired to give Sam the finest send-off possible.

The service was touching. Sam's eldest daughter sang a tearful "Ave Maria" and his wife, Diana, said the eulogy. Jo had tears running down her face as she gripped his hand, and it was all Rob could do to keep it together.

The rest of his team were there, along with most of the police force. Sam had worked with and been respected by a lot of people. Even the Deputy Commissioner showed up.

"I'm so sorry for your loss," Jo said to Diana afterwards. "He was a wonderful man and an incredible boss. He'll be sorely missed."

"Thank you," she said, from underneath her pillbox hat and veil.

Rob went to talk to Mallory, his old sergeant, who was there with a slender brunette with a heart-shaped face and chocolate-brown eyes. She looked familiar, but he couldn't place her.

He shook Mallory's hand. "Good to see you."

"And you," said Mallory. "You remember Sylvia?"

The woman smiled, which made her eyes crinkle. "How do you do, Detective?"

"Very well, thank you." Then it hit him. She was one of the people they'd questioned in the Katie Wells disappearance. It had been Lawrence's last case.

He grinned at Mallory.

"I was sorry to hear about the Chief. Do you know what happened?" Mallory asked.

"We're looking into it."

Superintendent Mayhew walked past with the Deputy Commissioner.

"And how's that going?" Mallory knew him too well. "Do you have any suspects yet?"

Rob glanced at Sylvia.

"I'll be over here," she said to Mallory, touching his arm. "Good to see you again, DCI Miller."

"Rob, please."

She smiled and moved away.

"How long has that been going on?" Rob asked his old colleague. In all the years he'd known Mallory, he'd had never mentioned a girlfriend — or anyone, for that matter. He was an intensely private person.

"A while. Now, are you going to answer my question?"

"We've got too many suspects, that's the problem," Rob said. "We have three different leads we're looking into, and all three of them have a motive."

"I didn't think the Chief was that unpopular," muttered Mallory.

Rob chuckled. "Ever heard of a guy called Kenny Holloway?" Mallory had started at Putney MIT a few years ago and might recall being told something about it. He had an amazing memory — never forgot a detail.

Mallory thought for a moment. Rob knew he was sifting through the filing cabinet in his brain. "You know, that name is familiar."

"Apparently, Lawrence put him away on a possession with intent charge. He got fourteen years."

Mallory snapped his fingers. "That's it. I remember now. There was talk about that."

"What talk?"

"This is only a rumour," said Mallory, "but shortly after I started, I heard a couple of guys talking about that drug bust. That's the one where they found a fortune worth of crack in his vehicle, right?"

"That's the one." Mallory's memory was incredible.

"Okay, so the word at the time was that the perp was beating his wife senseless. She'd been in and out of hospital for months, and now she was pregnant. There were very real fears for her safety and that of her baby."

Rob gave a terse nod. "She said her son was nearly fifteen."

"Yeah, so around the same time, a stash of crack went missing from the evidence locker."

Rob stared at him. "No way. You're not suggesting—"

Mallory held up his hands. "I'm not suggesting anything, I'm just telling you what I heard at the time. The evidence goes missing, and the next thing you know, a similar amount is found in this guy's car."

"I can't believe the Chief would do that," said Rob, stunned.

But would he?

He thought about the fragile, ethereal beauty. Pregnant. Unable to escape her abusive husband.

"Like I said, I'm just repeating what I heard."

"Was there an investigation?" asked Rob.

"Into the missing evidence, yes, but nothing came of it. They installed cameras in the evidence room after that."

Rob whistled. "Well, that definitely puts an interesting spin on things."

Mallory patted him on the shoulder. "Glad to help."

Rob let Mallory go back to Sylvia, while he made his way over to Jo, who was talking to Galbraith's wife.

"I think we need to take another look at Kenny Holloway," he said to the Scot.

Galbraith frowned. "What makes you say that? I thought we'd cleared him."

"I just found out that he could have been framed."

"By the Chief?" He shook his head. "No way."

Rob told him what Mallory had said. The DCI's eyes got bigger and bigger. "Well, I'll be . . ." He stared at Rob.

"It was never proven," Rob said, "but if it's true, Kenny was framed, which means he's got a serious motive to have wanted Lawrence dead."

CHAPTER 21

Mike was in Chantelle's apartment, staring out the window at Block D. He had a perfect view of the entrance. He knew he was playing with fire, and if Torch ever found out he was sleeping with his girl, he'd be a dead man.

"You want a drink, babe?" She came up behind him and put her arms around his waist. He turned and kissed her on the forehead.

"A cuppa wouldn't go amiss."

She smiled. "Coming right up."

Damn, she was beautiful. She made him catch his breath every time he looked at her. A foolish distraction, his mama would say. And she'd be right. He was risking his job, the operation and both their lives by being here, and yet he couldn't seem to help himself.

How could something so wrong feel so right?

The radio at his shoulder crackled and a voice said, "Torch and his two cronies are back. They're driving in now."

Chantelle shot him a worried glance. "Maybe you'd better go."

He'd walked onto the estate disguised in jeans and a pulled-up hoodie. He knew his way around, the place was so familiar to him. The smells, the rain-drenched car park, the paranoia. It was like he'd never been away.

He could get off just as easily. He knew how to melt into the shadows cast by the looming tower blocks. He even remembered where the easiest place was to clamber over the wall.

He focused on the area in front of Block D. Torch's CR-V pulled in and the gangster got out, along with Ali and Shane. They were always with him when he left the estate.

They waited outside the block, talking. Torch looked at his watch.

"What's going on?" Mike muttered to himself.

Chantelle handed him a cup of tea. "It's his first Tuesday meeting."

"First Tuesday? What's that?"

"First Tuesday of the month. They all get together and have a meeting. I'm not sure what it's about. I was never invited." She pouted prettily. "'Plausible deniability', Torch always said."

"Where do they meet?" he asked.

"In Block C, but not his flat. There's one upstairs they use. I think it's someone's grandma." She shrugged.

He kissed her on the lips. "You are an absolute gem."

She glowed. "Have I told you how happy I am that you interrogated me?"

"You can tell me later. Right now, I've got work to do." He squeezed her hand.

She pretended to be disappointed, but he could see by the gleam in her dark brown eyes that she was pleased. "Okay, my sexy policeman. Do your thing, but be careful, okay? Remember, he can't know you're here with me."

"I remember."

That was a sore point. He did not like the fact she was still with Torch, but to feed information back to him, she had to be. It was a complicated mess. But if this went according to plan, they could bust Torch for drug trafficking, child exploitation or even murder, and put him away for a long, long time. Which was no less than he deserved.

It was men like Torch who were at the heart of the rot of these estates. The kids looked up to them. They wanted to be in their gangs. They hung out with them, ran errands and began dealing. He'd seen it happen. It had happened to his brother.

Mike gritted his jaw. He was going to bring this motherfucker down if it was the last thing he did.

A few more guys had accumulated around Torch. Mike counted seven of them, including the two in the car. He sipped his tea and watched as more ambled up. They walked casually, jeans low, hoodies up, furtive expressions on their faces. Some of them were even glancing around, making sure there were no cops around.

Finally, when there were about fifteen guys, all standing around the entrance, Torch beckoned them to follow him inside.

Mike watched them walk into the block, then he reached for his phone.

* * *

Rob was about to climb into bed when his phone buzzed. He glanced at it.

Mike.

It must be important. His colleague was still on surveillance detail, and he wouldn't call this late if it wasn't an emergency.

"Yeah, what's up?" Rob said. Jo stirred beside him. He listened for a moment, then threw back the covers. "I'm on my way."

Jo groaned. "What now?"

"Something's going down on the estate," he said. "I've got to go. I'll be back later."

"Be careful," she murmured, as he pulled on his jeans and a shirt.

"I will." He kissed her on the head and rushed out the door.

The drive took twenty-five minutes. When he got there, he saw two cop cars hovering outside the estate. The surveillance van was parked up against the perimeter wall, with one officer on the roof gazing through night-vision binoculars.

"Where's Mike?" Rob asked.

"He's inside," the officer standing by the van told him.

"How'd he get inside?" Rob frowned. "Isn't that dangerous?"

"He's got a contact," the man explained. "He's been keeping tabs on Torch from inside one of the blocks."

Rob raised an eyebrow. Was this an old contact, from when he'd lived here, or was it a newer, prettier contact? He kept his suspicions to himself and pulled out his phone.

"What's happening?" he asked when Mike answered.

"They're still inside," he said. "Flat eighty-six, eighteenth floor. Fifteen gangbangers. Dodgy as hell."

"Do you know what it's about?"

"I'm guessing it's drug-related. It happens on the first Tuesday of every month like clockwork."

"Must be," murmured Rob.

"Are we going in?" Mike asked.

"Negative. We don't have the authority." He'd called Mayhew on the way and given her an update. He'd asked if they could raid the flat, with the help of the Firearm division, but she'd said no. "Not without hard evidence."

"Shit. What if they've got drugs in there? We could bust them."

"I'm sorry, Mike. I know how you feel. We need more before we go bulldozing in. Let's get proof of what's going down and we'll work with the NCA to bring them in."

"Argh." Mike cursed and hung up the phone.

Rob felt his frustration.

"They're coming out," said the man with the binoculars. "Torch is heading towards Block D."

Mike texted. *They're gone.*

He replied. *We're going in. Coming?*

Meet you out front.

* * *

Rob hardly recognised Mike when he stepped out of the darkness at the side of the tower block. His face was hidden by a dark hoodie, his jeans hung loosely over his hips and he had flat, nondescript trainers on.

"Jesus, you gave me a fright." Rob thought one of the gangsters had come back.

"Sorry, guv. I'm undercover. Been watching from a mate's apartment."

"So I heard." He didn't ask who and Mike didn't say. "Why don't you lead the way?"

Mike gave a curt nod and entered the tower block. "Eighteenth floor," he said, pushing the button for the lift.

Rob gestured for the two coppers to take the stairs. They didn't complain, they simply disappeared into the darkened stairwell and started climbing.

The lift shook and trembled, but eventually got them to the eighteenth floor. As the doors jerked open, they peered out before stepping into the corridor. It was cold. The wind cut around the curved edges, whistling like a banshee.

Rob suppressed a shiver. "Come on. Let's go."

They approached flat 86. Rob peered over the balcony and wished he hadn't. It was bloody high. The trees looked like tiny broccoli sprouts far below. He'd hate to live up here. If anything happened, like a fire, you'd be fucked.

The two coppers finally made it and slunk along behind them down the corridor, their breathing laboured. "Thanks, guys," said Rob, acknowledging their effort. If they'd been ambushed, the two coppers would have had to come to their rescue.

But the corridor was empty.

Rob knocked on the door. There was no answer.

"Knock again," said Mike. "There's an old lady that lives there."

Rob did, and eventually they heard a voice call out, "Go away."

"It's the police," he called back.

They heard the sound of the chain jingling and the door opened. A wrinkled face looked out. "Did you say police?"

"Yes, ma'am. May we come in?"

"Of course. I thought it was those naughty boys back again." She shook her head. "They give me such a hard time."

"That's why we're here, ma'am." Rob followed her into the living room and looked around. It was warm and cosy, and well lived-in. He could see the old woman had been here for some time, possibly her whole life.

The dining room table, however, was covered in beer bottles, cigarette wrappers and ring marks. "Sorry about the mess," she said, rushing to clear it up. "I wasn't expecting any more company."

"Let me do that for you," Rob said. Mike helped as they cleared the table and put the bottles and wrappers into a plastic bag that they would take with them. The two coppers stood guard, one outside the flat and one just inside.

"Did you invite those men inside your flat?" Rob asked.

She shook her head. "Oh, no. I never do, but they don't listen to me. They just come in anyway."

"They shouldn't do that," Rob said. "It's illegal. You can report them."

The thought seemed to overwhelm her. "I don't want any trouble," she whimpered.

"What do they do here, ma'am?" asked Mike.

She glanced up at him. "They talk, count their money, drink beer and leave. It's no bother."

She was scared now. Rob could see the fear fluttering across her face. "Ma'am, would you give your consent for us to search your flat? We think they may have left some things here."

"Like what?" she asked.

"The money they were counting. Maybe drugs." *Guns.*

"Oh, I don't know. What if they come back?"

"Then we'll arrest them," said Mike.

Her eyes widened. "Well, I suppose if you must, then go ahead."

"Thank you."

Rob nodded to Mike, and they pulled on their gloves. As the coppers kept an eye out, they systematically searched the entire apartment. They were careful not to make a mess and to put things back the way they'd found them. It was when Mike was searching an overhead cupboard in the kitchen that they found what they were looking for.

"Fucking hell!" Bundles of cash toppled out and rained down on him. He stepped back and waited for the deluge to stop.

The old lady stared in shock.

"Did you know that was there?" asked Rob.

She shook her head in a daze. "That's my best china in there," she mumbled. "Don't use it anymore."

Clearly.

They bagged the cash, then finished the search. By the end of it, they'd appropriated two pistols, a revolver and a shotgun. The old lady's eyes were popping out of her head. "I swear, I didn't know," she kept repeating.

"That's okay," Rob told her. "We know."

They left her mouthing after them and took the stash back to the waiting police cars. Everyone was on high alert, but they hadn't spotted anyone lingering around. If Torch and his cronies knew what had happened, they were too smart to come out.

Rob noticed Mike kept his hood up the entire time he was on the estate and only relaxed when he was safely in the car.

"Good work," said Rob, as they pulled away. "We'll get this lot checked in and debrief tomorrow morning."

Mike's eyes were on the tower blocks as they drove away, and Rob got the feeling that part of him wished he could have stayed behind.

CHAPTER 22

It felt like he'd only been asleep for a minute or two when Trigger woke him up.

"What is it, boy?" He patted the Labrador's head to try and stop his frantic barking.

Jo sat up beside him. "Do you smell smoke?"

Rob sniffed the air. Yep. The unmistakable smell of fire.

He threw back the covers. "Get Jack."

She slid out of bed and darted to the door. The smell was stronger now it was open. "Oh my God. It's coming from downstairs."

Rob pulled on his shoes and ran down the stairs. Trigger howled behind him. "I know, boy." He disappeared into the smoke-filled hallway.

It was coming from the living room. He took a breath and crept in. The smoke was thicker in here, but it seemed to be emanating from one point on the floor. It was then he noticed the window was broken. Someone had thrown a Molotov cocktail through the glass.

The rug was on fire, and it was spreading to the curtains. They didn't have much time.

He charged out of the room and back up the stairs. "We've got to get out of here," he yelled. "Grab what you need."

Jo was clutching Jack. "How bad is it?"

"We can get out, but we have to go now."

She grabbed her handbag and threw it over her shoulder, then ran back into Jack's room, picked up his fluffy bunny and a blanket and waited on the landing. Rob scrambled for his wallet and phone, looked around but figured everything else could wait.

"Follow me," he said, but Jo knew what to do and was right behind him, her hand on his shoulder. Jack was wrapped in her arms, a blanket over his head. Rob grabbed a trembling Trigger by the collar and together, they descended the stairs.

Smoke billowed out of the living room, making it hard to breathe. Rob held his breath as they rushed along the hallway towards the front door. He could feel Jo's hand on his shoulder. Steady. Determined. Thank God she was so level-headed. He pulled back the latch and yanked the door open. They stumbled out into the night, coughing, with tears pouring down their cheeks. Jack gave a little splutter and began to cry, but the fresh air got rid of any lingering smoke in his lungs.

"He'll be fine," Rob said at Jo's worried look. "Crying is probably the best thing he can do right now."

They stood together in the street watching the living room go up in flames. Rob felt his gut wrench. The sofa, the table, the television, the few books and CDs he'd collected over the years, all destroyed.

Then he looked at Jo jiggling Jack, who was gazing at the orange flames mesmerised, and Trigger, whining against his leg, and felt a surge of gratitude. They were safe. That was the most important thing.

He was about to pull out his phone and dial 999 when they heard sirens blazing down the street. Seconds later, two fire engines pulled up in front of the house. The firemen jumped out and shot into action. Hoses were prepared and connected, and men in protective gear sprayed heavy plumes of water into the ground-floor window.

"Is this your residence?" asked a firefighter, coming up to them.

"Yes, it is."

"Is there anyone still inside?" His tone was clipped, urgent.

"No, we're all out."

He nodded. "Stay back until we get this under control."

Rob did so, content to let them do their job.

It took less than half an hour to bring the flames under control.

"You're lucky you got out so quickly," the firefighter said. Through the broken window, they could see the charred remains of furniture, the carpet a smouldering mess. "The damage is limited to the living room, but the rest of the house should be fine."

"Thanks to Trigger." Jo fondled the dog's ears. Jack's eyes were as big as saucers as he stared at the red fire engine and the men with helmets on.

"Great dog you have there," the firefighter said.

"Any idea what started it?" Rob wanted confirmation for what he already knew.

"Yeah, this was an arson attack. We retrieved the device that started the fire." He went back to the truck and brought out a broken bottle stuffed with a petrol-drenched rag, or what was left of it. It was in an evidence bag, ready to be sent off for analysis.

"I thought so." He gazed at the bottle. So basic, anyone could make it. So potentially deadly.

"Know of anyone who might want to harm you or your family?" asked the firefighter.

Rob nodded slowly. "Yes. Yes, I do."

He looked at Jo.

Torch.

* * *

"Rob, are you sure you should be here?" asked Jenny, when he walked in the next morning. The entire department knew what had happened last night. After the firefighters had got the blaze under control, the police had arrived and taken a statement. Rob had identified himself and told them he suspected it was connected to a case he was working on.

Retribution for a drugs raid. Things were getting personal.

"Yeah — the sooner we catch this bastard, the better. This is payback for the raid last night." He was tired, his eyes felt gritty and he could still smell smoke in his hair, even though he'd showered at the hotel they'd gone to early this morning.

"I'm sorry, mate," said Mike, his jaw tense. "I didn't know it would go down like that."

"Not your fault." Rob patted him on the shoulder. "It was a legit bust. We found the money and the stash of weapons. It was a win for us. He's just a sore loser."

Mike nodded, his broad shoulders hunched. It was clear this played heavily on his conscience. Rob went to speak to the Superintendent.

"Go home, Rob," Mayhew said. "Be with your family."

"I need to be here," he said. Jo had gone to her place in Bermondsey with the baby and Trigger. She hadn't wanted to, but he'd persuaded her — just until Torch was behind bars. "I'm going to speak to Pearson today," he'd told her. "We have enough evidence for them to take him in."

"Please be careful, Rob," she'd implored him, her eyes bright with concern. "I couldn't bear it if—"

"Don't worry, I'll be fine," he'd told her. "Nothing's going to happen to me."

In front of him now, Mayhew rolled her eyes. She'd learned not to argue with Rob. When he set his mind to something, he was unmovable. "As you wish. Are we sure this is Torch's work?"

"Yeah." He gave her a hard look. "We raided his place last night." He told her what they'd found. "Nearly sixty grand in cash and a small arsenal of weapons. They've gone to the lab for testing. Hopefully, his fingerprints will be all over them."

It was a long shot. Torch was careful. So far, nothing had linked back to him.

"Perhaps one of the handguns killed Lawrence, or the boy?" she suggested.

He shrugged. "Maybe. If that's the case, we've got him."

"But you don't think he did it?"

Rob sighed. "I can't be sure. He has an alibi, remember. The supplier they call 'the Albanian'. And he doesn't own a motorcycle. Our only hope is to get him on a possession with intent charge and child exploitation. It's time to call in the NCA."

"Agreed," Mayhew said, like he knew she would. She wasn't one for taking on more than they had to. This was the crime agency's remit, not theirs. "I'll set up a meeting for this afternoon."

As much as Rob wanted to nail Torch for murder, he had no proof. They could put him away for the rest though. It was time he was taken off the streets.

He told Mike, who gave him a fist bump. "Yeah, that's what I'm talking about."

"Any sign of the missing kid?" Rob glanced around at his team.

Galbraith shook his head. "No, God only knows where the wee lad is hiding."

"*If* he's hiding," said Jenny. "He might have been kidnapped, or worse."

There was a pause. Nobody wanted to consider that option.

"Okay," Rob broke the silence. "Let's keep looking. Make sure all the local stations have his photograph and it's at the top of their priority list. This missing child could be a key witness in getting this exploitation gang behind bars — and finding out who killed the Chief."

* * *

The meeting with the National Crime Agency was tense. Rob, Galbraith and Superintendent Mayhew sat opposite Neil Pearson, Jo's old boss, and a serious, sharp-eyed detective called Ridley, who had a permanently pained expression like she was barely tolerating them.

Pearson wasn't happy that MIT had been conducting the investigation without their knowledge.

"It's a murder inquiry," explained Rob. "Once we became aware of the drug angle, we informed you."

"Except you knew a week ago when you found out they were using asylum seekers as couriers. You should have brought it to our attention then."

"We were under the impression that you were already aware of Torch's activities."

He scowled. "Who told you that?" Then his forehead cleared. "Ah, of course. Jo Maguire."

"Is it true?" Mayhew asked them. "Did you know about his county lines connection?"

"Yes and no. We were aware he was getting product from the Albanian gang — almost everybody in that area does — and that he was dealing on the estate, but we didn't know about the kids."

Rob nodded. That tied in with what Jo had said.

"We questioned Torch about his alibi for the night the shooting took place. Once we established he was unlikely to have killed the Chief, we decided to bring you in."

"Why, thank you," Ridley said dryly.

"You're welcome." Rob flashed her a thin smile. "Now regarding Benny, the dead boy in the river . . . He came from the same children's home that the drug runners were recruited from, so we've got some crossover. We think whoever silenced the Chief and Ant Price, the informant, probably killed the boy too."

Pearson studied him. "We'll be conducting our own investigation into the Pavićs."

He'd suspected as much. This is where it got tricky. "If they're involved in the murders, then it's our case."

"But if they're recruiting unaccompanied asylum seekers to distribute drugs, that's ours," Ridley replied.

"I suggest we work together on this one." Mayhew's voice rose above both of theirs. "We all agree that this child exploitation has to stop, and if the same person or persons who killed DCS Lawrence, his informant and the restaurant owner also shot Biniam Yemane, then we've solved our murders."

She gazed at Pearson. "You can charge them with whatever you want, as long as the shooter goes down for murder."

Pearson sat back in his chair but nodded.

Rob agreed with her. Pearson was an idiot, but the exploitation had to stop before any more children were hurt, and the Chief's killer had to be brought to justice.

He looked at the NCA boss and his sulky colleague across the table. "Welcome to the Major Investigation Team."

CHAPTER 23

Rob emerged from the meeting.

"You're never going to guess what I've found," Jenny hissed.

He held up a hand. "Guys, this is Superintendent Neil Pearson and Detective Chief Inspector Ridley from the National Crime Agency. They're going to be working with us to put Torch and his crew behind bars and track down who is responsible for the recruitment and exploitation of the child refugees."

Both NCA detectives nodded. "Ridley will remain here," said Pearson. "I've got to get back to the office."

"Right. Well, you can take Evan's old desk." He pointed to where the American detective used to sit.

"Thank you." Ridley carried her laptop bag over to the vacant desk and put it down.

"Let me know if you need anything," said Jeff, who was closest to her.

She nodded and sat down.

Pearson shook hands with the Superintendent. "We'll be in touch."

There was an awkward hush in the room, but then the usual activities started up again. Phone calls, printers working overtime, the low murmur of detectives discussing their leads. Ridley opened her laptop and got to work.

Jenny gestured to Rob, who followed her into the tiny kitchenette next door.

"What is it?"

"I've been looking into Kenny Holloway's background, and you'll never guess who he's related to."

"Who?" Rob didn't have time for games.

"Mickey Holloway. Mickey is Francine Holloway's husband. Remember her? She runs that escort agency out of the West End, the one where Jo went undercover."

"Holy shit. Really?" Now she had his full attention. That case had nearly cost Jo her life.

"Yes, he's her brother-in-law. Didn't you say Francine worked as an informant for Vice?"

"That's right. She'd be able to give us the low-down on Kenny."

"You want me to bring her in?"

Francine wouldn't like that. She was fiercely protective over her reputation. Besides, there was no need. She wasn't a suspect. "No, I'll go and see her. Great work, Jenny. Thanks."

She grinned. "Sure, guv. Do you want me to come with you?"

He thought for a moment. Francine was no pushover. "No, I think I'll take Mike. She needs to feel intimidated before she'll offer up any information."

Since Kenny didn't have anything to do with the drugs or the asylum seekers, Rob didn't bother mentioning it to Ridley.

"Make sure she's kept in the loop," he told Jenny before they left. "Anything you can give her that will help build a case around Torch would be useful. We need to bring his network down."

"Yup." Jenny knew his safety and that of his family depended on it. Mike, so far, was in the clear. Torch had no idea he was the one who'd turned one of his crew into a snitch.

* * *

Mike and Rob drove to the West End.

"Tell me honestly," Rob said. "Who's your informant on the estate?"

Mike glanced at him. "To say would be to compromise *her*."

It was as he thought. "Fair enough. Just be careful. You've seen what Torch is capable of."

"I will be." Mike's face was stony. "The sooner he's arrested, the better."

Rob couldn't agree more.

They pulled up outside a newsagent. "Where is it?" asked Mike.

"Between the newsagent and the Galaxy nightclub." Rob nodded at a glossy black door. There was nothing to say what it was other than a buzzer on the wall. There was no name, no plaque, no nothing.

"Not big on advertising, are they?" remarked Mike.

"Don't need to be," Rob told him. "It's all online. This is their admin office."

They rang the buzzer. A throaty female voice said, "Who is it?"

"The police."

There was a pause and the door clicked open. They went inside. The hallway was as Rob remembered. A musty smell and bad wallpaper.

"They're on the first floor." He took the stairs two at a time.

Mike followed. "This is a bit different from down-stairs," he said, glancing around at the white walls, polished floorboards and glass door. It was like a completely different building.

Rob pushed a second buzzer, and they were allowed in. He approached the receptionist. "Hello, Ruth. How are you?"

The woman sitting behind the desk had a hard face and a guarded expression. "Hello, Detective. I'm good, thank you."

Her tone was clipped, professional. She nodded at Mike, her gaze roaming over the silver scar along his jawline and his muscular physique. He nodded back.

"Francine in?" asked Rob.

"Yes, she knows you're here. She'll be out in a moment."

They sat down to wait.

The phone didn't stop ringing. "Hello, Daring Divas. Yes, Kimberley's available. What service do you require?" Mike, who hadn't been here before, stared at Ruth as she listed the various options.

He glanced at Rob. "What's—?"

Rob shrugged. "Don't ask me."

The door to the back office opened and a middle-aged woman with dyed blonde hair came out. She was smiling, but it didn't meet her astute, blue eyes. "DCI Miller, how nice to see you again."

Yeah, right. He forced a grin. "Francine, thank you for seeing us."

She gestured for them to follow her. "What's it about this time?" she asked, once they were in her office. She, too, checked out Mike, as he eased his bulk into one of the chairs opposite her desk.

"This is DC Mike Manner," Rob said. The room smelled faintly of printer paper, and he put a hand on the shredder. It was warm.

Francine gave Mike a brief nod, then turned back to Rob. "Detective?"

"It's actually to do with your brother-in-law." He sat down next to Mike.

Her eyes widened. She hadn't been expecting that.

"Kenny?"

He nodded.

"Yes, I understand he's recently been freed from prison."

"That's right." She frowned. "Why are you interested in him?"

"Well, as you might know, it was my ex-Chief Superintendent who put him away."

"Yeah, that trumped-up possession charge. He still maintains his innocence."

Rob wasn't going to get into that. "Be that as it may," he said, "the Chief was gunned down last Friday night in Clapham, days after Kenny was released."

Her chin rose. "Ah, I see. And you think he had something to do with it."

"Did he?"

Her eyes narrowed. "You'll have to ask him."

"I'm asking you."

"How would I know?"

"Come on, Francine. You're well-connected. Your husband's Kenny's brother. Was he with Kenny at the pub on Friday the third of October?"

"Look, I'm sorry, Detective, but I can't help you. I don't keep tabs on Kenny's movements, neither does my husband. Kenny is the black sheep of the family, if you like. He's been in trouble with the law since he was a teenager. Mickey's always bailing him out. This last time, he couldn't help him. He went away for fourteen years. If Kenny gunned down your chief, he wouldn't tell us about it."

Rob studied her. As usual, she was wearing a tight-fitting dress a couple of sizes too small for her, but she looked good. Her nails were manicured, her skin as smooth and unblemished as he remembered, and she had a shiny Apple laptop on her desk, rather than the PC she'd had several years ago. Business must be good.

"Could you ask around?"

She rolled her eyes. "Jesus. I can't just ask him if he took out the Chief Superintendent."

"But you could poke around?"

She sighed. "I'll see what I can find out, but I'm not causing a family rift over this. Why don't you go and speak to Kenny yourself?"

"We will. We've already spoken to his wife. She's not too pleased at having him home."

"I can imagine." Francine didn't elaborate. She didn't have to. The woman knew full well what kind of man her brother-in-law was. "Lucy cut herself off from the rest of the family when he went to prison. Didn't want anything to do with us."

Rob couldn't really blame her. Francine's husband had ties to organised crime in the West End. She'd been feeding the police information for years. A snippet here, a titbit there. Not even her husband knew. Francine worked both sides with equal finesse. But this way, the police left her and her girls alone. Mostly.

Rob slid his card across the desk. "Call me if you hear anything."

She didn't pick it up.

"Is that all?" she said. "I've got to get back to work."

CHAPTER 24

The case against Torch and his gang was coming together. Ridley had spoken to Declan and convinced him to testify. He'd been promised witness protection for himself and his mum if he cooperated. A new start, somewhere Torch and his gang would never find him.

He'd jumped at the chance.

"We have the old lady upstairs where the guns and money were found," Ridley added. "She could testify that Torch took advantage of her, used her place to hide his cache. It's a strong case."

"She won't do it," said Rob. "She's too afraid, and it wouldn't be fair to move her into the protected persons programme at her age. That's her home."

Ridley's expression hardened. "We can issue her with a summons."

"I don't think that's wise," he insisted. "Leave her out of it, if you can. Wait and see what the lab has to say about the weapons and cash."

Ridley reluctantly agreed. "If we get prints, we can leave her out of it. We also have the other child — what was his name again?"

"Imad," supplied Jenny.

"Yes, Imad. According to the translator who spoke to him, he was given the drugs by a big man who fits Torch's description. He could probably pick him out of a line-up."

"Also, let's only use that if we need to," Rob said. "The boy's been through enough."

By the frustrated expression on Ridley's face, she didn't have much in the empathy department. "Noted, DCI Miller."

"I've been looking at camera footage in your area the night of the fire." Will stood up. "Torch's Honda CR-V was picked up on an ANPR camera on Upper Richmond Road at three thirty a.m. I know it's circumstantial, but it will show he was in the area at the time."

"Great work." Rob rubbed his hands together. He doubted they'd find enough hard evidence to prove Torch was responsible for the petrol bomb, but the rest should be enough to put him away for a long time.

"Right, I'm going to speak to the Crown Prosecutor," Ridley said. "If he thinks we've got enough to charge him, we'll bring him in."

* * *

The CPS agreed and Ridley issued a warrant for Torch's arrest.

"You might want to wait on that." Mike held up his hand.

Rob turned in surprise. "I thought you wanted Torch behind bars."

"Yeah, but my informant has just told me the boys have been discussing a big deal. A major shipment coming in from Europe. Pure-quality coke, lower prices. They can undercut the market. The Albanian is bringing it in."

"When?" Ridley asked.

"Next few days."

The NCA agent's eyes gleamed. "You think we should wait?"

"It's up to you," said Mike. "But if you do, you could get the Albanian too. Bring down the entire network, not just Torch's piddly end of it."

She tapped a pen against her teeth. "Let me speak to Pearson. Is your informant reliable?"

"Very."

"Can they get some more information on the shipment?"

"I'm not sure. I can ask." He grimaced. Rob knew he didn't want to put Chantelle at risk. It would be a huge feather in their cap, though, if they could bring down the whole trafficking organisation. The Albanian drug gangs had the coke trade tied up in London. This would be a major setback for them. Not to mention how many international connections they could bring down if Torch or the Albanian talked.

Ridley got on the phone.

"Okay," she said, after a long conversation with her boss. "We're going to wait. Mike, let us know what you find out about the shipment. In the meantime, we'll put a tail on Torch and see where it leads. If nothing transpires by next week, we'll bring him in."

Mike nodded. "Works for me."

* * *

The house was strangely empty. Rob stood in the burned-out lounge and stared at the damage. It could have been a lot worse. The curtains were ruined, as was the carpet, but those could be replaced. The walls needed stripping and repainting, and the furniture was charred and stank of smoke, but other than that, it was largely intact.

The windows had already been replaced by a team who'd worked throughout the day under the watchful eye of a uniformed police officer and the neighbour, Mrs Winterbottom, who was shocked and outraged by the attack.

"It's because you put yourself on the line every day to protect us," she said, proudly. She'd popped round to see if he needed anything, since he was on his own now.

Not for long. As soon as Torch and his gang were arrested, Jo, Jack and Trigger could come home. He called Jo and updated her on the investigation.

"Ridley's a hard case," she said, "but she's super focused. She'll get the job done."

That was good to know. The sooner they had the drug traffickers behind bars, the better.

"I miss you." His words echoed in the blackened-out room. Now that they weren't there, he realised how attached he was to his new family. It was strange to think that six months ago he'd been sitting here wondering if he was making a mistake by asking Jo to move in with him. Now he wouldn't have it any other way.

"I miss you too," she said. "Not long now."

* * *

"Why so glum?" Rob asked when Will stomped into work the next day.

"I've just got a call from Ballistics," his sergeant said. "They were unable to pick up any fingerprints on the weapons or the money. Those guys are so careful."

Shit.

He'd been hoping they'd slip up and leave a print on a barrel or a bank note. But no such luck.

"We need this bust," Rob murmured. "It's the only way we're going to get the fucker."

"We will," said Mike in his deep voice.

Galbraith had been made SIO on a domestic in Wandsworth. A man had stabbed his wife and his wife's best friend in the garage, before sitting down on the pavement and calling the police. He'd admitted to the whole thing. Jeff and Celeste were on their way there now.

"He thought she was having an affair," Galbraith told him before he left.

* * *

Rob was reading up on the background information Jenny had put together on the Pavićs when his phone buzzed. He glanced at the screen.

Francine.

"Miller."

"I can't talk for long." She sounded a little breathless. He guessed she was at home rather than at work. "Mickey was at the pub with Kenny last Friday, the night your chief was shot. He said Kenny was legless by the end of it. He's not your man, Detective."

Rob felt a sinking sensation in his gut. For a while there, he'd thought he may have underestimated Kenny Holloway, but it appeared he really had just gone out and got drunk.

"Okay. Thanks, Francine."

But she wasn't done. "There's something else," she whispered. "He's been hanging out with a Dutch guy called van den Berg. Do you know him?"

"No, should I?"

"He's a big weed trader," she said. "I wouldn't be surprised if Kenny's looking for a new sideline. He's skint. Mickey had to lend him a grand to get him back on his feet."

"Why are you telling me this?" asked Rob. She didn't have to. Kenny was family, after all.

"I like Lucy," she said, after a beat. "She deserves better." And she hung up.

* * *

Rob gave his contact, DCI Bryson in the vice squad, a ring. Despite being called the Human Exploitation and Organised Crime Command, or SCD9 for short, most people still referred to it as Vice.

"Hey, Bryson, what do you know about a Dutch national named van den Berg?"

The drug squad detective cleared his throat. "That fucker. He's a dodgy geezer. He's got contacts all over the UK and sells some of the best dope we've come across. Can't catch him though. Never puts his name on a thing. Squeaky clean."

"I've had a tip-off that an ex-con called Kenny Holloway is negotiating a deal with him. Setting himself up for a profitable side hustle. You might want to put a team on him."

"Who's the tip from?"

"Someone close to Kenny." He wasn't about to name names. "It's in our best interests to put this guy back inside. He's a bit too liberal with his fists, and his wife and kid are in the firing line."

"Gotcha," said Bryson. "Okay, thanks for the tip. We'll put some surveillance on him and see where it leads. It might finally give us something on van den Berg."

Rob thanked him and hung up. If he could get Kenny off the streets again, his wife and teenage son could live in peace. He'd call that a result.

He was about to pack up when Mayhew came out of her office. Her face was grim.

"I'm afraid I've got some bad news," she said.

They all looked up.

"Another body has washed up on the South Bank."

CHAPTER 25

Rob's blood ran cold.

Not Dawit.

"Do we have an ID?" His voice was strained. Everyone was thinking the same thing. Was this Benny's younger brother?

"No, they're waiting for you to get over there. Cranshaw just called it in."

"Well, it couldn't have been Torch." He looked at Ridley. "He's been under surveillance since yesterday."

"That's right. I can tell you where he was every minute of the day, and it was nowhere near the South Bank."

"That rules him out, then." Jenny grabbed her gear.

As much as he disliked Torch, it was a relief to be able to take him off their list of suspects.

Jenny and Will took the specialist homicide vehicle and set off. Rob logged off and packed up. He'd follow in his own car, then pay Jo and his son a visit afterward, if it wasn't too late.

"Mind if I tag along?" Ridley said, before he left.

"Sure." Rob forced a smile. "But you'll have to catch a ride back with the others. I'm not coming back this way."

"Suits me."

They left together and drove across London, hugging the Thames, until they got to the South Bank. The body had washed up beside Festival Pier, so Rob parked as close as he could, outside the Southbank Centre delivery entrance. From there it was a short walk to the river.

The plaza in front of the Royal Festival Hall had been evacuated and a cordon put up at each end of the walkway where the body had been discovered. A diving team was pulling it from the water.

Forensics hovered in white suits, waiting. Rob saw Cranshaw standing at the railing looking down. "Excuse me," he said to Ridley, and made his way over to the Southwark detective.

Cranshaw managed a wry smile. "Good to see you, DCI Miller."

They shook hands. Cranshaw winced.

"You okay?" Rob asked.

"Yeah, sprained it apprehending a suspect."

Rob gave a nod. It was a common injury if the suspect tried to twist out of your grasp. It had happened to him once too. "Who found the body?"

"A Japanese tourist spotted him from inside one of the pods." Cranshaw nodded up towards the now stationary wheel. "She called emergency services from four hundred feet up."

Rob looked down to where a young boy was being lifted onto a stretcher. He was covered in mud and debris, his wet hair swept over one eye, the other open and staring blankly up at them. Will and Jenny were keeping onlookers back, while Ridley spoke to an officer in uniform, who was no doubt giving her the same information Cranshaw was giving him.

"Another kid." Rob suppressed a shiver.

Cranshaw nodded. "Yeah, similar age. I'd say sixteen, maybe seventeen."

Not Dawit then. Rob felt some of the strain dissolve, although it shouldn't have. Any murdered child was tragic.

Why was it any better that it wasn't Dawit? Perhaps he couldn't fathom a mother losing both her sons.

It was overcast and there was a heaviness in the air as if the humidity was pressing down on them. Rob took a slow, deep breath as the forensic techs carried the stretcher up the uneven stone stairs to the walkway.

When they reached the top, he held up his warrant card. "Can I have a moment, please?" They stopped. Rob was wearing gloves, but he hadn't bothered to suit up since this wasn't the place where the boy had been killed, so there was no danger of contaminating evidence lying around the body. That would have been washed away already. He studied the boy, taking in his old, stained clothes, his waterlogged jacket, the bruises on his neck and his dark eyes, gazing up at the clouds. "No gunshot wound?"

"Not that we can see," said a forensic technician. "There are ligature marks around his neck, so he could have been strangled prior to being thrown into the river, but we can't be sure about the cause of death until the post-mortem."

Rob reached for the boy's hand. The forensic techs watched him as he turned the hand over and studied the wrist. His pulse leaped. Yep, there it was. The circular stamp with a design in the middle that he couldn't make out.

"It's the same as Benny's," he said to Cranshaw, who was peering over his shoulder. "Identical stamp."

"Do you know where they're getting them?" Cranshaw asked.

"We think it's at the children's home," Rob replied. "They're earmarked for recruitment as drug runners and couriers. Of course, it could be even earlier than that, at the processing centre, but I don't think so. The stamps would have worn off by then."

Cranshaw raised his eyebrows. "It looks like a club stamp."

"Yeah, but it's not used for that. Trust me."

Rob stood back and the stretcher was taken to a waiting ambulance. From there it would go to the lab where one of the Home Office pathologists, probably Liz Kramer, would do the PM.

"Second refugee in as many weeks," remarked Cranshaw. "What the hell's going on?"

"That's what we're trying to find out." Rob rubbed his neck. "We've interviewed the couple who own the children's home, and even searched the premises. We found nothing. The boys are free to come and go, and they don't keep tabs on them. They have no control over where they are at any given time."

"Hard to trace their last movements," said Cranshaw.

"Exactly. Now we've got another body, and there's still a missing boy out there."

"We're on the lookout for him," said Cranshaw. "David, isn't it?"

"Yes, Dawit. He's the first victim's younger brother. We'd like to bring him in alive." He shook his head. Losing one child was an intolerable thought. Two would be impossible to get his head around.

"We'll do our best. All our officers have been alerted."

Rob gave a terse nod. "Thanks. I just hope he's not also lying in the river somewhere."

Ridley fought her way over through the wave of reporters who'd suddenly descended on them. "Jesus, who let the cat out of the bag?" she barked.

"Any comments, DCI Miller?" said a female reporter from the *Mail*, thrusting a microphone in his face.

He ignored them.

"Do you have an ID on the body?" asked a guy he recognised from the *Guardian*.

"Any leads at all?" asked someone else.

Will and Jenny came over and shoved them back. "We'll issue a statement when we know more," snapped Ridley.

Rob sighed in frustration. He couldn't answer them because he didn't know. They were no wiser than after Benny's body was discovered. Torch was out, which left the children's home staff or maybe a third-party recruiter that they didn't know about yet.

The man with the wolf tattoo.

"Let's head to the children's home," said Ridley.

So much for seeing Jo and Jack, although he should have expected it wouldn't end here. It had been wishful thinking, really. "Okay." He turned to Will and Jenny. "See you back at the station."

They nodded. It would take them some time to talk to witnesses and those first at the scene.

* * *

More clouds had accumulated overhead, and it looked like it might pour down at any moment. At least it would break the stifling humidity. They walked into the largely deserted house.

"It's probably supper time," Rob said.

The woman at the front desk glanced up. "Can I help you? Oh, it's you again."

"Yes, good evening." Rob forced a grin. "Please can you tell Margaret we're here."

"One moment."

She fired off a text, then went back to reading her magazine.

"Excuse me." Ridley went up to the glass window. "What exactly do you do if the boys can come and go as they please?"

"They have to check in," she said with a sulky pout. "We don't just let anyone in here. I have to make sure the boys are on the list."

"Do they check out too?" she asked.

The girl shrugged. "Supposed to, but most of the time they just wave and I do it for them."

"Pity we don't have an ID on the body," she hissed to Rob.

Margaret came striding down the passage. "She might be able to help us," Rob muttered back.

"Hello, Detective." She gave him a small nod. "You wanted to see me?"

Her gaze turned to Ridley.

"DCI Ridley, National Crime Agency," Ridley said, in a voice that had said it a thousand times before.

Margaret nodded. "What's this about?"

"You've got another missing child," Rob said. "Because we've got another dead body."

"Dear God. Not another one?"

He nodded. "I'm afraid so. We don't have an ID on the boy yet. Could you tell me who's not here who's supposed to be here?"

"How do you know it's one of ours?" her eyes narrowed.

"He's got the same stamp as Benny," said Rob.

"I told you, we don't stamp them here."

"Still, someone might be doing it. Could you check your records?"

She glanced at the girl at the desk. "Claudia, anyone check out today and not come back?"

"Felix and Harry are still out," the girl said. "But that's not unusual."

"The rest of the boys are in the dining room having supper, if you want to come and see for yourself," said Margaret.

Rob glanced at Ridley, who nodded.

They followed her through the living room and out a door on the other side that led to the next door property.

Ridley's eyes widened. "It's connected."

Rob nodded. "They own both houses."

The dining room was a large reception room that had been converted for the purposes of feeding lots of hungry children.

Rob counted. Ten kids.

"No one is missing," said Margaret. "That poor boy you found wasn't one of ours."

CHAPTER 26

"If he wasn't from here, then where was he from?" asked Ridley.

"You could ask Karin. She's one of the social workers assigned to the unaccompanied minors who arrive. She might know the other children's homes in the area."

"How old are these kids?" he asked.

"It varies. Our youngest is eight, and it goes up to sixteen."

The boy in the river had seemed older than that.

Ridley was obviously thinking along the same lines. "Where do they go after that?" she asked.

"Semi-independent accommodation," Margaret said. "They get some support there, help cooking and applying for jobs, that sort of thing."

"Who decides where they go?"

"If they're here, we usually send them to St Joseph's, providing they have space. There can be a waiting list. It's the closest and run by a Christian charity. Most kids like to stay in the same area. It gives them a sense of familiarity."

Rob could understand that. "Okay, thanks," he said. "Is your husband here?"

"No, Bruno's at the processing centre. We're taking one more this evening. An eight-year-old who came over with his older sister, but she died during the journey."

Christ.

"They're inundated down in Kent."

"Is that where they come from?" Ridley asked.

"Yes, mostly."

Karin came over. She had a friendly face with creases at the corners of her eyes. "They come over on boats or stow away in vehicles crossing the Channel," she said. "They're assigned a social worker at the asylum intake unit in Kent. From there, they get sent to children's homes if they're unaccompanied minors, or semi-independent accommodation if they're over sixteen."

"Did you know Benny?" Rob asked.

Her face clouded. "Yes, sweet boy. Joker of the group. I was devastated to hear what happened to him. Did you manage to catch the people who did that?"

"No, we're still working on it." Rob ground his teeth together.

Margaret moved away to talk to one of the kitchen staff.

"Karin, you haven't noticed anything strange going on here, have you?"

"Strange?" She frowned. "In what way?"

"Children coming and going at odd times, unexplained cash, disappearances."

"Is this because of what happened to Benny?"

Rob nodded.

"Well, now that you mention it, I did hear something odd the other night."

"You did?"

"Yes, I was falling asleep when I heard the sound of a window being opened. I looked out but couldn't see anything. The next thing, I heard a car drive off."

"You didn't think to say anything?" asked Ridley.

"Well, I would have done, but the next day, everything appeared normal. No one was missing, so I figured no harm done."

"You live on the premises?" Rob asked.

"Yes, three nights a week. The little ones like to know there's someone they can call in case they need something."

"Who else comes to the children's home?" asked Ridley.

"Oh, lots of people. Apart from social workers, there's a legal representative who helps the children with their asylum claims, there's a district nurse who checks up on them twice a week, kitchen staff, cleaners . . ." She shrugged.

Rob sighed. Anyone of those people could be recruiting them for the night-time activities. Promises of extra cash, threats of being sent back home . . . Who knew what tactics they employed to get the boys to do their bidding?

They said goodbye to Karin and Margaret, and Rob dropped Ridley back at the station car park. "Let's call it a night," he said. "We can look into the older kids' accommodation tomorrow." There was still time to drive to Bermondsey.

Ridley gave a stiff nod. "Goodnight, DCI Miller." And instead of going to her car, she strode back into the building.

Rob didn't care. He needed to see his family and that took priority.

* * *

Mike parked in the residential street and climbed over the wall to the Beaufort Estate. He was a dark figure merging into the shadows. The clouds blotted out the stars and the moon, which meant he could skulk around undetected. Anyone looking would need night-vision goggles to pick him up.

He ducked as he rounded the perimeter and approached Chantelle's block from behind. It was a muggy night, and he could smell rain in the air. There were thunderstorms forecast for the early hours.

He took the stairs, creeping up floor by floor until he reached hers. He checked the corridor. Empty.

Chantelle was expecting him, so he didn't anticipate any nasty surprises once he got to her flat.

Need to see you, she'd texted. *Urgent.*

Be there at midnight, he'd replied.

It was late, but he hadn't wanted to risk running into Torch or any of his crew. It was a weeknight, so he didn't think much would be going down, but you never knew who was watching in a place like this.

He knocked on the door. Three times. Then once. Then twice. Their signal.

It opened straight away and he was engulfed in her soft body, inhaling her exotic scent. He breathed in deeply. "Let's get inside first," he chuckled, closing the door behind him.

"I'm so happy to see you." She kissed him on the lips.

He responded. "Likewise, but we have to be careful. Torch doesn't suspect anything, does he?"

"I don't think so." Her face fell. "I've done everything you've said. I'm acting normally, not avoiding him. Although I wish I could."

"It's important not to give him any reason to suspect us," Mike said.

"I know." Then she brightened. "Come. I've missed you." She pulled him into the bedroom. He went willingly, but not before checking the lock and chain were on.

Afterwards, lying propped up in bed, Mike said, "So what was so urgent that you had to see me?"

She ran a hand over his bare chest. "You mean other than this?"

He grinned.

"I've got news. I overheard Torch talking to Ali this afternoon. He didn't know I was listening. They're arranging a meeting, an important one."

"Do you know who it's with?"

"Some Albanian guy, I think."

Mike nodded. "What did they say?"

"It's tomorrow night at eleven o'clock at the warehouse. I don't know where that is. I've never heard him mention a warehouse before."

"Okay, that's good. Anything else?"

"He's taking Ali and Shane. He told them to be ready to leave at ten. He said this is the big one. That everything will be different after this."

"He said that? 'The big one'?"

"Yeah. What's going on, Mike?"

He shook his head. "It sounds like a deal of some sort. I can't be sure."

"Will you use it to catch them?" He didn't miss the hope in her eyes.

"If we can, yes." He squeezed her hand. "Then this will all be over, and you'll be free."

She sighed and wrapped a long, smooth leg over his. "I can't wait. No more pretending."

He turned back into her arms. "No more pretending."

CHAPTER 27

"We'll put a team outside the estate," Ridley said once Rob had told her what Mike had discovered. "When they leave, we'll follow them to the warehouse."

"Keep in touch," Rob said. "We'll meet you at the warehouse." At her look, he added, "Obviously, we'll follow your lead."

This was an NCA operation, but it was their informant who'd provided the intel. After keeping Torch under surveillance for so long, they deserved to be in on the arrest.

"I'm going to check out the semi-independent accommodation that Karin the social worker told us about. You coming?"

Ridley shook her head. "I have to set up tonight's op and brief Pearson. Let's liaise when you get back."

Liaise? He didn't think he'd ever used that word in his life.

He nodded curtly and beckoned to Will. "Come on, Sergeant. Let's go."

* * *

St Joseph's House was a large Victorian semi-detached home within walking distance of Streatham tube station.

174

"It has six bedrooms," Will read from the website as they pulled into the driveway. "Four double rooms with an adjoining shower room, two single rooms with separate shower room and toilet, lounge, kitchen–diner, utility room, garden, staff office and CCTV."

Rob turned off the engine. "That's for ten kids."

"Apparently the home is fully staffed twenty-four hours a day," Will continued. "To enable young people to receive the necessary support that they need."

"Doesn't sound too bad."

They walked up to the front door and Rob pushed the buzzer. It peeled out an offbeat tune and then the door clicked open. They went inside.

A middle-aged woman sat in a side office, looking out over the counter. She had a lacklustre expression and thin lips pulled into a hard line. "Can I help?"

"DCI Miller and DS Freemont, Putney Major Investigation Team. We'd like to speak to whoever's in charge?"

"That would be me today," she said.

A gum-chewing teenager in a tight skirt and a short top showing her midriff sauntered past. "Sign out, Arabella," the woman called.

The teenager blew a bubble and stopped in front of the desk. She scribbled her name on a sheet of paper, looked the two detectives up and down, then turned and walked out. She didn't say a word to anyone.

The woman shook her head. "What do you want?"

"We need to talk about a boy that went missing from here a few days ago." Rob held up a photograph of the dead boy taken at the morgue. He lay on his back, hair off his face, a nasty cut above his left eye.

The woman gasped. "That's Claudio." She stared at the image. "Is he . . . Is he dead?"

"I'm afraid so."

Her hand flew to her mouth. "Oh my God. What happened?"

"We were hoping you could tell us that."

175

She leaned over and unlocked the office door. They went in. There were two chairs behind her desk and she swivelled around to face them.

"He — he went missing a couple of days ago," she said, taking big gulps of air between words. "When he didn't return home, we called the police and reported him missing."

"Who did you speak to?"

"I notified the duty sergeant," she said. "That's what we usually do if one of them doesn't come back."

"And what do they do?" asked Will.

She scoffed. "Nothing, usually. They keep an eye out for them, sometimes they bring them back, if they can find them. But mostly we never see them again."

"Does it happen often?" Rob asked.

She shrugged. "Not so much. Every now and then one of them disappears. Claudio was the first in almost a year." She smiled ruefully. "We've had a good run."

"When last did you see Claudio?" asked Will.

"The day before yesterday. He signed out early that morning. Said he was going to look for work. I didn't see him come back, so I checked with the care staff. No one had seen him since that morning. I waited the obligatory twenty-four hours, and then I called the cops. No point in doing anything before that."

She'd clearly been down this road before and knew the drill.

"Where did you find him?" she whispered.

For all her toughness, Rob could see her hands were shaking. She was genuinely shocked by the news.

"In the river, on the South Bank," he told her. "He'd been strangled and possibly drowned."

"Oh, sweet Jesus." Her eyes moistened. "He was a good boy. One of the more dedicated ones. He wanted to learn, wanted to get out of here."

"How long had he been here?" asked Rob.

"Four months, give or take. He's originally from Eastern Europe. Ukraine, I think. He came over by himself with a letter claiming asylum. His parents put him on a plane. He wanted to get a job so he could send money home."

Fucking hell. Now Rob was responsible for telling Claudio's parents that their son had been murdered.

Rob showed her a picture of the stamp on his wrist. "Do you know what this means?"

She stared at it. "No, I'm sorry. I haven't seen that before."

Rob glanced at Will. Somebody was targeting these boys, and he had to find out who. "Could you give me a list of everybody who works here?"

She scratched her head. "It'll be a long list. We have advisors, social workers, medical staff, legal representatives, cleaners, kitchen staff . . ." She trailed off.

"I need all of their names." Rob wasn't taking no for an answer. "Even the shift workers."

She chewed on her lip. "Do you think someone here was responsible for his death?"

"That's what we're trying to determine," he said. Once they had a list, they could compare it to the staff at the children's home and see if there were any commonalities.

"Okay. It'll take some time. I can have it for you in an hour. Do you want to come back?"

"Email it to me." He handed her his card. "Do you mind if we take a look around?"

"Not at all. I'll get Sophie to give you a tour."

She picked up her mobile phone and tapped the screen. "Sophie, I've got two police officers here who want to have a look around. Can you come down?"

She hung up. "Sophie is one of our long-term residents. She's been here for almost two years now. She's training to be a social worker at the local college." Her mouth creased into a watery grin. "One of our success stories."

A fresh-faced teenager — Rob put her around nineteen — came bounding into the office. She had bushy brown hair and naturally arching eyebrows that gave her a permanent expression of surprise.

"Hiya," she sang. "I'm Sophie."

Rob got to his feet. "Pleased to meet you, Sophie. I'm Rob, and this is Will."

"Thanks, Soph," said the woman behind the desk.

"Sorry, I didn't catch your name." Rob turned back to her.

"Nicola," she said. "Nicola Burkes."

Sophie led them away to show them around.

"How do you like it here?" Rob asked.

"It's okay." She shrugged. "I've learned a lot. When I got here, I didn't know what I was going to do. Then Nicola suggested social work, and it clicked."

"You're English?" asked Will.

"Yes, this accommodation isn't just for unaccompanied asylum seekers," she said. "It's for anyone who doesn't have a place to go."

"I'm sorry," said Rob. "What happened to your parents?" He didn't like to ask, but she was so bubbly, he didn't think she'd mind.

"They died when I was little," she said. "There was no one else, so I was taken into care. I jumped around most of my childhood, and when I turned sixteen, I came here."

"How old are you now?" Rob asked.

"Eighteen."

She showed them the recreational room, the lounge and the dining room — all downstairs. An extension had been built on the back to create more space. Several teenagers were lounging on sofas, glued to their phones. Upstairs were the bedrooms and bathrooms, with two double rooms in the attic.

"Did you know Claudio?" Rob asked.

"Yes, do you know where he is?" Her expressive eyes searched his face.

His gut twisted. "I'm sorry to tell you that his body was found on the South Bank yesterday."

She stopped and gripped the railing. "What? You mean he's dead?"

"Yes."

There was a pause.

"Did you know him well?" Will asked.

She seemed to be fumbling for words. "Yes. W—We were close." Her eyes filled with tears. "I'm sorry. I just can't believe he's gone."

She hugged herself, her back to the wall for support. "I'm sorry, I need a moment."

"Okay, why don't you point us in the direction of Claudio's room and we'll take it from here."

She nodded and pointed down the corridor. "Last on the left."

Claudio had one of the single rooms. It was surprisingly neat, with a couple of books on the desk, a few forms in a pile, a cup containing a pen and a pencil, and a toothbrush.

Rob opened the cupboard. "Not much here."

"He probably didn't have a lot of possessions." Will checked in the drawer beside the bed. "Nothing of note."

"Nicola said he was going to a job interview," Rob said. "I wonder for what job."

"Perhaps Sophie knows." Will went to the door. Sophie was still at the end of the passage, wiping her eyes.

"Sophie, do you know what job Claudio was applying for?"

She walked towards them, her nose red. "I think it was a sales job." She sniffed and swiped at her eyes. "He was quite excited about it. He said it was his ticket out of here."

"Do you know who he was meeting?"

"No, sorry. He didn't say."

Will thought for a moment. "Did Claudio have a mobile phone?"

"Yes, of course."

"Do you have the number?"

"Yeah, sure." She reached into her back pocket and pulled out her iPhone. She scrolled for a moment. "Do you want me to send it to you?"

"Please." Will gave her his number and she shared the contact. His phone beeped in his pocket.

Will looked at Rob. "We can pinpoint his last moments with the phone," he said. "And get his call records."

"Good idea."

Finding nothing suspicious in his room, they thanked Sophie and left. When Rob turned around, he saw her standing there, staring at the space he'd occupied, tears streaming down her cheeks.

CHAPTER 28

The list was waiting for Rob when he got back to his desk. Fifty-three names in total. He printed out a copy and sat down to study it. Nicola had categorised the names, which helped. Social workers, legal, advisory, kitchen staff, cleaners and the like. Rob didn't have to look very far before he found a name he recognised.

Karin Gutowski.

Was that the same Karin they'd spoken to at the children's home?

He rang Margaret and asked. Yep, same person.

They had a link.

He got Karin's number and called her, asking if she'd come in for a chat. "I can't right now, Detective." Her voice sounded hollow and distant. "I'm on the motorway heading towards Kent."

"Tomorrow, then." He glanced at the luminous blue digits of the digital clock. She'd never make it today. "First thing, if possible."

"All right." She ended the call.

His phone rang almost as soon as he'd put it down.

It was Jo. His heart skipped a beat. Jo never called him at work unless it was urgent.

"Jo? Everything okay?"

"Yes, we're fine. I've got some news about your missing boy."

"Dawit?" His pulse spiked.

"Yes, my contact at the crime agency came through. It took a few days, but she traced him to a homeless encampment by the railway line in Elephant and Castle. A uniformed officer has picked him up and is taking him to St Thomas's hospital."

"Hospital? Is he injured?" Rob was almost too afraid to ask.

"I understand he's been badly beaten, but he's alive. That's the main thing."

Yes! He exhaled. That *was* the main thing, and they'd still be able to talk to him. "Thank you, Jo. And please thank your contact for me. This is great news."

"Happy to help."

They said goodbye and Rob turned to Jenny. "Let's go! We've found Dawit. He's alive."

She grabbed her jacket and handbag. "Where?"

He was already out the door. "Some homeless encampment. He's been worked over but he's alive. He's being cared for at St Thomas's."

"Alive is good." She charged down the stairs behind him.

They blue-lighted it across town to St Thomas's hospital, a sprawling complex on the banks of the Thames near Waterloo. While they were moving, Jenny rang Samira the interpreter, and asked her to meet them there as soon as possible.

Rob pulled into the hospital car park and skidded to a halt in an emergency bay outside the entrance to the Evelina London Children's wing.

They announced themselves at reception and were told to proceed to the fourth floor. He was in the trauma unit.

"The detective who called said he'd been beaten," Rob told Jenny outside the lift.

"Just like Benny," she murmured. "It must be connected to the drug running."

"I just hope he can tell us what happened," he said. "And who this mysterious man is with the wolf tattoo."

The doors opened. They walked down the passage to the ward, when Rob saw a figure he recognised. "Cranshaw?"

The Southwark detective turned, surprised to see them. "DCI Miller, what are you doing here?"

"Our missing boy's been found," he said. "We're going to talk to him now."

"He's here?"

"Yeah, what about you?"

"I had a few questions for a paediatric nurse, a witness in another case I'm working on."

"Okay, well, we'd better get in there. See you."

Cranshaw nodded. "Glad you found him."

Dawit was in worse condition than Rob had expected. One side of his face was badly grazed, and he had a cut lip and a black eye. A doctor hovered over him, checking his vitals.

"How is he?" Rob showed the doctor his warrant card. "I'm in charge of the missing persons case."

The doctor glanced at Rob. "He's badly dehydrated, undernourished and has obviously been in some sort of fight. We've done some blood tests and are waiting for the results. I think the worst of his scars will be mental. He's had a tough time, by the looks of things."

The boy lay there, eyes closed, his thin chest rising up and down in an even rhythm.

"Is he conscious?" asked Jenny.

"Yes, but very tired. He needs to rest."

"We're waiting for an interpreter," Rob explained. "Then we'd like to ask him a few questions. It concerns the people who kidnapped him and possibly murdered his older brother."

"Oh, I wasn't aware he had an older brother."

"Yes, we pulled him out of the Thames two weeks ago. He might not even know he's dead yet."

The doctor grimaced. "Be gentle with him, he's been through a lot."

"We will."

Samira was shown into the room when she arrived. She tapped Dawit on the shoulder. Eventually, he opened his eyes.

Fear. Wild, terrified fear.

His world had become a hostile place.

"Selam," said Samira, in a soft voice. She was speaking Tigrinya, the most widely spoken language in Eritrea.

The boy's gaze jerked from Samira to Rob, to Jenny and back again in rapid succession. His pulse rate increased, the monitor beeping in protest. He seemed to be in the midst of an anxiety attack. Rob glanced at the door, half expecting a nurse to rush in and ask them to leave.

Samira continued to talk in a reassuring tone, but the boy remained agitated. He shivered, his eyes wide, the whites showing. He reminded Rob of a terrified horse about to bolt. Eventually, a nurse did come in.

Samira walked out with them. "He's too traumatised to talk right now," she said. "He understood me when I said we weren't there to hurt him, or to take him back, but I don't know if he believed me."

"Whoever threatened him must have done a number on him," Rob said.

"He may even have seen his brother get shot," Jenny pointed out. "In which case, I don't blame him for not trusting anyone."

"I'm going to put a watch on the door," Rob said. "Whoever silenced Benny might want to do the same to Dawit."

"Good idea," Jenny agreed. "We don't know how far their reach is."

Samira promised she'd be available whenever he was ready to talk.

"Thank you," Rob told her.

He and Jenny waited at the hospital until two uniformed officers arrived. Rob gave them specific orders not to leave Dawit unguarded for even a minute. It might be overkill, but he didn't want to take any chances.

"No one goes near him, you hear?" The poor boy had been through enough.

The two officers nodded sombrely.

Rob and Jenny had just got back to the car when their phones started beeping.

Rob glanced at the screen. "We're on! Torch has just left the estate with his two henchmen."

They pulled on their vests and took the batons and stun guns from the boot of Rob's vehicle.

"Ready?" he asked.

Jenny nodded. "Let's go get these bastards."

CHAPTER 29

Torch led them to an abandoned warehouse on the outskirts of Peckham. Industrial wasteland, by the looks of things. It was surrounded by a vibracrete wall covered in graffiti. The barbed wire on top was rusty and entangled with litter. A rickety gate hung off its hinges, just wide enough for a car to pass through.

Rob pulled over and killed the lights.

"What's happening?" he said into the radio.

"We're on foot," Ridley replied. "Positioned on the left of the warehouse. Torch has just driven in. No sign of the Albanian. Where are you?"

"Outside, on the approach road. We're keeping a respectable distance."

"Okay, let me know if you see anything."

"Will do."

They didn't have to wait long. Ten minutes later a black SUV drove down the road towards the industrial wasteland. It turned in through the broken gate, tyres crunching as they left the asphalt and hit the dusty gravel.

"Coming towards you," Rob whispered into the radio.

"Gotcha," came the brusque reply.

Rob nudged Jenny. "Let's go."

They left the vehicle and crept towards the gate, sticking to the shadows. It was almost dark, the sky a deepening indigo. The first few stars were coming out. Rob glanced around but the street was deserted. The factories and businesses on the other side of the road were shut or empty.

They slipped through the entrance and into the desolate grounds, hugging the wall. "Let's try and get a visual," whispered Rob.

Jenny nodded and they proceeded forward, careful not to make a sound.

He raised his hand and they stopped, then hunkered down behind a mound of gravel and sand. Keeping his body low, he peered out from behind a chunk of rock. Jenny crept around the side, completely hidden by a lopsided buddleia bush that had still managed to bloom despite the derelict surroundings.

Mike was here too. He'd come with Ridley and her team, but Rob couldn't see him. The tough South London copper wasn't going to miss an opportunity to see his nemesis put away.

The black SUV stopped, and two men got out. Rob strained his eyes to see through the near-darkness. As they cut in front of the headlights, he got a good look. They were wearing jeans and T-shirts. One had a grey beanie on, the other a maroon cap, and both sported gold watches.

Torch got out of the car, flanked by Ali and Shane. His stature was upright and confident, but Rob could see by the way he kept his hands flexed by his side that he was ready for action. His gun would be tucked away in the back of his jeans.

Conveniently, they met in the glare of the headlights. They thought they were safe. There was nothing here but a large, rusty hangar, empty for decades, waiting for some property developer to turn it into another slick, silver office block like those a few roads back.

There was the murmur of voices, but Rob couldn't hear what was being said. They talked for a few minutes, then Grey Beanie gestured for Torch to follow him.

The gangster left his two sidekicks and walked to the boot of the SUV. Grey Beanie opened it and stood back, while Torch and Maroon Cap peered inside.

Rob was betting the drugs were in there. He wiped a bead of sweat from his forehead. Not long now.

A fox cried out, breaking the silence. Torch glanced up, but then Maroon Cap said something and they went back to inspecting the merchandise.

Satisfied, Torch gestured to Ali, who took a silver attaché case out of the car.

Payment.

The other guy had his hand behind his back now, most likely on his gun, just in case the whole deal went south. Or maybe he was just jumpy.

This is the big one. Everything will be different after this.

Torch's man laid the case on the edge of the SUV's boot and flipped the latch. Maroon cap opened it and reached inside. A few tense moments passed, until he nodded and closed the case.

Rob exhaled. The deal was going ahead.

Torch reached into the boot and took out an old-style suitcase. He was carrying it back to his car when all hell broke loose.

"Armed police!" A loud voice severed the quiet.

Several black-clad men erupted from the shadows, rifles drawn. "Put down your weapons!"

If they were expecting an easy surrender, they were mistaken. Grey Beanie and Maroon Cap drew faster than cowboys at high noon and opened fire while simultaneously ducking behind the SUV. Two more armed men sprung from the back seat and joined them.

The armed police scattered, scrambling for cover, but not before one of them clutched his thigh and went down.

"Officer down!" came an urgent cry. "Need urgent medical assistance."

Fuck. It was all going tits up.

Torch dropped the case containing the drugs on the ground and reached for his gun. Ali and Shane were already firing at the police, crouching behind their car. Bullets pinged off the two vehicles and the metallic shell of the hangar.

Rob and Jenny, unarmed, could only watch.

There was a guttural yell and Ali fell to the ground. One of the firearms officer's bullets had found its mark. He rolled around clutching his chest, then lay still.

Not waiting to be cut down, the other two Beaufort gangsters scampered around the vehicle and took off like track runners down the side of the hangar.

"Cover me," yelled a deep voice and Mike charged through the gap between the cars in pursuit. He wasn't going to let Torch get away.

Fucking hell. He was totally exposed.

Luckily for Mike, a switched-on SCO19 officer fired frantically at the SUV.

Jenny took off after Mike, keeping to the wall.

Shit. None of the others saw her go.

There was a shout as a ricocheting bullet hit one of the men from the back of the SUV. He went down, rolling on his back, holding his gut. It didn't look good.

Sirens could be heard approaching, getting louder with every ear-splitting peel. Ridley had obviously called for backup. The fight continued until three police vehicles raced into the grounds and more armed officers piled out.

"Wait! Wait!" cried the other uninjured SUV passenger and knelt on the ground, his hands in the air. It was then that Rob noticed that Grey Beanie and Maroon Cap had vanished. They must have scarpered over the wall during the chaos.

"Hold your fire," came a clipped order, and the shooting stopped.

Rob slid down the mound. "They went that way," he shouted, taking off in the direction Mike and Jenny had gone. He was almost at the end of the hangar when he heard gunshots. His heart skipped a beat. Please let that not be a member of his team.

He rounded the corner to find Mike on the ground, holding his shoulder. "They're heading for the fence," he gasped. "Jenny's gone after them."

Hell. "Are you okay?"

"Yeah, fine. Go get them."

Rob took off again, aware he was running blind into deepening darkness. He could barely see what was up ahead, but his torch would only serve to make him a target, so he kept it off.

He heard a bark behind him and spun around. A police dog raced past him faster than a thoroughbred racehorse. Another followed, close on its heels.

He heard a terrified cry, then another shot was fired.

To hell with it. He switched on his flashlight and saw Jenny standing over Torch, pointing a gun at him. The gangster must have dropped it when the dog attacked. The K-9 hero had Torch's arm in a ferocious grip and was shaking it back and forth.

The gangster tried to pull his arm free.

"Stay where you are," she warned. "The dog will only hold on tighter if you try to wriggle away."

"Get it off me," he yelled. The dog was growling, spittle flying from his jaws.

Rob stopped beside her. "Where's Shane?"

Jenny didn't take her eyes off Torch. "Didn't see where he got to, sorry guv."

Then there was a petrified scream and more growling up ahead.

"Don't worry, I think we've found him."

Two K-9 police officers ran past. Soon, he too was in handcuffs.

Rob helped a bleeding Mike off the ground and back to the front of the warehouse, where three ambulances were waiting. The injured firearms officer was being stretchered into one, while a lifeless Ali was carried into the other.

"I'm not going on a stretcher," Mike growled.

"Get in there, tough guy." Rob handed him over to a paramedic, who immediately put a dressing on the wound to stop the bleeding.

"Apply pressure," the paramedic ordered, "and sit down before you fall down. You've lost quite a bit of blood."

Mike grudgingly agreed, but he still didn't lie down.

The two remaining drug dealers from the SUV were bundled into a police van and taken away. Torch and Shane were transported to the nearest police station in separate vehicles.

"Good call on the dog squad," Rob said as Ridley came over.

"Thanks. We had them waiting, ready to go. I had a feeling they'd run for it. Pity those other two got away."

"Yeah, maybe the others will talk."

She shrugged. "Maybe." But he could see she held little hope. They had more to fear from ratting on their drug bosses than the police.

The ambulance taking Mike to hospital was ready to leave.

"Excuse me." Rob walked over to Mike. "Good job tonight."

"We got him." Mike grimaced through the pain. "We fucking got him."

CHAPTER 30

Nothing was ever that simple. When Rob got into the office the following morning, he was greeted with frustrating news.

Torch wanted to make a deal.

"He raised holy hell all night, demanding to speak to his solicitor," the custody sergeant told him. "Didn't go down well with the other suspects in holding."

"Okay, prep him for interrogation," Rob said. "Let me know when his legal representative gets here."

"Yes, sir."

"What deal can we give him?" Jenny asked. "He was caught red-handed doing the drug deal with the Albanian gang. Mike will be devastated if we let him go."

Rob kept his expression neutral. "Let's see what he has to offer before we decide anything," he said. "I'm not going to make him any promises."

Jeff came over. He'd been working on the stabbing with Celeste and Galbraith and had only just heard of the shoot-out last night. "How's Mike?"

"He's okay." Rob had stopped by the hospital on his way to work. "He's grumpy as hell at being shot, but he's ecstatic we arrested Torch and his sidekick."

Making a deal with Torch would not go down well. Not after all they'd been through to catch him in the act.

Rob got the call just before lunchtime. "Solicitor's here," the custody sergeant told him. "Torch is asking for you."

"Here we go," Rob muttered. He and Will went downstairs to the interrogation rooms.

"I hear you want to make a deal?" Rob said, once they were all seated. Torch was using the same solicitor as before. This time, she was in a red skirt suit with matching heels.

"Yeah, man. I got information," he drawled, leaning back in his chair.

"You realise you're facing some very serious offences? I'm not sure how much of a deal I can offer you."

"Wait till you hear what I've got to say."

Rob studied him. He was a big man, easily filling the cold metal chair in the interview room. Tattoos covered his arms, his smile revealed a gold tooth and he had bulging biceps that put Mike's to shame. He also exuded a casual confidence, which was worrying.

"What is it?" Rob also leaned back and crossed his arms. This better be good.

"I can tell you who shot your chief." He leered at Rob. "And Ant Price and the other dude."

Rob paused. Was he for real?

"Haven't we gone down this road before?" he said. "You claimed not to know anything about that."

"No," he snapped. "I said I didn't do it. I didn't say I didn't know who did."

Will was staring at Torch.

They had to hear what he had to say, even if he was full of shit. "Okay, who did it then?"

"Deal," Torch insisted.

"My client wants full impunity from prosecution if he gives you this information," said Okorocha.

Rob was shaking his head before she even finished her sentence. "No can do, I'm afraid. The Crown Prosecutor is never going to allow that. I might be able to get you a reduced sentence, but impunity? No."

Torch jutted out his chin. "I guess you don't want to know that badly then."

He was playing hardball. Rob clenched his teeth. Two could play that game. "I'm sorry, it's out of my hands. You were caught with fifty grand's worth of coke on you. That's heavy shit. You're looking at the maximum penalty for possession with intent. That's twenty-four years, give or take."

Torch's gaze hardened. "Fuck you, man."

Rob turned to his solicitor. "Let me know when he's willing to accept my deal of a reduced sentence. Otherwise, we're done here."

They left the interrogation room.

"Do you think he'll cave?" Will asked.

"I don't know. If he doesn't, we're in trouble. I'll have to speak to the Superintendent, but it would suck if we had to let him go."

"Surely they won't go for that?"

"It's the Chief," said Rob. "One of ours. Don't you want to find out who did it?"

"Yeah, but not at the expense of letting that scumbag go free. We also don't know if he's telling the truth."

"We'll figure that out after we hear what he has to say."

The afternoon stretched on. Rob got the post-mortem report back from Liz Kramer on the second victim, Claudio Stepanenko. According to Border Control, he was from the Donbas region in Ukraine.

"He died from asphyxiation," he told Jenny. "There was no water in his lungs, suggesting he was dead before he entered the water."

"Strangled?" she said.

He nodded. "Looks that way. He had ligature marks on his neck and conjunctival petechial haemorrhage."

Jenny had worked for the murder squad for long enough to know the signs. "Poor kid."

"He also had abrasions on his legs and knees, and bruises on his arms where he was held down."

"Two perpetrators?"

"Must be. One to hold him down, the other to strangle him."

"Any DNA?" Jenny asked hopefully.

"No, not this time. The water removed all forensic evidence. Even his nails were washed clean."

She sighed. "No leads there, then."

It didn't look like they were getting any closer to find out who killed the Thames boys. Or Lawrence.

"Still no word from Torch?" asked Will, at about four o'clock.

Rob shook his head. "Doesn't look like he's going to go for it. We'll charge him with what we've got. The CPS has given the all-clear."

Weary, he got to his feet. He was just about to go downstairs when his phone buzzed. He glanced at the screen, then grinned. "We're in business. He's agreed to give us the name in exchange for a reduced sentence."

Will leaped out of his chair. "Excellent. Let's go find out who killed the Chief."

* * *

The casual smirk was gone from Torch's face. He now wore a deep frown that made his eyebrows arch together.

"I want everything in writing," he said, trying to maintain some level of control.

Rob took his time sitting down. "Until we hear what you have to say, we're not authorised to take even a month off your sentence."

His solicitor whispered something in his ear. Encouraging him to cooperate, no doubt.

He sighed. "Okay, so there's this guy, right."

"What guy?"

"This guy. He runs a trafficking racket. I don't know where he gets the kids from, but you can hire them for jobs. He drops them off and picks them up again when they're done."

Rob frowned. "What jobs?"

"Drug couriers, runners, burglaries, sex. Anything you want, they provide."

Rob stared at him. "Is that who you used to distribute your coke to clients in the suburbs?"

He shifted in his chair. "I wouldn't know about that."

Right. "Tell me more about this man." said Rob. "Does he have a name?"

"They call him the Wolf."

Rob glanced at Will. The man with the wolf tattoo.

"That it?" he scoffed. "If you think that's going to get you anywhere, think again."

"He's a white guy," Torch said. "English. I've spoken to him on the phone, that's all."

"How do you pay?"

"Cash. I leave it at the mobile phone shop where I pick up the kids."

Rob thought back to the manager of the mobile phone shop.

They just order phones from me. I swear.

Lying shit. "And you've never seen who picks it up?"

"No, I've never needed to know. He provides a good service. The boys always follow through. We've never had any problems, not until the other night when you bust Declan at the station."

If Torch was aware he'd incriminated himself, he didn't give any sign. Not that it mattered. They had more than enough to charge him with anyway.

"What other services does he offer?"

"The kids do burglaries," Torch glanced at his hands. "They're experts. In and out in under five minutes."

"What else?"

"There's the girls, too."

Rob froze. "Girls?"

"Yeah, man. He runs a brothel. You can get anything you want there. Strictly off the books, you know?"

Rob did know. Unfortunately, he knew exactly what Torch meant.

Underage girls made to have sex with strangers, kept against their will. Unfortunately, it was fairly common with unaccompanied girls. Frequently their passports were taken away from them and they were threatened and drugged if they didn't comply.

"Where is this brothel?" Rob asked, his voice coarse.

"I don't know. That's not my thing."

"How do we know you're telling the truth?"

"'Cos he asked me if I wanted girls. I said no. I got a girl. I ain't into those doped-up bitches."

At least he has some morals. "I need a name, Torch. If you want me to cut you a deal, I need a name."

"I don't know his name."

The dark eyes flickered. He was scared of this guy.

"I know you know," Rob said. "You don't strike me as the kind of guy who would do business with someone they hadn't checked out."

Torch acknowledged that with a small nod of his head. "Still can't tell you," he said. "I wish I could, believe me, but if he found out . . ." The rest didn't need explaining.

"If you give me his name, we can arrest him," Rob said. "He'll be behind bars. You'll be safe."

"I'll never be safe," Torch said. "He'll know I ratted him out. Not many people know who he is, yeah? I won't be safe anywhere, not even in prison. He has guys everywhere."

"We can protect you." The words sounded hollow even to his own ears.

Torch sniffed. "No, man. You can't protect me from the Wolf. No one can."

CHAPTER 31

Rob threw a pen down on his desk. "Get that mobile shop owner in here," he barked.

No matter how much they'd pushed, Torch had refused to give up the name of the Wolf.

"Who can he be?" Will said. "Who has that kind of power?"

"Organised crime," said Rob. "It has to be." Child trafficking, sex trafficking, exploitation. This guy had developed quite the little empire.

"How come we've never heard of this guy before?"

Rob shrugged. "We don't usually deal with these kinds of crimes."

"I wonder if the NCA has heard of him," said Jenny.

"That's a good point. I'll speak to Jo."

He got her on the line. After asking how Jack was, he told her it was a work-related call. "Have you ever heard of a man called the Wolf?"

There was a pause.

"This is confidential information, Rob. Why do you want to know about him?"

His pulse leaped. "We think he's behind Sam's murder, and the murder of these two young boys."

"Oh, shit."

"Who is he, Jo?"

She sighed. "We don't know. Nobody does. He's part of an organised crime group linked to the trafficking of women from Eastern Europe and Africa for prostitution, and children from Vietnam as low-level drug workers. OCGs are not confined to one industry anymore."

"He's not the top man?"

"We don't think so, but he's pretty high up. He must be to be running multiple rackets. Does Ridley know of the connection?"

Rob thought for a moment. "I don't think so. She wasn't there when it was mentioned the first time and I don't think the Superintendent has said anything to her about it."

"If she thinks he's involved, Pearson will try to take the case off you. They've been trying to find out who he is for years."

"Not going to happen," Rob said. "This is a homicide investigation."

"Be careful, Rob. I know I keep saying that, but I mean it. We want you to come home. We miss you."

A longing surged through him, so strong it took his breath away. "I miss you too," he rasped. "I can't wait to wrap this up so we can all be together again."

He heard Trigger bark in the background.

"Trigs agrees with you." She laughed. "I'll let you go now, but call me later."

"I will."

He hung up and stared at his computer, processing what Jo had told him.

"Any luck?" asked Will.

"Nope. They don't know who he is either. Part of an organised crime syndicate. He might not even be the top guy."

"Shit," said Will. "Do we want to get involved in this?"

"No. But I want Sam's killer, and if this character is our man, he's going down. The NCA can go after the rest of the OCG. That's not our remit."

Will gave a worried nod. "Let's just hope Ridley doesn't get wind of it."

* * *

The hospital rang while Rob was preparing to interrogate the mobile phone shop manager.

"Dawit is feeling much better," said the nurse. "You might be able to talk to him now."

Rob hesitated. He needed to hear what Dawit knew. He phoned Samira and got ready to leave.

"You take the mobile shop manager," he told Jenny. "I'm going to speak to Dawit. He's being discharged today."

Jenny looked up. "The shopkeeper's here now?"

"Yep, he's downstairs with a legal rep."

"Okay, guv." She nodded to Will. "Coming?"

"Absolutely."

Rob drove to St Thomas's hospital. He was pleased to see the police guards still at the door.

"Any trouble?" he asked.

"No, sir."

Samira was already there. "He's doing much better," she said. "I think he's beginning to accept we aren't going to hurt him or send him home."

"Do you think he'll talk?" Rob asked.

She shrugged. "I hope so."

Rob had insisted on a private room due to the security measures in place. Dawit was sitting up in bed drawing a picture. He looked up as Rob and Samira entered.

"Hello, Dawit." Rob smiled.

The boy's gaze flew to Samira. She said something in Tigrinya and he glanced back at Rob.

Not wanting to spook him, Rob sat in the chair away from the bed. "Will you ask him if he's up to answering some questions?"

Samira relayed the message. The boy's face clouded but he gave a small nod.

Great. "What happened to you?" Rob directed the question at the boy, leaving Samira to translate.

Dawit shook his head, his mouth quivering.

"Who hurt you?"

"A man," came the translated reply. "He beat me up for sleeping in his place."

Rob frowned. This must have been after the boy escaped.

"Why did you run away from the children's home?"

A pause, then, "I didn't want to, but they took me and my brother away. They wanted us to break into a house and steal. I didn't want to do it. My brother said no, and they shot him." His eyes filled with tears.

Rob felt his gut wrench. "I'm sorry about your brother."

The boy bit his lip, trying not to cry.

"You're very brave," Rob said. "If we find the people who did this to your brother, we can punish them."

Dawit's head jerked up. "You can?"

"Yes, I'm the police."

The boy thought about this for a moment.

"Who took you from the children's home? Who told you to do this? Was it Bruno?"

The boy shook his head.

"Was it Margaret?" Another shake.

"Who was it, Dawit?"

"A woman. She told me we had to do it or else they'd send us back." His face crumpled. "I said I wanted to go home, and she got very angry."

"A woman? Which woman?"

He shrugged.

"He doesn't know her name," Samira said.

"But she works at the children's home?"

The boy nodded. Shit, if only he had photographs of the staff. Karin Gutowski came to mind. She was the only person who had a connection to both the children's home and the semi-independent accommodation where Claudio had gone missing.

201

He googled her on his phone but couldn't find a photograph. He couldn't find any reference to her at all. Nothing. Not even a social media page. That was strange.

He put the phone away. "Okay, what happened next?"

"A man came and picked us up. He put us in a van and drove us somewhere. Then another man took us to this big house. He told us to break in and steal jewellery. That's when my brother said no. He told me to run and fought them—" The boy's voice broke. "But they shot him."

Samira took his hand and spoke soothingly to him.

"He saw the whole thing," Rob murmured.

She nodded. "Yes. It's no wonder he was so traumatised. He's been sleeping rough ever since."

Alone, terrified, grieving his brother and then beaten up by vagrants. What a nightmare. He studied the boy, who was gripping Samira's hand. At least it was over now.

Rob thought of his own son, safely at home. "Have you told him he's safe? No one is going to hurt him again."

"I did, yes." She smiled. She obviously cared for the boy.

"What will happen to him now?"

"He'll be taken back to the children's home," she said. "Unless a foster family can be found. Given his age, it might be more suitable."

"Given what's been happening at the children's home, I think the relevant authorities need to be informed. There'll be some sort of investigation."

"They won't close it down, will they?" Samira frowned and caressed Dawit's hand.

"Not unless the couple who run it are arrested," Rob said. "But we have no evidence that suggests they're involved."

"Good, because where would all those children go? That is their home."

"Do you have children?" Rob asked.

She shook her head. "Oh no. I've never found anyone I like enough to have children with." She smiled ruefully. "I'd like to foster one day, though. Once I have a place of my own." Catching Rob's curious glance, she added, "I live with my mother. It's not the most ideal circumstances to raise a child."

"It might be worth asking." Rob looked at Dawit. "He's very attached to you."

"I'm very fond of him."

Rob asked Dawit if he could draw a picture of the woman who threatened him. He nodded and picked up a pencil.

The doctor came in and called him over.

"Excuse me," Rob said to Samira.

"The boy can go home." The doctor smiled. "He's much improved. He may have trouble sleeping at night, or have nightmares, but that's understandable given what he's been through."

Rob held out his hand. "Thanks for everything, Doctor. We'll arrange for someone to pick him up."

The doctor shook his hand. "Good luck." He marched off.

Rob returned to the bed.

The woman in the drawing was a brunette with a very round face. Frankly, it could have been anyone.

"Given what's happened, I don't like the thought of him going back to the children's home. The person who coerced him into doing the burglary might want to silence him."

"You think they'd harm him?"

He could hear the fear in her voice. "I think they might try, yes. That's why I put a guard on his door."

She studied Dawit's face, her eyes roaming over his curling locks, and bruised skin.

"I wonder," she murmured.

Rob raised an eyebrow.

"I could have a word with Children's Services. They might allow him to stay with me." She flushed. "Temporarily, I mean, just until a foster family can be assigned. I don't like the thought of him going back there."

Rob nodded slowly. "Actually, that would be great. If the woman involved is a social worker, she'd be able to find out where he was, but if you asked them to keep it off the books, for his own safety, that would be even better."

Samira gave a determined nod. "I'll see what I can do — just until you catch whoever is doing this."

She fetched her phone from her bag and stepped out the room. After a few minutes, she came back in, beaming. "All sorted!"

Rob turned to the boy. "Dawit, would you like to go with Samira?"

She translated and his eyes lit up. He reached over and hugged her.

Rob smiled. "I think that's a yes."

CHAPTER 32

"He said it was someone from the children's home," Rob told the rest of the team when he got back. "A woman."

"Margaret?" asked Will.

"No, he said not. I think it might be Karin, the social worker. She visited both the children's home and the accommodation where Claudio stayed. She's the only link to both places."

"She seemed so . . . nice," Will said.

"I know, but I want to put a tail on her. Jenny, will you arrange it?"

"Yep."

"But first, tell me what happened with the mobile phone store owner."

Will shook his head.

"What?" said Rob.

"He wasn't very cooperative," Jenny said. "He denied anyone dropping off cash at the store. Said he didn't know anything about it. Refused to budge, no matter how hard we pushed him. He's still in a holding cell, but we don't have anything to hold him on."

"Bloody hell." Rob drummed his fingers on the desk. "He could potentially identify the Wolf."

"He's not going to talk," Will said. "He'd rather die first."

"What is it about this guy that puts the fear of God into everyone?" Rob mused. "The only person to take him on was a twelve-year-old boy."

"And look what happened to him," Jenny pointed out.

Rob sighed.

"At least his brother is still alive."

"Do we have Karin Gutowski's home address?" Jenny asked. "For the surveillance team."

"Fuck it. I'll do it." Rob got to his feet.

"Are you sure, guv? Don't you have to get home?"

"Jo's at her flat with Jack and Trigger," he said. "She's staying there until this is tied up. I don't have anywhere to go. I may as well make myself useful and save some money."

Jenny shrugged. "Suit yourself. Give us a shout if you need any backup."

"Will do."

* * *

Karin Gutowski lived in a Victorian end-of-terrace in Wandsworth. It was a surprisingly nice house for a social worker. He watched her come home and park her Volkswagen Tiguan in the driveway. She certainly wasn't short of money.

His research told him she was divorced, lived alone and had owned the house in Wandsworth since last year, according to Zoopla.

Before that, she'd stayed in a one-bedroom flat above an off-licence in Clerkenwell. This was quite a step up.

It was possible that she'd inherited money from a deceased family member, but he was banking it was something else. Something to do with organised crime.

The lights went on inside. He saw her close the curtains, then watched as her shadow dissolved into the interior. Had she settled in for the night?

He glanced at the time on the dashboard: 6.52 p.m. He'd give it a couple of hours and then call it a night. If she hadn't gone anywhere by eight, then she probably wasn't going to.

He called Jo and listened to Jack's unintelligible garble on the phone. He was dying to give them a hug. "What do you say I come through there tonight?" he said, unable to keep the longing out of his voice.

"We'd love to see you," Jo said.

Knowing he was going home to his family, he was impatient for eight o'clock. Perhaps he should have let Uniform do the surveillance.

It was almost eight when the front door opened and Karin came out.

What now?

He watched as she got into her car and backed out of the driveway. She was wearing jeans and a hoodie, strange attire for a night visit. His gut told him something was going down.

He followed at a distance, careful not to get too close. She drove towards town, keeping within the speed limit. She was a good driver, if nothing else. He followed her through Clapham and into Lambeth. Where was she going? Back to work?

She turned into a narrow road off the Cut and pulled over about halfway down. Rob parked further up, not wanting to draw attention to himself. She got out of the car, looked up and down the street, then entered an apartment next to a barber's.

What was she doing here?

He got out of the car and approached the apartment's door. It was dark now, the only light coming from the streetlamps and the bars and cafés across the road. There was no sign on the black-painted door, only the number 38 in gold stuck to the wall and an intercom system. He glanced up. A camera stared back down at him.

He immediately turned his back and walked across the street to one of the cafés. As he did so, he checked his phone to see what the name of the street was. Lime Grove.

Rob took a seat by the window and ordered a coffee. Then he texted Jo and told her he might be late. His target was on the move. She sent him two kisses in reply.

A man walked up the street and rang the buzzer beside the black door. It opened and he disappeared inside. Rob frowned. Was this a meeting of some sort? A clandestine get-together of the members of the OCG?

Another man rang the buzzer. He was allowed in. The door shut instantly. Rob never got a look inside.

A short time later, the first man came out. He hurried away, like he didn't want to be seen there. Another man went in. Karin still hadn't emerged.

Rob ordered another coffee. "Do you know anything about that place across the road?" he asked the man serving him.

"Very bad place." The man shook his turbaned head.

Rob watched as another man went in, and one came out. He hadn't seen him before. He must have gone in before Rob arrived.

He began to get a sick feeling about this. He waited until he saw Karin leave. She was clutching her handbag tight underneath her arm. There was something valuable in there. Money? Had she just been paid for her services?

He paid for his coffee and crossed the street. This was a bad idea, he knew that. But he was going to do it anyway. He had to know.

He knocked on the door. A camera positioned on the wall eyeballed him for a long moment, then the door buzzed open. He pushed it inwards and entered the building to a small entrance hall with nothing but a flight of stairs in front of him. He walked up, a ball of dread tightening in his stomach.

A man greeted him at the top. He took out a wad of twenties and said, "How much?"

"Fifty quid."

Rob handed over the cash.

"This way."

The man led him down a squalid passageway to the second door on the right. He unlocked it with a key, then said, "You have twenty minutes." Rob walked in. The door shut behind him and he heard the key turn in the lock.

Rob froze.

In front of him was a bed. Lying on it was a semi-naked girl. She couldn't have been more than sixteen. Her legs were bare, but she was wearing a white T-shirt, stained with what looked suspiciously like vomit.

Her eyes were huge, her skin blotchy, and make-up was smudged under her eyes. She stared at him with a scared resignation.

He walked over to her. "What's your name?"

"Maria."

"Maria, I'm not going to hurt you. I'm a policeman and I'm here to help."

Her eyes lit up, just a little. A small flicker of hope.

"How long have you been here?"

She shook her head. He looked around the room. Apart from the bed, there was nothing in it. No carpet, no rug, no dresser or drawers. Just the filthy mattress and a pillow. Time would stay still in a place such as this. The days would blur into one another until it became one endless nightmare.

"Who put you here?" He took a step closer.

She shimmied to the top of the bed, hugging her knees.

"What's his name?"

She stared at him with wide eyes. Could she even understand what he was saying? She looked Eastern European. Olive skin, dark hair, brown eyes. She would have been pretty once. Before this.

"Maria, do you understand me?"

She gave a small nod.

"Give me a name. Who brought you here?"

"Anton," she whispered. "The man who picked me up was called Anton."

Anton. That was a start.

"Did he bring you here?"

She nodded.

"From where?"

"The airport."

Rob pulled out his phone. "Okay, listen to me, Maria. I'm going to go now, but I'll be back. I'll be back to get you, okay?"

"No." She reached for him. "Don't leave me here. Please."

He hated doing it, but he stepped back. "I have to. I can't take you with me now. I promise I'll be back soon, with more police officers. We'll get you out of here."

"No, take me with you."

He banged on the door.

"Please, don't leave me here." She was crying now. "Please . . . help . . . me."

The door opened. She skimmed back onto the bed.

"Yes?"

"I'm done." He walked out, leaving her sobbing behind him.

CHAPTER 33

Rob called Galbraith the second he walked out into the street. Jenny and Will had both left the office for the day. One of the other major investigation teams was on call, but Galbraith was still there finishing up some reports.

"I've found the brothel. We have to raid this place tonight," said Rob. "They've got young girls here. Jesus, Gav." He shuddered as the image of Maria cowering on the filthy bed flashed through his mind.

The Scot jumped into action. "Aye, I'll get hold of the Super and clear it," he said, in his no-nonsense brogue. "Stand by."

Rob went back to his car. He felt dirty just being in that place. It was unthinkable what those girls were going through. Locked up, used as sex slaves.

Needing some normality, he called Jo and told her what had happened. She was horrified.

"Get them out of there, Rob," she told him. "Do whatever you have to but get them out. Do not leave them in there for a second longer than you have to."

He promised, then waited for Galbraith to call back.

* * *

The Armed Response Unit assembled up the road. Twelve well-trained men under one command. That should be enough. He'd counted four adult men in the building, excluding the punters. There may be more, but they were out of sight.

Galbraith handed him a vest. "You ready?"

"Yeah, let's do this."

The armed officers smashed the door down, then systematically filed into the building. There were shouts and screams, but thankfully no gunfire. It took them a little under fifteen minutes to secure the premises.

Rob, Galbraith and four female officers moved in. They passed the men being led out in handcuffs. The man Rob had spoken to when he'd first arrived glared at him on the way out. Rob marched past, ignoring him. He was scum. Ruthless, inhumane and unfeeling. They had to be to treat other human beings like this.

The girls were released and wrapped in blankets before being led out of the building. Most were in shock. One or two had been drugged into compliance. One sported a nasty bruise across her face, and another had scratch marks all over her body.

"I can't imagine what they must have been through," a shocked female officer told him. "They thought they were coming here to start a new life and ended up chained to a bed."

* * *

"There were eleven in total," Rob told the rest of the team the following day.

He'd never made it to Jo's. The traumatised women had been taken to the hospital where they were being treated for shock, as well as any injuries they might have sustained over the course of their captivity. After that, they'd be housed in a place of safety until they were well enough to manage on their own. Most would need counselling to get over the ordeal. Some would never get over it.

The men running the brothel had been arrested and remanded in custody. Rob was planning on interrogating them when he'd calmed down. He'd yet to get his head around the conditions in which the girls had been kept and the abuse they'd suffered.

"On second thoughts, perhaps I'm not the best person for the job."

"I'll do it." Jenny's voice was hard.

Will nodded. "You can count me in."

"And me," said Galbraith, whose eyes blazed with Gaelic passion.

"Thanks," Rob nodded at his colleagues.

* * *

He watched on the video link as the men were interrogated. They were Eastern European — Romanian, according to the guy Rob had spoken to. He seemed to be the one in control.

As the team worked through the suspects, Rob waited for an answer to one question. Who was in charge?

"We are," the Romanians said. It turned out two were brothers, one was a distant cousin and the other a family friend. "It's a family business." He seemed almost proud of it.

Forensics had searched the brothel and taken all the files, laptops and documents they could find. The Finance team were looking into it as they spoke. If they were being bank-rolled or were paying someone dues or protection money, they'd find out.

"Do you know this woman?" Jenny slid a photograph of Karin Gutowski across the table. She'd managed to get her driver's licence from the DVLA and blown it up.

"No," came the answer every time.

Except Rob knew they were lying. He'd seen her walk into the building with his own eyes. She'd stayed half an hour then left again, carrying something in her bag.

What weren't these guys telling them?

* * *

Karin Gutowski arrived of her own volition early the next morning. "I hope this won't take long," she said. "I have to get to work."

"Why don't we go this way?" Rob led her down the hall to an interview room. "We just have a couple of questions."

They sat down, then Will arrived and joined them.

"You remember Sergeant Freemont?" Rob said.

Karin nodded, a guarded look appearing in her eyes. "Am I in trouble?"

Rob fixed his gaze on her. "I don't know. Have you done something wrong?"

She frowned. "Not that I know of."

"Then you have nothing to worry about."

The frown didn't leave her face.

"Okay, Karin. We want to ask you what you were doing at 38 Lime Grove, Waterloo yesterday evening."

The colour drained from her face. "I don't know what you mean."

"You were seen entering the premises at eight thirty and you left half an hour later at nine."

She clasped her hands together in her lap.

"I think I should speak to a solicitor," she whispered.

"I thought you said you had nothing to hide?" Rob hadn't taken his eyes off her.

She fidgeted. "I don't."

"Then what were you doing there?"

She had every right to a solicitor, but if he could get something out of her now, before she lawyered up, it might help them. "I was visiting a friend."

"At a brothel?"

She swallowed.

"We know all about what goes on there," Rob said. "In fact, we raided the property about an hour after you left. The Rusescu family is in custody. Who exactly was your friend?"

"Florin and I grew up together in a little village in Romania," she said. He could see she was thinking fast. "He lent me some money."

"Did he give it to you last night?"

She nodded. "That's why I went there, to pick it up."

"Why do you need money?"

She chewed on her lower lip. "I have a large mortgage and my salary doesn't quite cover it. Florin helps me out from time to time."

"And what do you do for him in return?"

"I do his books for him." Her words flew out in a rush.

Was that true? "You mean you cook the books for him?" Like hell the brothel was paying any tax at all. In fact, they would be listed as some sort of shell company, a nondescript name with untraceable directors. He'd seen it before.

"Are you a qualified accountant?" Rob asked.

She shook her head. "No, but I trained as a bookkeeper before I went into social work."

"Okay, fine."

Will made a note. They'd look into that.

"How long have you been in England?" Rob asked.

"Since I was four. My mother brought me over when I was little. She worked as a cleaner." Rob heard the resentment in her voice.

"Where is your mother now?"

"In a nursing home in Berkshire. She has advanced dementia."

"I'm sorry to hear that."

She gave a terse nod. "Her life hasn't been easy."

Rob took a deep breath. "Karin, have you heard of a man called the Wolf?"

She went very still. "No."

"Are you sure?"

Another nod, but he saw a flash of fear in her eyes.

"Are you recruiting young boys from the children's homes and other accommodations you work at for an organised crime group?"

Karin turned to stone. "I want a solicitor," she croaked. "I won't say another word until I get one."

"Fair enough." Rob slid his chair back and got to his feet. "Karin Gutowski, I'm arresting you on suspicion of child trafficking. You do not have to say anything, but it may harm your defence if you do not mention when questioned something which you later rely on in court. Anything you do say may be given in evidence."

She stared at him with wild, defiant eyes.

"You'll be transported to the Wandsworth Custody Suite, where you'll be processed and held until your solicitor gets there. We'll continue this conversation when you have the appropriate legal representation."

He nodded at Will, who took out his handcuffs. Karin was silent as Will secured her wrists behind her back and led her from the room.

CHAPTER 34

"Guv, we have the information back from Claudio's mobile phone. The last tower it pinged was the T-Mobile Tideway Switch in Battersea."

Rob scowled. "That's upriver from where he was found."

"He could have been swept downriver on the outgoing tide," pointed out Jenny. "It's pretty tidal around there."

She had a point. Was Battersea where Claudio had been killed and thrown into the water? "Let's go check it out," he said.

Will grabbed his rucksack. "What about Karin?"

"She can stew for a while. It'll take some time for her solicitor to arrive, anyway."

"I'll look into the financials from the brothel," Jenny said. "See if I can find the payments to Karin. Or any other third-party organisations," she added.

* * *

There was a large construction site off Nine Elms Lane in Battersea close to the river. A brick wall ran along the road-side, breaking off where a metal section had been erected to allow lorries and construction vehicles to enter the area. The makeshift gate had steel rods that went into the ground and a chain keeping it shut.

"Not much of a deterrent," muttered Will. "Anyone with a crowbar or wire cutters could gain access."

The site seemed deserted, and the office, which resembled a shipping container, was empty. It took Rob less than a minute to cut through the chain and pull open the gate. They walked in on foot, leaving the car ramped on the pavement outside. Judging by the posters on the side of the office, it would one day be a luxury apartment block with views over the Thames, but right now it was little more than a muddy hole in the ground.

A crane stood to the side, stretching upwards into the clouds. A long wire rope hung from it, taut and unyielding, fastened to a steel rod. It looked like the work had been discontinued and the crane operator had simply left the rod there and walked away.

"Where is everyone?" asked Will.

"No idea. Perhaps they've put it on hold for some reason. It certainly looks like it's been this way for some time."

Large puddles had formed in the muddy foundations, and a sad digger stood to one side, facing away from the rectangular hole like it couldn't bear to look.

"Perfect site for a killing," Will murmured.

Rob had been thinking the same thing. There were no site lights, nothing to illuminate the area. The streetlamps wouldn't have extended over the wall, or if they did, not by much.

They walked towards the river, careful to avoid the edges of the hole, which had been smoothed out by rainwater and looked like they might cave in at any moment.

"It would be pitch dark down here at night," said Rob.

Will glanced to the left and right. "The towpath doesn't continue along here. There's no riverfront access. It's perfectly secluded."

"And a body thrown in here might float down to the South Bank if the tide was right."

They looked for signs of a struggle, but the recent rains had washed away anything that might have remained of the altercation.

Rob paced up and down the riverfront. The bank was stony and exposed, thanks to the low tide. "It must have been high when he was killed," Rob mused. "Otherwise, the body wouldn't have floated out until the tide came in."

"No one to see it here anyway." Will peered down onto the mud and stones.

That was true. They could have just dumped Claudio on the rocks and let the tide do the work for them.

"What about Benny?" Rob thought out loud. "Was he killed here too?"

"Could have been," replied Will. "If they were killed by the same person or group. His body made it further down the river, but not by much."

"Benny was shot." Rob paced up and down the riverfront, eyes glued to the ground. The concrete path that ran along the embankment had a low railing on the river's edge but nothing on the side of the construction site. That would presumably be landscaped after the apartment block was built.

"I don't see any blood," Will said, also surveying the area.

Rob kept looking, working his way inwards in a grid pattern.

"Here!" He pointed to a spot on the damp ground.

Will ran over.

"Look at that. It could be a bloodstain."

Will crouched down and studied the spot where Rob was pointing. "Could be," he said, "It's darker than the rest of the earth, but it may just be a redder type of mud."

"Let's get SOCO out here anyway," Rob decided. "That way, we'll know for sure."

Will pulled out his phone.

Rob straightened up and gazed out over the windswept water. Small white crests were flicking up on the surface as it danced downstream. The tide was going out now — in fact, it was almost all the way out. Soon it would turn and come surging back in, filling up the banks to the brim. In some places, like where he worked in Putney, it would seep over the bank and cause localised flooding. He'd even known parked cars to be swept away by unsuspecting visitors to riverside bars and pubs.

That's how Benny's and Claudio's bodies had been taken. Left on the stony bank, then drawn into the swollen river and washed downstream to the South Bank. He shuddered as an icy wind sliced through the empty construction site, chilling him to the bone. What a desolate place to die.

Will hung up. "They're on their way."

* * *

Once the crime squad on call had arrived to secure what was now a potential crime scene, the area was cordoned off and plastic steps were laid across the muddy ground to prevent contamination and anyone slipping into the hole.

Rob got a message that Karin Gutowski had been processed and was ready for interrogation. Her DNA swab had been sent to the lab for comparison with that found under Benny's fingernails. "It's unlikely she was the one who assaulted Benny," he told Will on the way there. "But we'd better make sure."

Jenny rang while they were en route. "Guv, Karin doesn't have a mortgage. She bought her house outright two and a half years ago. Cash purchase."

Wow. He shook his head. "So Florin Rusescu lending her money was bullshit. He was paying her for services rendered."

"What services?" Jenny asked.

"That," Rob said, "is what we need to find out."

Karin Gutowski wasn't nearly as composed now. Instead of her work attire, she was wearing a standard-issue police tracksuit a size too big for her. Her face was pale and she seemed smaller, as if she'd shrunk into herself.

A stocky man with a short beard sat beside her. Her solicitor. He nodded as they walked in.

"Right, let's get to it." Rob sat down opposite them. Will started the recorder and informed them that the interview was being recorded and filmed.

"I'm going to pick up where we left off during our last discussion," Rob began. "Karin, are you recruiting unaccompanied asylum-seeking children on behalf of a criminal organisation?"

She glanced at her solicitor.

"My client would like to cooperate with the police," he said. "We'd like her compliance to be noted."

"Of course." Rob turned his steely gaze onto her.

Her solicitor nodded and she began to talk. "It started three years ago," she said, her lip quivering. "Florin Rusescu approached me and asked if I wanted to make some extra money. At that point, I was struggling financially. My mother was still living with me in a small flat, and she was unable to look after herself. I was finding it very hard to cope." Her voice broke.

Rob didn't respond. He wanted to keep her talking.

"He said he knew a guy who would give me five thousand pounds a month if I did some extra work for him." She glanced up at Rob, her eyes shining. "I didn't want to, but my mother was so unwell. I needed to put her in a home."

He didn't react. Everyone had choices, she'd made hers.

She exhaled shakily. "All I had to do was earmark certain boys for delivery jobs. They weren't going to be hurt. They'd even get paid, which would give them some spending money. It didn't sound too bad."

You could spin it anyway you wanted, it was still child exploitation.

"Who was this guy?" he asked.

"I don't know. I never met him."

"Was he a friend of Rusescu's?"

She frowned. "A business associate, I think. They weren't friends."

"What makes you say that?"

"The way he talked about him — with respect and maybe a little fear."

The Wolf. "Go on."

"I only chose the older boys, the ones who could understand what they were doing. Most of them wanted the work. They didn't care if it was illegal."

Rob pressed his lips together.

"It worked well, until . . ." She faded off.

"Until Benny put up a fight?"

She nodded. "Yes. Benny and his brother were different. They were from a strict, religious family. I didn't know that at the time. Florin said this man wanted two boys for a burglary job. It would be easy. The owners were away, and the boys would be in and out in five minutes."

"Why did they go along with it?"

"I think Benny wanted to make some money to look after his brother, but when they got to the house, he changed his mind."

"He couldn't go through with it?"

She shook her head. "I don't know what happened next. I wasn't there. Florin told me there was a fight. Benny said he was going to the authorities, and whoever was in charge shot him."

She bit her lip. "I didn't know that was going to happen. I swear. I'd never have knowingly hurt any of the boys."

"Who was in charge?" Rob asked. "Was it the same man who paid you?"

"I don't know." Her voice was strained.

"Who collected the boys from the children's home?"

She hesitated.

"Karin, if you know, you should tell me."

She sighed. "There was this man, I don't know his name. I never asked. He had short hair, a buzz cut. He picked up the boys, took them away in the van and then brought them back the next morning or whenever the job was done."

"Did he have an accent?" Rob asked.

"He sounded English."

"What about tattoos?"

"I don't know." She looked away. "I didn't notice any."

It made sense that the Wolf wouldn't do his own dirty work. He'd have an enforcer for that. He took in Karin's stiff shoulders, defeated expression and moist eyes. She was telling the truth. If it hadn't been vulnerable children, he may even have felt sorry for her. She was a victim herself, in a way. The Wolf had taken advantage of her financial situation, her mother's illness, and coerced her into working for him. She wasn't by nature an evil person, she'd just convinced herself that what she was doing wasn't hurting anyone.

"One last thing," he said. "Do you know a man called Anton?"

"Anton is Florin's cousin. He's younger, in his late twenties. I've met him at the . . . the brothel."

That made sense. Anton was the one who picked up the girls from the airport. The sweet-talker. The one who lured them in.

"Okay, we'll leave it there for now."

"What will happen to me?" Her voice quivered.

"You'll be remanded in custody for the time being." Rob sighed. At the very least, she'd be charged with child exploitation and abusing a position of power. He couldn't see her getting away without jail time. She was a decent person who'd made some bad choices, but those choices had resulted in two kids dying — and that was unforgivable.

Rob and Will were leaving Wandsworth Police Station when an alarm sounded.

"Is that a drill?" Will glanced around.

People were running towards the custody suite, including a medic with a first-aid kit.

"Something's happened," Rob muttered.

They turned around. The alarm seemed to be getting louder, drowning out the other noise.

"Torch is being held down there," his sergeant breathed.

They took off at a run.

223

God, no. Rob forced his way through the group of officers to where a cell door was wide open.

Inside, Torch lay in a pool of his own blood. His throat had been slashed.

CHAPTER 35

"What the fuck happened?" growled Rob.

"W—We found him like this a few minutes ago," stammered the red-faced custody sergeant.

"Why's the cell door open?"

"I don't know."

"Lock down the entire building," Rob barked. "Nobody is to leave. Do you hear me?"

Will took out his phone and issued several commands. The officers in the custody suite stared at each other, stunned. Rob guessed nothing like this had ever happened to them before.

"Someone got to him," Rob hissed, when Will had hung up.

Everyone was still staring at the dead man. No one had moved away from the body.

"Whoever it was got out before we got here," agreed Will. He turned to the sergeant. "Do you have CCTV down here?"

He nodded, mutely.

"I want to see it. Now."

The sergeant turned and Will followed.

Rob stared at Torch's lifeless body. His eyes were open, gazing at the door as if daring anyone to come in. His big, brawny body had crumpled like a rag doll, the strength ebbing out onto the concrete floor. The gaping slit in his throat glistened under the fluorescent lighting like a contorted grin.

Rob shuddered. "Get Forensics in here. This is a crime scene. I want it sealed off. Nobody is to go in or out, understood?"

The officers lingering behind him nodded.

"You!" Rob grabbed a young, uniformed officer by the shoulder. "Get some tape and seal this area off now."

He blinked, snapping out of his shocked stupor. "Yes, sir."

Rob turned away. *Shit. Shit. Shit.*

The only person who could tell them who the Wolf was had been killed. And right under their noses. It was audacious. It was dangerous. It was risky as hell. It had also opened up a whole new possibility. That the Wolf had law enforcement connections.

* * *

"Do you really think so?" Jenny gasped.

They had assembled in the briefing room, standing around the eight-seater boardroom table.

"It's a possibility. Think about it. He managed to get to him inside the custody suite. That means he had an inside man. Will, you looked at the CCTV. Anything?"

Will shook his head. "The cameras were off in that corridor at the time of the murder."

Rob grimaced. "That backs up my theory. If the killer was a cop, he'd have known how to disable the cameras."

"What about the other cameras in the block?" asked Jenny.

"No, they were all operational. It was just the cameras in that particular corridor and that specific cell that were out."

"I've got the camera footage from the rest of the building," said Will, his face grim. "I'll trawl through it and see if I can spot anyone acting strangely. We might still be able to figure out who it was."

Rob nodded. If anyone could spot the perpetrator, it was Will. He had a keen eye for detail and wouldn't give up until he'd exhausted all options.

"Rob, my office!" He glanced up to see Mayhew beckoning from behind the glass.

"Excuse me," he said to the team, and left the room.

"What's this I hear about a murder in the cells at Wandsworth nick?"

He sank down in the chair opposite her desk. The beginnings of a headache prickled around his temples. "It's true. Shamar Williams had his throat cut this afternoon."

"Torch? Our prime witness?"

"Correct, ma'am. He was one of the few people who could identify the Wolf for us."

"And this Wolf, he's in charge of the OCG?"

"We're not sure, ma'am. He's definitely involved. We know he's running the child trafficking ring, and also the brothel where the girls were found, but whether he's their top man . . . " He shrugged.

"You mean there could be someone else, higher up, pulling the strings?"

"It's possible, but that's not our problem. With all due respect, we're only interested in finding DCS Lawrence's killer, and the person who murdered those two boys."

"I agree, the OCG isn't our remit." She thought for a moment. "What does Pearson have to say about this?"

"He doesn't know yet, ma'am."

Her eyes widened. She was picturing the shitstorm that was bound to go down. "Well, I suggest you fill him in ASAP."

"Yes, ma'am."

"What are you going to do now?" she asked, in a rare moment of humility. Torch's death had shocked them all. "How will you find this Wolf character?"

"We still have a few leads to follow up," he replied. Weariness pressed down on him. "There's the blood at the crime scene in Battersea. It may belong to one of our victims, and there might be DNA or other evidence from the man who shot him."

It was a long shot, and the Superintendent knew it. He could tell by the withering look she gave him. "What else?"

"I want to go and talk to the girls at the brothel. One of them might have seen or heard something."

She nodded. "What about the Romanians?"

"They're adamant it was a family business," he said. "They've refused to implicate anyone else. We're looking into their finances. There might be something there."

Again, a long shot.

Mayhew sighed. "We need to tie this up quickly, Rob. We're way over budget and it's getting messy. I've had the Police Commissioner on the phone wanting to know what's going on. She's worried about police misconduct. That death in the cell. It doesn't look good. People are going to be asking questions. The papers are going to have a field day."

It was pretty messy for Torch too. "Ma'am."

"Okay, I'll let you get on. Keep me posted."

"Will do, ma'am."

* * *

"Come on," Rob said to Jenny when he got back to his desk. "Let's go speak to the girls. They've been put up in a bedsit in Pimlico."

Jenny drove. "The only accounts I could find for the brothel was a book of cash payments," she said. "Room numbers and a cash amount. They didn't even use names."

"Any outgoing payments?"

"That's where it gets interesting," she said. "Once a month there's a cash payment to 'Lupus Holdings'. It works out to be exactly twenty-five per cent of the monthly takings."

"The Wolf," murmured Rob. "Isn't *lupus* 'wolf' in Latin?"

"Oh my God. Yes, you're right." Jenny stared at him. "Why didn't I think of that?"

"The Wolf owns a quarter of the business." Rob rubbed the stubble on his chin. "Perhaps he was an initial investor, a loan shark. Or maybe it's protection money. We won't know if they don't tell us."

"At least we can confront them with this," Jenny said.

"Yep, and we will, first thing tomorrow morning. Right now, I want to get to the bedsit while the girls are still there. In a few days, they'll move on."

* * *

Rob had elected to question each of the girls privately in their own rooms. He started with Maria because he knew her — sort of. She looked much better now. Clean, dressed in a sweatshirt and trackpants, her hair brushed. It was only her eyes, nervous and uncertain, that hinted at what she'd been through. Jenny had taken one of the other girls, a Swedish national called Olga.

"I don't know who was in charge," Maria said.

"You don't remember anyone important coming to the brothel? Someone the others looked up to?"

She shook her head. "I was confined to my room. I wasn't allowed out. They brought me food. They brought me water. I was prisoner." She flinched as if he'd raised his hand to her. The mere memory of what had happened would haunt her for ever.

"Did you overhear anything? An argument, perhaps? Yelling?"

"Only the screams of other girls."

Feeling raw, Rob moved on to the next girl. Her name was Imani, and she was seventeen years old. She'd crossed into Spain from Algeria and then made her way to the UK. She had long black hair and pale green eyes, a striking combination, but there were lines in her face. Lines that shouldn't have been there. Lines that would never go away.

Despite her ordeal, she sat upright, her hands in her lap. He sensed a strength in her, a defiant will to survive despite what had happened. Her spirit wasn't broken.

"Do you speak English?" Rob sat on a chair opposite where she perched on the bed. The bedroom door was wide open and there were people milling around outside in the corridor. He wanted the girls to feel safe.

She nodded. "A little."

"Imani, we're trying to find the man who was in charge of the place you were kept. Can you help us with that?"

"The boss man?" she asked.

"Yes, that's right. Did you see or hear anything that could help us identify him?"

She thought for a moment, her gaze shifting off Rob and onto the wall behind him. "I don't know. There were several men there, but I don't know if any of them were the boss man."

"What makes you say that?"

"They all acted the same. No one gave orders. They took money, they showed in the men, they argued among themselves." She shrugged.

"You saw this?"

"Yes, my room was closest to the stairs, and I could hear what they were saying. I looked through—" She made a circular motion with her finger.

"The keyhole?"

She nodded.

"Okay, that's good. Thank you, Imani. Is there anything else you saw or remember? Anything that could help us?"

Her eyes flickered. "When I first arrived . . . there was this man." She took a deep breath.

"Yes?"

"He was English, I think. He told the men I was special. He told them he wanted to be the first one to have me." She cringed. "He came back every day for a week. Nobody else came into my room. Only him."

Rob frowned. "Do you think he was the boss?"

She shrugged. "Maybe an important client? I don't know." Her face fell. "Then one day, he stopped coming."

Rob knew what that meant. That's when the other men came. Lots of them.

"I know this is hard for you." He tried to keep the urgency out of his voice. "But is there anything you can tell me about that man? What did he look like?"

"He was shorter than you." She studied Rob. "He had lighter hair too, but thinner, like he was losing some of it."

"How old was he?" he asked.

"Maybe forty or fifty." She shrugged. "I don't know. Older than you."

Rob felt a surge of adrenaline. They were getting somewhere. This could be a description of the Wolf.

"What else?" he asked. "Any markings or tattoos?" He held his breath.

She shook her head. "No, but he had an injury." She tapped her forearm.

"An injury? What kind?"

"I don't know, but there was a bandage on his arm."

Rob's blood ran cold.

"A bandage, are you sure?"

"Yes, I'm sure."

"How long ago was this?" he whispered.

"A few weeks ago. I only arrived in the UK a month ago. I am one of the lucky ones. I wasn't there for a long time."

Long enough. In that place, every day must have felt like an eternity.

"Okay. Thanks, Imani. You've been very helpful."

He ran from the room.

"Jenny!" He took the stairs two at a time. "Let's go!"

"What's the hurry?" she asked. "Did you find something?"

"I know who it is," he rasped, his chest heaving. "I know who the Wolf is."

CHAPTER 36

Galbraith gaped at him, as did the rest of the team. "Cranshaw? Are you sure?"

"No, but it fits. Think about it. He's in law enforcement, he'd know how to get into the Wandsworth precinct. He's been at Southwark nick for close to twenty years. He'd know Torch, the Albanians, the Pavićs. Everyone."

"He was the one who notified us about the boys in the river," said Jenny. "Why would he do that if he was the one who put them there?"

"He wanted to divert suspicion," Rob said. "Besides, homicide wouldn't necessarily fall to CID. He probably thought Barking MIT would handle it, but then it was given to us. Maybe he knew someone at Barking? Had them on the payroll? Who knows?"

There was a long pause as the team digested this information.

"We need proof," Will said. "A bandage isn't going to be enough."

"The girl, Imani, could identify him. She'd do it too, I'm sure of it."

Galbraith shrugged. "It would be his word against hers. She was drugged, under duress, not thinking clearly. The defence would come up with a hundred reasons why she's not a reliable witness. He's a respected officer of the law."

"He must have had the wolf tattoo removed," Rob mused. "That's why he was wearing the bandage. When I shook his hand the other day, he winced. Said it was a strain."

"Even so, it doesn't put him at any of the crime scenes," Will pointed out.

"It could be his DNA under Benny's fingernails." Rob's brain was whirling. "What if we could get his DNA and compare it?"

"How are you going to do that? Come right out and ask him?" said Jenny.

Rob pursed his lips. "Maybe I will."

"I was kidding. You can't just waltz into Southwark Police Station and confront him."

"Why not? He won't be expecting it."

"He's dangerous." Jenny shot Will a worried glance. "If it was him, he put the hit out on the Chief."

"He can't do anything at the station," Rob argued. "And if he's innocent, he won't mind me taking a DNA sample."

Will frowned. "Well, I'm coming with you."

* * *

They arrived at Southwark Police Station and asked the duty sergeant to let DCI Cranshaw know they were there. A few moments later, a young detective came downstairs to greet them.

"I'm DC Tremayne." She flashed them a cautious smile. "I believe you want to see DCI Cranshaw?"

"Yes, DCI Miller and DS Freemont from the Putney Major Investigation Team. It's in connection with the two boys found on the South Bank."

"Oh, yes. That was just awful." She brushed her auburn hair off her face. "Come with me, please."

She led them up a flight of stairs to an open-plan squad room, a lot like theirs, except about half the size. "This is

CID." She gestured with her arm. "Cranshaw's office is down the hall."

So he had a separate office, did he? They walked past the squad room, and Tremayne knocked on a door with DCI Cranshaw's name on it in gold lettering. It was old-school but seemed appropriate in the busy police station.

"Come in."

Tremayne opened the door. "DCI Miller and DS Freemont here to see you, sir."

"Thanks, Tremayne. Send them in."

She smiled and stood back, allowing them to enter.

Rob was impressed she'd remembered both their names and ranks. "Excuse me," he said, before she could walk away. "Would you mind hanging around?"

"Me?" She frowned.

"Yes, if you don't mind. We have something to ask your boss and we'd like you to be a witness."

"Uh, okay."

Cranshaw stood up. "DCI Miller, what's the meaning of this?"

Rob walked into the room while Will stood next to an awkward Tremayne just inside the doorway. "I'm sorry for the interruption, but we have something sensitive to discuss with you, and we thought it would be better if we did it here, in your office."

"I don't understand. What's this about?"

"I'm sure it's a mistake, but your name has come up in connection with an illegal human trafficking operation."

Tremayne gave a little gasp.

Cranshaw's face coloured and his expression grew thunderous. "What? How?"

Rob cleared his throat. "We have a witness who said you repeatedly sexually abused her at an illegal brothel." Cranshaw opened his mouth, but Rob held up his hand. "Now, I'm sure she's mistaken, but in order to rule you out, we need to ask you for a DNA swab."

"A DNA swab," he spluttered. "Me?"

"Yes, if you don't mind."

"Of course I mind. This is ridiculous."

"I really am sorry for the inconvenience," Rob said. "It's a simple matter to clear this up. If your DNA doesn't match that found at the scene — which it obviously won't — you're in the clear."

Cranshaw fixed his gaze on Rob, and in that moment, Rob knew. He'd done it. He'd done it all. The bastard had killed Sam, Ant Price and Zhou, and he'd shot Benny and strangled Claudio. Perhaps not with his bare hands, but he'd ordered the hits.

"You have DNA from the brothel at Lime Grove?"

"You know about it?"

"I heard about the raid. It's in my neighbourhood. Of course I know about it."

"Did you know it was there?"

"Not before you raided it, no."

Liar. "We found DNA at the scene that didn't belong to any of the four men who ran the place."

"It could be anyone's. Why me? Any number of men would have been through that place."

"That's true," agreed Rob. "Except the witness described you, right down to the wolf tattoo on your forearm."

He froze.

Tremayne's eyes dropped to her boss's arm, where a bandage was visible under his sleeve.

"I don't have a wolf tattoo," he said. "I sprained my elbow making an arrest."

"Do you mind if we see it?" asked Rob. "It will help to rule you out."

"I've been told not to remove the strap," he said.

Tremayne narrowed her eyes.

Rob shrugged. "Okay, suit yourself. But if you refuse to show us your arm or give us your DNA, I'm going to have to take you in. I'm sure you don't want to walk out of here in cuffs."

"You wouldn't dare." His eyes blazed.

Rob didn't so much as blink. "I would much rather not."

Cranshaw sighed. "Okay, you win."

He slowly unravelled the bandage. All eyes were glued to his arm. Underneath the wrapping was a surgical dressing. Through it, they could see a faint yellowy-red stain.

"Doesn't look like a strain," said Rob.

Cranshaw took off the dressing. "It's a wound that got infected, okay? I didn't want to make a fuss, so I said it was a sprain. What's the big deal?"

The wound was infected. It looked like a strip of skin had been removed and become suppurative. A yellowish scab had formed over the top.

"How'd you do that?" asked Rob.

"I burned it on the grill in the oven. Anything else you want to know?"

Rob studied it. It could be where a tattoo had been removed. Unfortunately, there was no way of knowing. No ink that he could see. No markings.

He ground his teeth in frustration. "You should get that looked at."

"I have a course of antibiotics." He nodded to an open box of tablets on the desk next to an empty paper cup.

"Okay. Well, if you give us that DNA sample, we'll get out of your hair."

Cranshaw turned his back on them and gazed out of the window. His voice was calm, overly casual. "Without a warrant, I'm not giving you any of my DNA."

There was an awkward silence.

"Now I've had just about enough of this nonsense." Cranshaw turned back around. "You can't arrest me on a whim. Where's your warrant?"

He knew they'd been bluffing.

His eyes gleamed. "Tremayne, see them out."

"Yes, sir." She turned to the visitors. "This way please, gentlemen."

If that's the way you want to play it.

He gave Cranshaw a blistering look. "We'll be back. You can count on it."

CHAPTER 37

"I want a tail on Cranshaw twenty-four seven," Rob bellowed into the phone.

"The Superintendent won't allow it," came Galbraith's metered response. "I'm sorry, mate, she's put her foot down. We have no direct evidence implicating Cranshaw in the murders, and we're so far over budget, she's thinking about pulling the plug altogether."

"You've got to be kidding me?" Rob held the bridge of his nose. "She can't do that. We're so close. He did it. I know he did."

"We need a bit more than your gut feeling," Galbraith said.

"For fuck's sake!" Rob slammed his hand on the steering wheel. "I'll do it, then. He knows we're onto him, he's going to run."

"You can't tail him by yourself. Be sensible, Rob."

"Why not? Who's going to stop me?" He glanced at Will, who shook his head.

"Okay, but for God's sake, be careful," Galbraith said. "If he is the Wolf, then he's dangerous and unpredictable. In a tight spot, you don't know how he'll react."

"I think he's going to do a runner."

"Well, if he does, let me know. We'll send in the cavalry."

"Thanks, mate."

Rob hung up then looked at Will. "You need to get back to the station with the DNA. Put a rush on it. We need the results ASAP."

Will glanced down at the paper cup in the evidence bag on his lap. Rob had snatched it off the desk when Cranshaw had turned his back on them. He'd taken a chance, and it had paid off.

"You know it won't stand up in court," he said.

"It doesn't need to. We just have to prove it's his DNA under Benny's fingernails, then we can arrest him and get an official swab."

Tremayne had seen him do it but hadn't said a thing.

"If he's innocent, this will prove it," Rob had explained to her on the way out.

"I don't know what you mean, sir," she'd replied.

He decided he liked her.

* * *

Jenny texted him Cranshaw's vehicle registration number. It took him ten minutes to find the dark grey Mercedes A180 in the underground police car park. Then he positioned himself down the road where he could keep an eye on the exit.

At seven thirty, Cranshaw's Merc exited the car park. Rob slunk down in the driver's seat as he drove by, then pulled out and followed, keeping a safe distance between them. He knew Cranshaw's home address and figured he was probably going there to pack. He'd know it wouldn't take Rob long to get a warrant. That didn't leave much time to get out of town.

As expected, Cranshaw drove home. Rob pulled in behind a satellite installation van and cut the engine. Cranshaw parked in his driveway and climbed out of the car. He stood still for a moment and glanced up and down the street, but Rob was tucked in behind the van.

Satisfied, Cranshaw went into the house.

Rob settled down to wait. If the crooked detective was going to make a run for it, he'd leave tonight, probably under cover of darkness.

His phone rang.

"How's it going, guv?" It was Jenny.

"Fine. I'm in position outside his house. If he makes a move, I'll know it."

"We've got the DNA back from the blood you found at the Battersea crime scene," she said. "It's a match for Benny's."

Yes! That was something, at least. They had the primary crime scene. "Now, if only Cranshaw's DNA matches that under his fingernails . . ."

"How are we going to get him for the Chief's murder?" she asked. He heard the concern in her voice. That crime scene had been pristine. The shooter hadn't come in further than a few steps. Likely, Cranshaw hadn't even been there.

"Someone is doing the dirty work for him," Rob said. "We need to find out who. Look into the four Romanians again. See if one of them owns a motorbike."

"Okay, I'll get back to you."

Next, he called Jo and told her what he was doing.

"Alone?" she blurted out. "Are you sure that's wise?"

"I don't have a choice," he said. "Mayhew won't sanction surveillance. Not enough evidence — or budget."

"But Rob, you know what he's capable of. He killed Sam and the others. And those young boys. Oh, Jesus."

"Don't worry," he reassured her. "I've got the team on standby. If he leaves the house, I'll let them know. If he tries to flee, I'll call for reinforcements. I won't tackle him by myself."

"You promise?" she whispered.

"I promise."

It was twenty past midnight when the door opened and Cranshaw came out. The house was in darkness. He pictured Cranshaw's wife and kids asleep inside.

Was this it? Was this Cranshaw making his escape?

He was carrying a sports bag, quite a big one, which he dumped in the back seat of the car. Then he climbed in behind the wheel.

Imagine your whole life reduced to one sports bag. But that's what it boiled down to, really. He had to leave before he was arrested, and that's all he was taking. One bag from an entire life.

Did his wife know? Rob was betting not. She was probably fast asleep, oblivious to the fact that she'd never see her husband, the father of her children, again.

What a scumbag.

Cranshaw headed south on the A23 towards Croydon. He avoided the airports — they could be being monitored. Rob grimaced. They weren't. If Cranshaw boarded a plane, he would probably get away with it.

Was he heading to Dover? A port was much harder to police. Perhaps he was heading towards the Channel Tunnel?

Rob followed, keeping out of sight.

Cranshaw turned onto the M25 and then onto the M20 towards Dover. The port was looking more and more likely.

Rob called his team, all of whom were still at the office, and gave them an update. He knew by the echo he was on speakerphone.

"I'm driving down." Galbraith said tersely. "You'll need backup."

"I'm coming too. We're leaving now," added Will.

Their drive to the coast would take the better part of two hours. The big Scot checked in with him every half an hour. "We're thirty minutes behind you, mate," he said as Rob reached the final stretch of the M20. He and Will had evidently managed to make up some of the distance.

It felt good knowing they were coming, and he wasn't totally alone. Rob hadn't thought about what he was going to do when he got to the port. Probably flag down some uniformed officers or Border Control and enlist their help in apprehending his suspect.

Except Cranshaw didn't go to the port. He swung off the M20 just before Folkestone and turned towards the coast.

Rob hurriedly dialled Galbraith's number. "He's going to Folkestone," he yelled.

"He must know someone with a boat," the detective said. "Why else would he go there?"

Rob felt like slapping himself. "Of course he'd know people with boats. His business involves human trafficking. He must have contacts who bring immigrants across the Channel."

"That's how he's going to get out of England," Galbraith said.

"Not if I can help it," muttered Rob. "I'm ten minutes out. Gotta go."

Galbraith wouldn't make it in time. If Cranshaw had a boat waiting, he'd have no choice but to take him down alone.

The lights of the town flickered in the darkness. Rob glanced at the time on the dash. Just past two in the morning. The sky was impossibly dark, and the sliver of a moon, if you could even call it that, kept darting behind low-lying clouds as if it was afraid of what it might see.

Would Cranshaw realise the same set of headlights had followed him all the way from London? Hopefully not. There wasn't much traffic this time of the morning, but the roads weren't deserted. Delivery vans, postal lorries and shift workers would be going about their business.

Cranshaw didn't stop in Folkestone. He turned off before it and veered south until he got to the coast.

As they got to the narrower, windier lanes, Rob killed his lights, praying he wouldn't meet any vehicles coming the other way. He didn't. Not down here on this isolated stretch of beach.

He opened his window and smelled the sea. It was fresh and salty, and made his nose itch. He couldn't remember when last he'd been to the seaside. He and Jo had been talking about taking a holiday for months, but they hadn't got round to it yet.

Cranshaw's tyres crunched as the detective turned off the road onto a gravel track. Unwilling to risk it, Rob pulled over and cut the engine. He got out of the car, pulling on his stab vest, and taking his baton and stun gun with him. Sticking to the edge, he crept down the gravel track after Cranshaw's car.

He rounded a bend and saw the red tail lights go out. The Merc had stopped in a car park next to a small jetty. At the end of the jetty was a dark shape — a waiting motorboat. It was barely noticeable, but Rob spotted it because the person on board was smoking a cigarette and the amber light danced around like a firefly.

Shit. Now what?

Cranshaw climbed out of his car and lifted the sports bag from the back seat. This was it. He was going to board that launch and get taken out to a fishing trawler or similar vessel and disappear into the wide blue yonder.

No fucking way.

"Cranshaw, stop!" he shouted, shattering the stillness.

He spun around. "Miller? Jesus, you don't give up, do you?"

"No, sir. I'm arresting you on the suspicion of the murder of Chief Superintendent Sam Lawrence, Anthony Price—"

"I don't think so, Miller. This ends here."

He reached into his pocket, pulled out a gun and fired.

CHAPTER 38

Rob flew backwards and landed on the ground. He let go of the baton and the stun gun as pain radiated from his torso.

He'd been hit.

Shit, it hurt to breathe. He clutched at his chest, feeling for the hole in the vest. For the sticky blood. There was none.

Thank fuck.

The bullet hadn't gone through.

Relief flooded his body. He rolled onto his side. Cranshaw was hurrying toward the launch. The bastard was getting away.

Groaning, Rob tried to sit up. He'd got him right in the centre of his chest, over the sternum. He wheezed, then slowly got to his feet.

No way was he letting Sam's killer get away. Not now. Not like this.

There was a shout from the motorboat and Cranshaw turned and ran towards the pier.

"No, you don't!" Rob took off after him. His chest was burning, but as long as he could move, he'd keep going. The bruises would heal.

Cranshaw was almost at the end of the pier. Rob increased his pace, wincing in agony. He stumbled, gasping for breath. The dark shape with the sports bag kept moving.

"Come on," he panted. He couldn't give up now.

Cranshaw made it to the launch. He tossed his bag into the boat and jumped in after it. The driver pushed away from the pier and turned the tiller so they were facing out to sea.

Rob sprinted down the jetty, gritting his teeth against the pain. He had no idea what he was doing, only that he couldn't — wouldn't — let Cranshaw escape. Once the motorboat was out of range, there was nothing he could do other than call in the Coastguard, and he already knew that would be a pointless endeavour. By the time they'd mobilised, Cranshaw would be halfway across the Channel.

The boatman spotted Rob racing towards them and shouted a warning. *French*, Rob thought through the haze of pain. Cranshaw took another shot, but it went wide. Rob kept going.

More shots were fired, but they were wild, unfocused, and the motion of the boat didn't help. The gun clicked. He was out of bullets.

Gotcha.

The driver of the launch didn't appear to be armed, thank God. Rob reached the end of the jetty and launched himself into the air. He landed with a thud in the boat and threw himself at Cranshaw.

The driver tried to pull him off, and immediately the boat veered off course, twisting on the dark water in an ungainly pirouette.

"Stay on track," yelled Cranshaw. "I'll deal with this."

But he'd dropped his gun in the fight. Rob grabbed it and threw it under the seat, out of reach. No chance of reloading. Now they were even.

He pulled Cranshaw into a headlock and tried to force him into a kneeling position. "I said, you're under arrest," Rob growled.

Cranshaw elbowed him in the solar plexus, just underneath where he'd been shot. He felt a crack and doubled up, gasping for breath. Next, a fist landed in his face and he reeled backwards. A boot kicked him in the groin. Jesus, the pain was intense.

So was the rage. For Sam, for Ant, for the innocent restaurant owner and the two lost boys who would never have a life in their adopted country. Howling, Rob picked himself up and lurched at Cranshaw. He punched him in the face, then in the stomach.

It was the Southwark detective's turn to go down. Rob followed with a lethal uppercut to the chin. The crooked DCI's head snapped back. He groaned, barely conscious. Rob kicked him in the ribs for good measure. Hard.

"That's for the Chief."

Then he got out his handcuffs and restrained the groaning police officer.

"Turn this boat around," he ordered the driver, through an aching jaw. The man ignored him. Lights bobbed up ahead. They were close to the fishing trawler. Once there, Cranshaw would have help.

"I said, turn this boat around, unless you want to be arrested too." But without a weapon, he had nothing to drive home his words.

The driver let go of the tiller and dove overboard.

Rob stared at the white bubbles where he'd gone in. "What the—?" Now what? He couldn't dive in after him. He could barely stand up, let alone swim, and he was restraining Cranshaw by the arm.

The man swam towards the lights bouncing on the dark water up ahead. Securing a semi-conscious Cranshaw to a railing, Rob grabbed the tiller and turned the launch around. The boatman could go. He'd alert the Coastguard and hope for the best, but he had Sam's killer. That's all he needed.

He headed back towards the jetty. The sea breeze swept his hair back, and if he hadn't had to keep a watchful eye on his suspect, he might even have enjoyed the ride.

* * *

"I can't believe you did that." Jenny stared at him in wonder. It was midday and he'd spent the last six hours in A&E getting his chest X-rayed and arguing with the consultant doctor that he was well enough to go back to work. A fractured sternum was hardly life-threatening, and he had work to do.

"I had no choice," he said. "I couldn't let him get away."

"You could have been killed," grunted Galbraith. "Then what would I have told Jo and the bairn?" He and Will had arrived half an hour later than Rob, to find him stumbling out of the launch with a groggy Cranshaw in handcuffs.

Guilt washed over him. In the heat of the moment, he hadn't even thought of them. He'd been so intent on catching Sam's killer, he'd forgotten about everything else.

He should have, though. He had other people to think about now. People who needed him. A family. He couldn't go around putting himself in harm's way like that, playing the maverick. How would Jo support Jack without him? He didn't want Jack to grow up without a father.

A lump formed in his throat. "I know. It was foolish. I didn't think."

Galbraith patted him on the shoulder. "Well, no harm done, eh? But dinnae go doing anything like that again."

"I won't." He shook his head and he meant it. Never again would he go racing into danger without backup.

"We've had a few breaks in the case." Jenny turned to the folder on the table in front of her. "We looked into the Pavićs in more detail. Margaret is clean, but her husband, Bruno? Not so much."

"Yeah?"

"Yup, he was in the military in Croatia. He left after the war ended and immigrated to the UK."

"Why didn't we find this out before?" Rob asked.

"He changed his name," Jenny explained. "When he arrived here, he was Bruno Pavić. In Croatia, he was Goran Jurak. Took his mother's maiden name, apparently."

Rob nodded slowly. "Was he the one who pulled the trigger?"

"We think so. He has a motorcycle licence," she said, "although we didn't find one on the premises. We're still looking into lock-ups or garages where he may have hidden it."

Rob's eyes narrowed. "Have we picked him up?"

"Yes, he's at Wandsworth Police Station now. Kicking up a fuss, by the sounds of things."

"Good, let him sweat." Rob rubbed his chest. Karin had lied about the accomplice. When he'd asked her who'd collected the children, she'd said a man with a buzz cut, when all the time it had been Bruno. She'd been protecting him.

He ground his teeth. "We'll deal with him later."

"It was Cranshaw's DNA under Benny's fingernails," Jeff revealed. "Mayhew put a rush on the analysis. We got it back an hour ago."

"So he was there with Bruno," Rob surmised, picturing how it went down. "The two of them must have tried to persuade him to go through with the burglary. Threatened him and his brother. When the boys refused, it got ugly."

"Dawit said Benny attacked Cranshaw and told him to run for it," said Jenny, sadly.

"One of the men shot him," said Rob. "The gun Cranshaw used to shoot me is with Ballistics, as is the bullet lodged in the vest."

"We'll know soon if it's a match for Benny." Jeff shook his head. "I hope they go away for a very long time."

"They will." Rob gritted his teeth. "I'll make sure of it."

"You got him." Mayhew came out of her office. She was smiling, a rare sight. "Congratulations."

"Thank you, ma'am."

"The Police Commissioner sends her appreciation to the whole team."

The others nodded. It was nice to be appreciated.

"Rob, I'd like to have a word with you in private." She smiled around. "Thank you, everyone, for all your hard work. Now we have to make sure we have a fail-safe case for the prosecution."

"Yes, ma'am," they chorused.

Rob followed her into her office. His pulse beat a little faster. There was something in her expression that made him nervous. She couldn't possibly have found out about the mobile phone, could she? He certainly hadn't let anything slip, and he doubted anyone in his team had either. Still, she had that guarded look that he didn't like.

"Let's take a seat." She gestured to the two round back chairs and small coffee table at the other side of her office. A teapot and two teacups sat ready for use. Steam curled upwards from the spout. This comfy nook was usually reserved for informal chats or visits from the higher-ups. Despite his nerves, he felt strangely honoured as he sat down.

"Tea?" she asked.

"No, I'm good." She was pulling out all the stops. Perhaps this was a congratulatory chat, and he was reading too much into it.

"I was going through the case notes on the shooting at the restaurant." She carefully poured herself a cup of tea. "When something occurred to me."

"Yes?" His mouth went dry, but he tried to act nonchalant.

"I wondered how you made the jump from Lawrence's informant, Anthony Price, to Shamar Williams."

Rob reverted to the story he'd discussed with Galbraith. "Actually, it was Cranshaw who put us on to him. He gave us a detailed rundown on Torch's history and told us he was the one Ant was watching."

"I see." She contemplated him as she took a sip.

"It's in the report." Rob kept his voice even.

"I noticed that we requested Lawrence's phone records, along with those of Anthony Price and Raymond Zhou."

"We did." *Shit.*

"And yet Lawrence's phone wasn't found at the crime scene."

He tried not to tense up. "Only Ant Price and Raymond Zhou's devices were taken into evidence." That much was true, at least.

248

"What do you think happened to Lawrence's phone?"

She held his gaze. Was she watching for his reaction? He felt like he was in one of the interview rooms downstairs, but on the wrong side of the table. "I don't know," said Rob. "Maybe he left it at home?"

"Did you check?"

"We didn't need to. We had his phone records."

She frowned. "Not like you, is it, Rob? To leave a stone unturned? Especially in the case of Lawrence's murder."

Rob's heart was in his mouth. Was she trying to get him to confess? Should he? *Could* he? There was no way he was going to drop his team in it — if he took the fall, he was taking it on his own. But if he did, he'd lose everything.

He hadn't seriously considered the repercussions before, but now he was sitting here, wondering how he was going to support Jo and Jack.

He adopted a light tone. "Just trying to be more efficient, ma'am. I can go back and double check, make sure its whereabouts are accounted for." How the bloody hell he was going to manage that, he had no idea, but he was sure the team could come up with something. God, he should never have put them in that position.

He held his breath as Mayhew sat back.

Come on, he thought.

Her gaze lingered on his face, then fell to her cup of tea. "It won't affect the court case, I suppose," she said. "But it is a loose end. Please, be more thorough in future. We don't want to give the defence any chinks in our armour. We need this to be watertight."

"Yes, ma'am." Rob heaved an inward sigh of relief. They'd got away with it.

Mayhew took another sip of her tea. "I believe it was DCI Cranshaw's DNA under our first young victim's fingernails."

"Yes, ma'am. We also think it was his gun that was used to kill him. We're waiting on Ballistics."

"Good, keep me posted."

"I will do, ma'am." His heartrate was returning to normal.

249

"That's all, Rob. Once again, great work. You got justice for your guvnor."

Rob nodded.

It wouldn't bring him back, but it was something, at least.

CHAPTER 39

Rob elected not to interview Bruno Pavić, and let Jenny and Will take the reins. As senior investigating officer, he ought to take a more managerial role anyway, and leave the interrogations to his team. By conducting interviews himself, he wasn't allowing them the opportunity to get the experience they needed to advance their careers.

Galbraith's words were also fresh in his mind. He had to be more careful. He didn't want to end up like Sam, gunned down in a seedy restaurant in the small hours of the morning. He didn't want Jo to get *that* call. He didn't want Jack to grow up without him.

Bruno, who was being held at Brixton Police Station, had requested legal representation and had been allocated a solicitor. She sat beside him now, young and attentive, in a navy suit.

Rob settled himself on a stool in the observation room and studied Bruno Pavić on the screen. He reminded Rob of a sulky kid. He sat slumped in his chair, his lower lip sticking out, a petulant expression on his face. Everything about his body language told Rob he knew he was caught, and he was trying to wrestle whatever leverage he could from the situation.

Rob turned his attention to Will, who introduced everyone, then Jenny commenced with the questioning.

"Mr Pavić, how do you know DCI Cranshaw?"

Margaret had been in earlier, requesting to see her husband, but Rob had refused. He didn't want to give Bruno time to mount a defence. After talking to Margaret, he was confident she wasn't involved. She'd been as much in the dark as they had about her husband's extramural activities.

He felt sorry for her, though. Her face as she'd left the station was one of shock and betrayal. Her husband had kept secrets from her, terrible secrets. He'd exploited the children in their care. It was the ultimate betrayal. He doubted she'd ever forgive him.

"You do realise that we have DCI Cranshaw in custody?" Jenny said when he didn't reply. "In situations such as this, it's usually the one who fesses up first that has the easier time of it. The CPS looks favourably on those who are seen to be helping, and Cranshaw is a much bigger fish than you are."

Pavić thought about this for a moment, twiddling his fingers on the table. Rob noticed his fingernails were dirty and jagged, as if he'd been biting them.

"We met several years ago," Bruno began in his heavily accented English. "I was arrested after a fight outside a bar."

Rob exhaled. He was talking.

"DCI Cranshaw was the arresting officer?" Jenny clarified.

"Yes."

"How did your relationship begin?"

"What relationship?"

"Your business arrangement." She gestured with her hand. "How did you start working for him?"

Bruno glanced at his solicitor, who nodded.

"He approached me." This was where it would play in his favour. Putting the blame on Cranshaw would result in a shorter sentence. "He interviewed me after the fight. I was surprised when he let me go with a warning."

"That must have been a relief for you," Jenny said.

"Yeah, until he spoke to me outside."

252

"What did he say?"

"He said we could help each other." Pavić glanced down at his hands.

"And you agreed?"

A cautious nod.

"What did he propose?"

Pavić took a deep breath. "He needed young people for various jobs, and said if I could supply them, he'd pay me. We were struggling financially at the time — we'd just bought the next door property and the mortgage repayments were steep, so I said yes."

"Did you consult your wife?"

He shook his head. "No, Margaret would never have agreed."

Jenny leaned forward. "So you did it for the money?"

He nodded and stuck out his lower lip again.

"Did you think about what this would do to the kids? That you were putting them in danger?" Jenny's tone was casual, but Rob knew her well enough to know she was seething inside. This was a personal question, one *she* wanted to know the answer to. It wasn't for the record.

Pavić didn't reply. It was clear he hadn't spared a thought for the children, or how this might have affected them.

Jenny's voice hardened. "Is it true that you threatened them if they didn't comply? You told them they had to do this as payment for coming to England?"

His eyes darted up at her, then down at the table. "No comment."

That was a yes.

"Mr Pavić, did you kill Benny Yemane?"

Bruno's eyes jerked upwards. "No, I didn't."

"Do you know who did?" Rob glared at the screen. It was now or never. If he was going to turn the tables on Cranshaw, now was the time to do it.

His solicitor murmured in his ear. He looked stricken but nodded.

"Mr Pavić, do you know who killed Benny Yemane?"

He cleared his throat, his Adam's apple bobbing. "Cranshaw killed the kid."

Yes!

Jenny flashed a triumphant look at Will, who gave her a tiny nod. *Good job*, he was saying.

"Were you witness to this?" she asked.

"Yeah. I was with him." He paused, remembering the scene. "There was a fight. Benny launched himself at Cranshaw while the younger kid ran away. I went after him. That's when I heard the gunshot."

Jenny frowned. "You didn't see him pull the trigger?"

"I heard it. He was less than two metres away from me. When I turned around, the gun was in Cranshaw's hand and the kid was lying on the ground."

"Good enough," Rob murmured.

Jenny nodded. "Thank you, Mr Pavić." She took a steadying breath. "Now, I want to talk to you about Detective Chief Superintendent Sam Lawrence."

Rob held his breath.

"Who?"

Rob stared at the screen, a lump in his throat. Could Bruno really not know who the Chief was?

Thrown, Jenny took a second to regroup. "Mr Pavić, where were you on the night of the third of October?"

He shrugged, as if the date was inconsequential.

Rob ground his teeth.

"Is this your motorcycle?" Jenny slid a photograph of a black motorbike across the table. Just before the interview, Will had traced it via a bank payment from his wife's account to a lock-up in Lambeth where they stored a lot of their junk.

"It looks like it," he muttered.

"This is the registration?" She put another photo down, with the front of the bike visible.

He nodded. "Yeah, so what?"

"Your motorbike was picked up on CCTV camera outside the Thai Kitchen in Northcote Road on the third of October. Does that help jog your memory?"

He swallowed but said nothing.

"We also have a witness who can put you there just before one thirty in the morning, the time when the Chief Superintendent was gunned down along with two other men — Anthony Price and the restaurant owner, Zhou."

Neither the CCTV nor the witness had seen Bruno's face, but he didn't know that. Neither did his solicitor.

There was a loaded silence that dragged on. Jenny sat quietly, waiting for Bruno to speak. Eventually, he murmured, "Cranshaw ordered the hit."

Rob blinked. Had he actually said that? He fist-pumped the air while a shocked Jenny said, "Are you saying DCI Cranshaw ordered you to murder DCS Lawrence, Anthony Price and Raymond Zhou?"

"My client has already confirmed that," his solicitor said, her voice a little croaky. This was probably the biggest case she'd ever worked on. Child exploitation had suddenly snowballed into a murder charge.

Bruno nodded.

Rob hadn't been sure Bruno would go for it. Cranshaw put the fear of God in most of the people he worked with, but Bruno was only thinking of saving his own arse now.

Jenny pulled herself together. "Do you have proof of this?"

Not that Rob doubted it, but a jury might if they couldn't back it up with hard evidence. Some suspects would say anything to get a reduced sentence.

"Only the ten thousand pounds in my bank account," he said.

"Payment for the hit?" Jenny raised her eyebrows.

Pavić nodded.

It would have come in from Lupus Holdings, no doubt. That would do it — if they could prove Lupus Holdings was set up by Cranshaw. The financial forensic team had their work cut out for them.

Still, they had Bruno for the hit on the Chief and the others, as well as his role in the child exploitation ring. That alone would see him sent away for a long time.

CHAPTER 40

DCI Morris Cranshaw's interview came a few days later. This one Rob wasn't going to delegate. He wanted to look Sam's killer in the eye as he confronted him with murdering his mentor.

He stilled his breathing and opened the door to the interrogation room. Will followed, the thick case file in his hand. They'd been busy accumulating evidence, making sure every forensic report, ballistics analysis and witness statement was airtight.

Cranshaw looked up as they entered. Rob felt the hostility fly across the room.

Good. You're cornered, you bastard. There's no way out.

Rob took his time closing the door and sitting down. All the while, the bent detective's glare rested on him.

Will began the proceedings, and the recorder was switched on. Cranshaw's solicitor was a tense, slim man in a double-breasted suit that engulfed him. He sat stoically in the chair beside his client, a pen poised in his hand, a notebook open on the table in front of him. He looked more like an accountant than a lawyer, the complete opposite to the broad-shouldered, tight-fisted man bristling with barely concealed rage next to him.

"DCI Cranshaw, we're here to talk about the murder of Biniam Yemane and Claudio Stepanenko, the attempted murder of myself, DCI Miller, and the murder of retired Detective Chief Superintendent Lawrence, Anthony Price and restaurant owner, Raymond Zhou."

Cranshaw said nothing. This had all been made clear to his solicitor prior to the meeting, so there were no surprises.

"Why don't we start at the beginning?" Rob opened the folder Will had placed on the table. He took out a photograph of Benny, dark eyes staring apprehensively at the camera. It had been taken at the asylum centre in Kent where he'd been processed.

"Do you know this boy?"

Cranshaw kept his eyes on Rob. "No."

"Could you look at the photograph?"

His gaze didn't waver. "I said no."

Rob sighed internally, but then he hadn't expected this to be easy. Cranshaw knew the system, he'd been on the other side of the table many times, probably more so than Rob.

"We have two witnesses who put you at the building site in Battersea where Biniam Yemane was shot and killed." He watched the detective's face, but there was not even a flicker. He'd make a great poker player.

"According to them, you were the one who pulled the trigger. You shot the sixteen-year-old boy and then dumped his body in the river. What do you say to that?"

"Who are these witnesses?"

"I'm not at liberty to say."

Cranshaw scoffed. "Whoever they are, they've got it wrong. I had nothing to do with the boy who washed up on the South Bank."

"Two boys," Rob corrected. "Benny was the first. The second, Claudio, was also part of your little scheme."

"What scheme would that be?" Cranshaw was quick to turn the tables, but Rob wasn't having any of it.

"I'm asking the questions here," he snapped. "You ran an organised crime group that used asylum-seeking kids and trafficked youths for illegal activities such as burglaries, drug running and prostitution."

"Nonsense. I did nothing of the sort."

Rob leaned back in his chair. "You know, the problem with organised crime groups is that no one wants to take the fall for anyone else, so when you push the individual players enough, they crack. Bruno Pavić named you as the leader of the OCG."

"Bruno Pavić is a violent man with a criminal record. He'll say anything to get himself off."

"Are you saying he lied? That he was the one who shot those boys?"

Cranshaw shrugged. "How would I know? I wasn't there. All I'm saying is it wasn't me."

"How do you explain that the bullet we pulled out of Benny Yemane matches the slug you fired at me?" Cranshaw's gaze dropped to Rob's chest. "I'm fine, by the way. Fractured sternum, nothing too serious. The vest saved my life."

Cranshaw's jaw tightened. "I borrowed Bruno's gun in case I needed it."

That was clever. A simple explanation, hard to prove. "For your getaway, you mean?"

"No, because I have a dangerous job and I wanted a way to protect my family."

"The same family you left when you made a run for the Kent coast?"

Cranshaw's complexion reddened. Rob was getting to him. "I suppose Bruno will back this up?"

"I doubt you can believe anything he says."

"Oh, I get it. He's the criminal and you're the respected detective. Who's going to believe him over you?"

He shrugged.

"So why did you run? Why leave everything and race to the coast in the middle of the night to get on a fishing trawler crossing the Channel?"

"I was meeting with an informant, that's all. You've got the wrong idea."

"You packed a bag for that?" Rob's eyes narrowed.

"I was staying overnight. Of course I packed a bag."

"Who was this informant?"

"A fisherman who trafficked immigrants across the Channel. I was working on exposing the operation."

Rob frowned. "That's not your remit."

"I'm a detective, what can I say? I was following a lead. You got in the way."

Unbelievable. He was trying to spin the story so he came out looking like the good guy. Will cast Rob a worried look.

"You shot at me."

"I didn't know who you were. You could have been anyone."

"You called me by my name. You knew exactly who I was."

"I'm sorry, you must be mistaken. It was dark, the motor launch was behind me along with the crashing waves. I had no idea who you were. I was protecting myself."

Shit. This was beginning to sound plausible. He had to turn it around, and fast. Luckily, he had one more piece of evidence up his sleeve that was indisputable.

"An admirable story, DCI Cranshaw, but how do you explain your DNA under Benny's fingernails?"

Cranshaw stiffened. He hadn't known about the DNA.

"Juries love DNA evidence," Rob went on. "It's pretty damning in court."

Cranshaw scowled but didn't respond. Neither did his solicitor, who seemed to shrink further into his oversized suit jacket.

"You can't explain it, can you? Because that would place you at the scene of the crime. There's another witness, too. Did you forget about Benny's younger brother, Dawit? He saw you shoot his brother."

"He's a kid," growled Cranshaw. "How would he know?"

"Oh, he's a smart kid," Rob explained. "He told his social worker everything. Even drew a picture of you. It's quite good. Do you want to see it?" Rob took it out of the folder and passed it over. This time, Cranshaw did glance down. Briefly. A flicker of annoyance crossed his face.

"You tried to kill him, didn't you?" Rob kept pushing. Chipping away at the cracks. "That's why you were at the hospital the day he was brought in. Except we put a guard on the door so you couldn't get to him without being noticed."

"I don't know what you're talking about," Cranshaw gritted.

"We checked. There was no nurse who was giving you a testimony at the hospital that day. You were lying."

Cranshaw's hands clenched.

"Let's go back to the OCG." Rob changed direction. He wanted to keep Cranshaw on his toes, keep his mind working overtime trying to come up with plausible scenarios, hoping to catch him out. You helped the Rusescu family set up their brothel, didn't you?"

"I don't know who they are." The stoic expression was back.

"Well, they know you." The implication was that they'd ratted him out, even though none of the family had said a word against the Wolf.

Rob continued with his line of questioning. "Twenty-five per cent of their profits are paid to Lupus Holdings, a limited company that you set up. We checked with Companies House."

He smirked. "I don't own a company called Lupus Holdings."

Rob gave him a hard look. He knew they hadn't found anything at Companies House, hence the smirk. It just served to show they were on the right track.

"No, that's true. You didn't use your own name. Does the janitor at Southwark Police Station know he's the sole owner and director of a limited company?"

Cranshaw's gaze darkened.

"Not that it matters, those funds are confiscated now. As are the funds in the offshore account set up in the same name. Quite a sizeable nest egg you had there. Was that your going away money? When you left your family and fled to the Kent coast, is that what you were planning to live on?"

He was winding Cranshaw up now, he could tell. The muscles in the man's jaw were flexing as he ground his teeth.

"That's what Anthony Price was going to tell DCS Lawrence, wasn't it?" Rob homed in on the most crucial part of the interrogation. "He knew you were the Wolf, the head of the OCG. Somehow, he'd figured it out and he was going to tell his old handler, a man he trusted. You couldn't have that, could you? That's why you had him taken out."

Cranshaw went very still. "No comment."

Rob sensed he was close to snapping. "You hired Bruno Pavić, a man who was used to violence, to do the job for you. You paid him ten thousand pounds."

Ten thousand pounds. That's all three men's lives were worth. Rob swallowed over the bitter taste in his mouth. "Bruno has already admitted it, so there's no point in lying. His orders were to take out Anthony Price, your informant on the Beaufort Estate, along with Lawrence. The restaurant owner was collateral damage."

Cranshaw was breathing heavily now, his hands curled into fists. "Damn you, Miller. You think you're so smart, don't you?"

It was a small crack in the otherwise solid facade. Now he just had to prise it open.

Rob met his gaze. "You made it easy for me. You left a trail of evidence behind you. The bullets, the DNA, the bank accounts." He shrugged. "You should have been more careful. That's no way to run an OCG."

A growl came from Cranshaw as he launched himself across the table. He gripped Rob by the collar and yanked him forward. "I'm going to get you for this."

Will snapped into action and tried to pull Cranshaw off Rob, while the solicitor bolted from his chair and sandwiched himself against the wall.

"You mean you're going to kill me, like you did Torch?" Rob looped an arm around his neck, holding him close. Cranshaw hadn't expected that. He tried to pull back, but it was too late. Rob had him in a vice. "Are you going to slit my throat too?"

"Torch was a good-for-nothing gangbanger," Cranshaw croaked. "He deserved what he got."

"Sir!" yelled Will, as two officers burst into the room. They quickly subdued and handcuffed Cranshaw.

Rob shot the crooked detective a triumphant look as the officers marched him to the door. "You may have disabled the CCTV in the cell, but we still have you at the station that day," he hissed. "We know it was you."

Cranshaw spun around. "You think I'm the only one?" He snorted and shook his head. "You give me too much credit." The officers pulled him forward.

"Wait!" Rob barked.

The officers stopped.

Rob went up to Cranshaw. "What do you mean? Is there someone else?"

Cranshaw tossed back his head and snorted. "You're a dead man, Miller."

CHAPTER 41

"What did he mean, he's not the only one?" Jenny paced up and down in the squad room, a worried look on her face.

"There must be someone else involved." Will ran a hand through his hair, which was already standing up in messy spikes. "Someone we don't know about."

"Someone in law enforcement?" asked Jenny.

"Not necessarily." Rob leaned back in his desk chair. He was a lot more shaken up than he cared to admit.

You're a dead man.

"He could be bluffing," Will said.

"I hope so," Jenny breathed.

"It doesn't matter." Rob got to his feet. "That's not our remit. The crime agency's queuing up to interrogate him. Let them deal with it. We've got more than enough to charge him on multiple counts of murder, attempted murder and human trafficking. And now, thanks to the footage you found, we can place him at the station when Torch was killed."

"He was wearing a cap and sunglasses, which is why we didn't see him go in," Will explained. "But he removed them in the gents' on the first floor after he'd slashed Torch's throat."

"The building was in lockdown," said Jenny.

"Yeah, he couldn't get out, so he went up. He waited until it was safe to leave, and then slipped away unnoticed."

"Clever," said Rob.

"I can't believe he was at the hospital that day to kill Dawit." Jenny, who'd watched the whole interview on the video link, shivered. "What a monster."

"At least Dawit is safe with Samira. I heard this morning that she'd applied to foster him."

"I'm so glad. He deserves some happiness."

"And we deserve an end-of-case drink," said Will.

"Damn right," Jenny agreed. "Oh, I almost forgot. Bryson from Vice called. He said to tell you that they picked up Kenny Holloway and some Dutch guy, Van den . . . ?" Jenny frowned.

"Van den Berg?"

"That's it." She clicked her fingers. "They busted them doing a drug deal. Kenny had ten kilos of cannabis on him."

Rob laughed. "That's him going back inside, then. His wife will be relieved." By the time he got out, their son would be grown up and wouldn't have to endure seeing his mum slapped around.

Clapping broke out as Mike walked into the office, his arm in a sling.

"Hey, look who's back!" shouted one of the guys from across the squad room.

Rob strode over and shook Mike's good hand. "Welcome back, mate."

Jenny hugged him, while Will thumped him on the back.

He winced. "I heard you solved the case without me."

"We did. Glad to see you're out, though." Rob nodded to his bandage. "How's the shoulder?"

"Fine." He didn't meet Rob's gaze.

Being shot was no joke. Mike would be in pain for a while.

"It's great to have you back," said Jenny.

"Not for long."

They all stared at him.

"What do you mean?" Jenny asked. "Are you leaving us?"

He hesitated. "I've been giving it some serious thought," he said. "There's an opening at the Beaufort Estate community centre. They're looking for a general manager."

"Seriously?" Rob pursed his lips. "You'd go back there?"

"Raza Ashraf came to see me," he said. Rob's smile vanished. "He offered me the job and I'd be doing some good, you know."

"You going to live on-site?" Will looked slightly horrified at the thought.

"No, I'll keep my apartment, but I'm close enough to go in every day. Besides, with an ex-copper on the estate, things should calm down a bit."

It would give the residents peace of mind. Rob thought about those kids studying in the classroom, eager to get their qualifications. Having Mike there would give them a real shot.

"I think it's a great idea." Jenny got up to embrace him.

"You do?" Mike's shoulders relaxed.

"Yes, the timing's perfect. They need someone to fill Torch's boots, and I can't think of a better candidate than you."

He grinned. "Thanks, Jen."

"Well, I guess congratulations are in order," said Rob. "Have you told the Super?"

"Hell, no." He glanced worriedly at her office.

Rob chuckled and slapped him on the back. "No time like the present."

* * *

"I don't know whether to be mad that you went after Cranshaw by yourself or happy that you're okay," Jo said when he finally got home that evening. He'd had a couple of beers at the pub to celebrate with the team but hadn't stayed long. After the tumultuous last twenty-four hours, he wanted to get home to his family.

"I was worried sick."

"I know, and I'm sorry." He meant it. "I promise I won't do that to you again."

"You'd better not." She shifted Jack onto her other side. "I can handle the long hours. I can even handle some level of danger, but to take down a killer by yourself . . ." She shook her head.

"I know," he repeated. "It was stupid and dangerous, and I didn't think." He didn't mention Cranshaw's final words. It would just worry her even more.

She handed Jack to him, then put her arms around them both. "It's okay. I forgive you. But only because it was Sam's killer. To be honest, I'd probably have done the same thing myself."

He hugged her back. "You're way too smart for that."

She laughed. "Don't count on it."

"Even so, I'm taking more of a back seat now." He sat on the couch. Jack murmured contentedly. "It did make me realise how much I've got to lose."

She smiled ruefully. "Scary, isn't it?"

He took her hand. "I don't want to do anything to jeopardise this."

"Me neither, although . . ."

He glanced up. "What?"

"I've decided to go back to work."

"You have?" Her eyes were sparkling. He could see she really meant it.

"Yes, I spoke to a friend of mine today. She's in intelligence. There's an opening for a part-time analyst in Vauxhall."

Rob's eyebrows shot up. "MI5? MI6?"

"One of them. I'm never sure which is which."

"Jesus, Jo. Isn't that like jumping from the frying pan into the fire?"

"No, not really." She waved a hand in the air. "It's a desk job. I'll be coordinating different ops, doing analysis, that sort of thing. It's not out in the field."

He let out a relieved breath. But was that a hint of disappointment in her voice?

"Will it be enough for you?"

She squeezed his hand. He knew her too well. "It'll be enough for now. Like you said, we've got Jack to think about. We've got our family. A desk job will suit me fine."

"What about the NCA?"

"Pearson doesn't want me back. He'll jump at the chance to get rid of me."

Rob stroked Jack's hair. "If that's what you want."

"It is."

He broke into a smile. "Then I'm all for it."

She grinned.

"When would you start?" They'd have to think about childcare, rearrange their schedules.

"Well, I haven't got the job yet. My interview is next week. But I thought I'd give myself until the end of the year. Start in January."

Jack would be seven months old then. "That sounds reasonable."

She kissed him on the cheek. "You're the best, you know that?"

He grinned at her. "I always said we made a good team."

Trigger snorted in agreement and laid his head on Rob's foot.

"I've been thinking," Rob said, a moment later, "that it's about time we took a holiday. Together. As a family."

Jo's eyes twinkled. "Did you have anywhere specific in mind?"

"The seaside," he said. "I'd like to go to the seaside."

THE END

Thank you for reading this book.

If you enjoyed it please leave feedback on Amazon or Goodreads, and if there is anything we missed or you have a question about, then please get in touch. We appreciate you choosing our book.

Founded in 2014 in Shoreditch, London, we at Joffe Books pride ourselves on our history of innovative publishing. We were thrilled to be shortlisted for Independent Publisher of the Year at the British Book Awards.

www.joffebooks.com

We're very grateful to eagle-eyed readers who take the time to contact us. Please send any errors you find to corrections@joffebooks.com. We'll get them fixed ASAP.

Made in the USA
Las Vegas, NV
12 April 2022

47363506R00159